THE COLOURS
OF THE DANCE

THE
COLOURS
OF THE
DANCE

E J PEPPER

Matador
9 Priory Business Park,
Wistow Road, Kibworth Beauchamp,
Leicestershire. LE8 0RX
Tel: 0116 279 2299
Email: books@troubador.co.uk
Web: www.troubador.co.uk/matador
Twitter: @matadorbooks

ISBN 978 1800462 854

British Library Cataloguing in Publication Data.
A catalogue record for this book is available from the British Library.

Printed and bound in Great Britain by 4edge Limited
Typeset in 11pt Minion Pro by Troubador Publishing Ltd, Leicester, UK

Matador is an imprint of Troubador Publishing Ltd

For all my lovely Irish friends,
of every persuasion and none

ACKNOWLEDGEMENTS

A big thank you to all those who have given me their time and expertise, especially:

Linda Anderson, whose unflagging enthusiasm helped keep me going.

Talented fellow writer, Sarah Hegarty, for her invaluable input and suggestions.

The M. A. Creative Writing course at the University of Chichester, particularly Alison MacLeod for her generous insights.

Lorena Goldsmith and Robin Wade, judges of the First Novel Prize, for encouraging me to have confidence in the book.

Sue Rawlings for her helpful feedback. Also readers Ann Davies and Sally Lomax.

Juliet Mitchell and the Arvon Foundation.

Mary-Jane Holmes for her useful suggestions regarding the opening chapters.

Last, but by no means least, Andrew - for his constant love and support.

ONE

'TELL THE GIRL TO KEEP HER FEET STILL! THAT'S A good turkey rug.'

The voice is a reed brushing my skin – soft, but with a spike at the end of it.

I was practising my steps in my head, but when I look down, I see the mat is all wrinkled up, the way the pastry went when I helped roll it out.

Kate gives me a shove, so hard that I nearly fall onto the floor. Then she stoops down and straightens the mat. I can see why the lady likes it so well. It has all different colours to it – reds and orange and yellows and green. They come floating up at me, like a clump of wild flowers.

Kate seizes my hand again, and we step back onto the mat and stand, waiting.

The lady sits in a big chair, the light from the fire shining on her silky hair. Even from where I'm standing,

1

I can see that she's lovely looking, with creamy skin and big eyes. In her hand is the smallest teacup I've ever seen. It has a pattern of leaves on it. I take a step forward to see what kind they are, but Kate pulls me back.

The lady gazes across at us. For a moment, her face has a puzzled look, as if she's forgotten we're in the room.

'So, you have no family in the area?' she says.

'My parents and the rest of them were took by the sickness,' Kate says. 'All in this twelve months past.'

'And the child is your bastard?'

'Indeed she is not.' Kate's voice has a wobble to it. I reach for her hand again, but she slaps it away. 'She was my sister's.'

'I've heard that before.' The lady sighs. 'It's very tiresome. The last girl I saw had her bawling infant with her, and the one before that wasn't fit to lift a cushion.'

'I'm not afraid of hard work.'

'That's as may be. And you're how old?'

'Twenty-four, Missus.'

'And the child?'

'About ten years – but I'm not sure.'

'Of the work? Or the brat's age?'

I can feel Kate all of a tremble beside me. 'I learned how to cook in our last place,' she says, 'and I'm quick to learn.'

'That's all very well, but it doesn't take away from the fact you've no Testy Moan Yals.'

'That house had the sickness too, so they had to let us go,' Kate says. 'I'm willing to try anything.'

The lady lifts the teacup to her mouth, and takes a

swallow. Then she puts the cup down again. 'The last thing I want is to have to mollycoddle you or your child.'

'I'll see she causes no trouble. And when we're settled, you'll have an extra helper.'

'And an extra mouth to feed.' The lady sighs again.

'I'd work for nothing, Missus. If we could just have our board and keep.' Kate draws in her breath. 'I've heard it said that the Prod girls take time off to visit their families. So you'd have no worries on that score.'

The lady leans forward. 'You're not telling me you're Carth Lick? The Advert Eyes Ment states quite plainly Prods only.'

'*Please*, Missus. Give me a chance. I promise I'll not let you down.'

The lady holds up her hand. 'Just a moment. I need to think.' She sits, staring ahead of her.

In the silence, my belly gives a great rumble. Kate glares at me, but it's not my fault we had just the one piece of bread for our breakfast, and that was a good while ago.

I stare about me because this is the grandest house I've seen in my whole life. At the lady's elbow is a round table with a tray of tea things on it. The pot and jug have the same green leaves as the teacup. There's blue tiles round the fireplace, and the chairs have patterned covers, as if they've had their best frocks put on them. But best of all, facing us is a big looking-glass with a gold frame round it. I stand on my tiptoes so I can see into it, but Kate pulls on my arm.

After a while, the lady looks across at us again, and her lips are curled upwards. But it's not a smile for us – it's as if she's had a different thought to please her. 'Very well,' she says. 'It's risky, but we'll give it a go. A week's trial only. Your hours will be from six in the morning until ten at night. You'll have your food and a bed, and one Sunday afternoon a month off, unless I say otherwise. How would that suit?'

'Oh, thank you, Missus. It would suit very well indeed.' Kate takes a step forward, but the lady puts a handkerchief to her nose.

'Stand over there, would you.' She points to the corner by the door, so we step off the mat and move to where she says. Then she picks up a small bell and swings it backwards and forwards. The sound it makes is like the trickle of water. There are steps outside, and the door opens. A stout kind of a woman comes in.

'You rang, Missus Thompson?'

She's dressed in dark clothing, with a white apron over the top. She has a long, thin nose and grey, wispy hair that sticks out from under her cap.

'There you are, Nellie. How many times do I have to tell you to curtsey when you enter a room?'

From the way the woman dips her knees, I can tell that she's not a great one for the dancing.

'That's better. Now, did you get those errands?'

'I did indeed. Carrigans were clean out of butter, so I had to go to McDaids. Your sister, Missus Clarke, was in there, and she said to tell you that she and the children are fully recovered from the chicken pox.'

'Poor Nora.' The lady smiles. 'Is her face much marked?'

'It is. Though, God willing, the scars will fade with time.'

4

'Perhaps. Now, Nellie, I've a nice surprise for you.'

She steps forward. 'Yes, Missus Thompson?'

'You've been complaining long enough that you need more help about the place.' She waves a hand at us. 'So here it is.'

The woman turns. She has a face on her like a month of wet Sundays. 'But would you look at the state of them. Threadbare clothes, and covered in mud. And the smell!'

'Nothing that soap and water won't fix.'

'And Mister Thompson? What's he going to say?'

'Need I keep reminding you, Nellie, that I am the one running this household?' The spiky bit is back in her voice. 'Now, take these two through to the scullery, and see they get cleaned up. You'll find spare clothing in one of the closets.'

The woman sniffs, and moves to the door.

I wait for Kate to follow, but instead she lifts her skirts on either side of her, and gives a curtsey. 'I promise you'll not regret your decision, Missus Thompson.'

The lady's lips curl upwards again. 'Well, we'll see. Now, go with Nellie, and remember to do as she asks.'

'Certainly, Missus Thompson.'

We're almost out of the door when the lady calls after us, 'Oh, I forgot. What's your name again?'

'Kathleen O'Hagan, Missus Thompson, but people call me Kate.'

'And your daughter?'

'My niece here is Brede.'

The lady leans forward. 'So, Brede, I trust you're a hard worker too.'

5

I look down at the floor.

'I'm afraid you'll not get a word out of her,' Kate says.

'No matter. I like a quiet child.' She waves her hand. 'Well, off you go, then.'

Kate moves away, but I stand just where I am, looking across at that mat. Because what I'd like best in all the world is to lie myself down in the middle of it, pull the edges around me and close my eyes, knowing that nothing bad can ever happen to me again.

But Kate is giving my arm another tug, so I go stumbling out of the room after her.

TWO

'SOMETHING IN HERE'S BOUND TO FIT.' THE NELLIE woman reaches up to the press. Her stockings are wrinkled round her ankles, and she has on black shoes with a strap across the front. Above us is a whole row of presses, and there's one, two rails of washing hanging from the ceiling.

She drops a bundle of clothing onto the floor. 'The state you're in, you should be washing in the yard, but Mister Thompson's out there seeing to the pony.' She points to the corner. 'There's plenty of soap in that sink, so be sure to clean yourselves properly. Because I'm not having you in my kitchen in the state you're in! And that's final!'

'Thank you,' Kate says. 'We're really...'

But already she's out the door.

Kate lets out a great breath. 'We've done it, Brede. A roof over our heads.'

She walks over, and opens the privy door. It has grey walls and a big hook with squares of paper for wiping ourselves with. The seat is made of wood, and she waves her hand towards it. 'All these weeks using a ditch, and now we've our very own throne – like one of the queens of Ireland.' She gives a bow. 'After you, my lady,' she says, and we both get a fit of the giggles.

It takes a good while to get the dirt off. Kate stands me in the sink, and soaps me down, and the water's so cold, I squeal like a piglet, until she slaps my legs for me to stop.

Then she finds a lady's blouse that reaches down past my knees, and with a belt on it and my shoes on me again, I feel good as new.

Then it's Kate's turn to wash herself. I've no titties yet, but she says they'll grow, given time. Hers are smaller than my mammy's, but she has good arms and legs, although there's still a big, red mark from the bad thing that happened when we were walking past the farm that time. I reach out to touch the sore place, but she pushes me away.

'Stop it, Brede! That hurts.'

She chooses some clothes from the pile on the floor. Then she turns to me. 'Will we be able to find the kitchen, do you think?'

We go into the passage and stand for a moment, listening, but there's not a peep from anywhere. So I follow her to a door at the far end. As she pushes it open, a grey cloud comes rolling out towards us, so that we start coughing and spluttering for all we're worth.

Through the mist I can see the Nellie woman stooped over a range. The flames and smoke are fairly pouring out, and she flaps a cloth backwards and forwards in front of it.

Kate rushes forward, seizes hold of the cloth, lifts a big dish out of the oven and runs with it to the sink. She tips a pan of water over it, and there's a hissing sound. And then the flames are out.

The woman walks over to where Kate is standing. 'Now look what you've done, you stupid girl! That was a perfectly good cloth until you got hold of it.' Kate and I stare at the cloth. It has a big hole in the middle, with brown bits round the edges. 'Just wait till Missus Thompson hears.'

'I was only—' Kate begins, when a voice says, 'What's going on here, then?'

I never saw him come in, and now I squeeze myself behind the door. His boots are all muddy, and when I look at the rest of him, I see that he's a great big man, with a moustache and a load of dark hair. His shirt is open at the neck, with more hair sticking out of it.

He points to the sink, where the smoke still rises from the dish. 'I trust that wasn't my supper?'

His voice is like the scrape of a stone on rock. The table has a long cloth over it, so I creep forward, and tuck myself under it.

'I'm thankful to say it was not. Though it might just as well have been, given the state I'm in.' Her voice starts to go higher. 'As if it's not enough having to do all the cooking and cleaning myself, your wife has taken into her head to house two down-and-outs. No disrespect to her, Mister Thompson, but heaven knows where they're from and, what's more,' – her voice drops to a whisper – 'they're papists.'

His boots turn towards Kate's shoes. 'You're one of these women, I suppose? So where's the other one got to?'

I hear feet moving around, and Kate calling my name. Then her head appears under the table. 'Come out from there this instant,' she says.

I scramble up, and go and stand beside her.

'As you can see, Mister Thompson,' Nellie says, 'she's a child. So what earthly use is she going to be to us?'

'I promise she'll not be any bother.' Kate is trembling away beside me, and I just wish I could go back under that table again.

The man clicks his tongue. 'I've really no time for this nonsense.'

'I'm only trying to do my best, Mister Thompson.' The woman's forehead has gone all creased. 'For you – and for Missus Thompson.'

'And God knows how the place would get by without you, Nellie.'

The frown has gone from her face, as if someone's taken an iron to it. 'Well, I don't suppose the Carth Lick woman meant any harm,' she says.

'I certainly did not,' Kate says. 'Why, the whole place might have gone up in—'

'I'll put the pair of them in the outhouse, shall I, Mister Thompson?'

'Do what you like with them. Missus Thompson and I will take our supper at the usual time.' He jabs his thumb at us. 'You'd better give them some food, or they'll be fit for nothing.'

'Certainly, Mister Thompson.'

He goes out, and Kate moves to the sink, and starts to wash some dishes.

'I suppose you've sat at a table before?' The woman lifts out a loaf, butter and a slab of cheese. Just the sight of them brings the water to my mouth.

Kate pulls out two chairs, and the woman slices up the bread, and pours tea from a brown pot into three cups. 'Help yourselves,' she says.

I stuff a crust into my mouth, and then take a swallow. But the tea's so burning hot, I spit it out, along with the bread I've not yet chewed up.

'For God's sake!' The woman reaches for a cloth. 'Here.'

'Small bites now, Brede,' Kate says. 'And remember to close your mouth when you eat.' She puts the cloth on the side. 'You'll have to excuse her, Nellie, but we've had nothing since breakfast.'

'It's Missus Mack-Elroy to you.'

'Of course.'

Kate hands me another piece of cheese. 'You've worked here a good while then, Missus Mack-Elroy?'

'Over forty years. I cooked for Mister Thompson's mother, and for his first wife.'

I chew on my bread, wondering how many wives he's had.

'Mister Thompson must think the world of you,' Kate says.

'I like to think so. As did Missus Eileen Thompson. She's been dead these five years, God rest her.'

Kate blesses herself.

'And we'll have none of those papist goings-on in this house.'

In the silence the rain goes beat-beat against the window, and I'm thinking how grand it is to be all nice and snug here in the warm.

'Can I pour you some tea, Missus Mack-Elroy?'

'Well, I wouldn't say no.'

'So the present Missus Thompson's not been here long?'

She smooths a crease in the cloth. 'Two years come February. It's not like it used to be in the old days.' She sips her tea. Her smallest finger is sticking out, and I'm wondering if she's burnt it. 'Indeed, no.'

I've eaten one, two three pieces of bread, and finished my tea, and now my eyes feel as if someone's piled stones on the top of them.

Kate gives my mouth another wipe. 'Would it be all right if I put Brede to bed, Missus Mack-Elroy? I can then help you in here?'

'Well, it'll get her out from under my feet,' Nellie says. 'Though I will say for her that at least she's not a noisy one.'

Kate gives me a look, but I pretend not to see.

Missus Mack-Elroy gets up. 'You'll be needing some bedding.'

'That would be grand.'

'Well, don't just sit there catching flies, girl. I'm not doing your carrying for you.'

'Stay here, Brede,' Kate says.

The room is going all dim, so Missus Mack-Elroy lights a lamp, and the two of them go out of the kitchen. I wait a moment, and then I get up and follow along behind, because I'm not going to be left in the dark on my own. I walk down the passage, past the room with the privy and the big sink. Ahead of me is an open door. Missus Mack-Elroy puts her head round it, so I stay very still in the shadows. 'I'm just fetching some blankets from the upstairs press, Mister Thompson – for the Carth Licks.'

'As long as Missus Thompson here has no objections.'

'The pair of you can carry on as you like.' The spike is back in her voice. 'You always do.'

Kate and the Nellie woman go on down the passage, with me tiptoeing behind them.

But it's hard not to make a sound, and when a board creaks under me, she swings round. 'I thought you were told to stay in the kitchen?'

'Go on back, Brede,' Kate tells me. 'We'll be down in a minute.'

I move away, but the passage ahead of me is filled with dark shapes that I don't like the look of one bit. So when I reach the room with the open door, I have a peep inside. Mister and Missus Thompson are sitting on either side of the hearth. There's a good fire going, and the flames are dancing across the walls. He has his boots off, and his feet are stretched towards the blaze.

The heat comes out towards me, and I'm thinking I've not felt this warm since I lay in my bed by the range, with my mammy and da and brothers in the other room.

'That woman,' Missus Thompson is saying, 'never agrees with me on anything.'

'I'd have thought you'd be only too pleased.'

'Having her go against me all the time?'

'Must we go over the same ground?' He gives a laugh, and it's like her smile – you wouldn't know where you were with it. 'She's an old woman, Adelina, and a loyal one.'

'To you perhaps.'

'You shouldn't let her trouble you so much.' There's the creak of a chair, and then the sound of the fire being poked. 'But there's plenty round here aren't going to like your taking in these papists. Your mother included.'

'It was her I was thinking of.' The smile is back in her voice.

'Have a care, Adelina.'

'Well, at least William would approve. Did you hear what he said to Bob Drummond about giving Carth Licks the vote? I thought Bob would burst a blood vessel!'

'William can look after himself. Although it may be a different matter when his father dies. Feelings, and tempers, are running high, and…'

There are footsteps coming down the stairs, so I go running back. And I'm sitting at the kitchen table all nice and quiet when Kate comes in to tell me it's time for my bed.

I use the privy, and the seat feels all lovely and smooth under my arse – though I know that's not a word a queen of Ireland would use.

In the outhouse there are two straw mattresses side-by-side on the floor, with a brown rug between them, and a small window with bars across it.

'Isn't this great?' Kate blesses herself. 'The Sacred Heart is looking out for us, all right.'

I'm too tired to be thinking about any of that, so I flop

down onto the mattress. 'You're a funny one,' Kate says. 'I can never tell what's in that head of yours.' She pulls the blanket over me. 'But if you behave yourself, we'll maybe have a chance to go over your steps. You'd like that, wouldn't you?'

When she goes out, I lie in the dark, feeling the scratch of the blanket under my chin, and listening to one of the animals snuffling away to itself.

I'd like to be thinking of my dancing, but there's something else I can't get out of my head. It's Missus Thompson's talk of a vessel. Because my da's brother used to go out fishing in a boat. And ones that size must hold a deal of blood, and take a deal of strength to break.

But who in the world would do such a thing?

THREE

W HAT I LIKE DOING BEST WHEN I FIRST WAKE IS to watch the morning come in under the door. It creeps forward, like the line of water that licks away at the sand when the tide comes in. If the light's the colour of porridge, I know it's another grey old day, but if it's the yellow of my mammy's apron, then the two of us will be out in the sun, spreading the washing over the fewsher to dry.

She and my da sleep in the back room, along with the babby, who has a special box on the floor. My two brothers used to be in there, and my big sister shared the space with me by the range. But that was before the three of them took to their beds. And, even though it was wintertime, with a lick of frost over the ground, they were burning hot, and Mammy said the pain in their bellies was so fierce that they couldn't eat their food. And no matter how hard she shouted at them to get up, or how often my da swore he'd take his stick to them, they wouldn't shift. But the worst part was the shite that came pouring out of their backsides, and even with my mammy washing and wiping away for all she was worth, there was no getting away from the stink.

When they didn't wake up one morning, she cried and cried, which made my insides twist about. And the priest came and said it was God's will, which just made her cry the harder. So then I took to going in and out of her and my da's room when it was all dark, so I could shake her to be sure she was still there, but he would shout at me to for God's sake let a man get some rest, so now I've to stay quiet as a mouse by the range until I hear them stirring.

This morning, I listen for the creak that means Mammy's out of her bed. The first thing she'll do is put on the water for the tea and the porridge, and then she'll see to the babby. And sure enough, he's starting up his crying. There was a time when I'd want to give him a good slapping, but now I'm glad to hear him, because it means that any moment now, Mammy will be coming through the door.

So I get up and go tiptoeing over to the bedroom. When I push open the door, I see the two of them are still fast asleep. They're lying on their backs, but as I get nearer, I can tell my da isn't sleeping at all, because he's staring straight at me, with a very cross look on him.

'I heard the babby,' I whisper. 'Do you want me to lift him?'

He doesn't answer, so I creep round to Mammy's side of the bed. She's very white-looking, and her eyes are shut tight. I put a hand to her face, but her skin is all cold under my fingers. 'Wake up, Mammy!' I give her a shake, and her head rolls to one side, and then she lies still. My da hasn't moved either, and there's not a blink to be had out of his eyes, and I can feel the panic rising up inside me.

'It's morning!' I tell them, and now I'm shouting. I pull the blanket off, like they do to me when I'm too tired to get up. And it's then I see that they're lying in a whole load of blood. My legs go all of a tremble, because there's no breath coming out of either of them.

And then I'm shaking them for all I'm worth. 'Wake up!' I yell. And that sets off the babby. 'Wake up!'

*

'Brede!' Kate is bending over me.

I jump off the mattress, and go and press myself against the wall, to stop the shaking.

'Do you want us on the road again?' She heaves a sigh. 'Missus Mack-Elroy is upstairs, helping Missus Thompson dress, so we've to make a start on the breakfasts.' She points to my new clothes that are on a stool in the corner. 'There's an apron and cap for you as well. Quick as you can, now. You remember where the kitchen is? The second door on your straw-foot side.'

She goes out, but I stay right where I am, chewing on a piece of my hair, until the shaking stops. I pull on my clothes, and use the privy, and splash water from the sink onto my face. And all the time I'm thinking how I can be a help to Kate, so she's not cross with me anymore.

In the kitchen, she's lifting the bread from the oven. 'Stand back, Brede.' She puts the dish on the edge of the range, but as I turn away, my elbow knocks into it, and it goes clattering to the floor.

'For God's sake, Brede!'

I pick the loaf up, but it's so hot, it slips from my fingers, and into the basket of turf beside us.

Kate picks the loaf up, and gives it a wipe on her apron. 'I can't do anything with you hanging around me all the time.'

I reach for her hand, but she pushes me away.

She walks over, and pulls open the yard door. 'Nothing for you to knock over out there. You can practise your steps until I call you.'

It's a damp old morning, but I'm glad to be out in the air with the chance to look about me. At the far end of the yard, there's a pig-pen, with a load of grunts coming from inside. My da had a pig that my brothers called Mollie, but he had to sell her to pay for all their medicine. But I'll not think about them.

Beside the pig-pen is the coop for the chickens that are scratching and pecking about the place. Then there's the stable, where Mister Thompson keeps the pony and horse. They have their heads stuck out, and I see that the pony is brown with a white mark on its nose, and the horse is white all over. Beside the stable is a pile of manure. It has a crowd of midges over it, and lets off a powerful stink.

The yard is covered in big stones that will be just grand for my steps. So I put my arms by my sides, and hold myself very straight, like I remember my mammy telling me. She was a great one for the dancing, until the babby came along and she got too tired. *Head up, Brede, and point your toes!* I can hear her saying. *And be sure to count.*

Straw foot: hop, hop down,
kick up 1,2,3, over 2,3.
Other foot: hop, hop down,
kick up 1,2,3, over 2,3.
Or is it: *back 2,3?*

The horse gives a snicker, but if I know if I just try hard enough, I'll soon get the hang of it.

Straw foot: back 2,3, turn
Other foot: back 2,3, turn.

The clatter my shoes makes on the stones is really grand.

Hop 2,3,4,5, over 2,3,4,5.
Straw foot: jump hop, kick up 2,3.

'What in the name of goodness do you think you're about?'

I thought Missus Mack-Elroy was upstairs with Missus Thompson, but here she is, coming round the side of the house. She glares across at me. 'You come inside this instant. The way you're carrying on is enough to bring on one of my bad heads. And take that filthy piece of straw off your leg.'

Any eejit could tell you it's the only way to tell one foot from another, but even if I had the words, I doubt she'd listen. I put the straw into my pocket for safe-keeping, and follow her into the kitchen.

Kate is still at the range, cooking off the bacon, and the smell of it is really grand.

Missus Mack-Elroy pulls out a chair. 'I'm surprised at you, allowing the child to behave like that.'

'I thought she'd come to no harm out there.'

'Making all that rumpus? It's a wonder the chickens are still laying.'

'I'm sorry, Missus Mack-Elroy. It'll not happen again.'

'It had better not.'

All the while they're talking, I'm noticing a box right beside Missus Mack-Elroy, with a cat curled up inside. It's lying very still, with no breath coming out of it, so I walk over and give it a poke. It leaps up with a great screech, and goes running out the door.

'How would it be,' – Kate's words come out all of a rush 'if I start on the fry for your breakfast?'

'I'd have thought you'd have it already done.' Missus Mack-Elroy points her finger at me in a way I don't care for at all. 'And keep her out of my way. I've never come across a child as Agree Vating.'

Kate hands me my cap. I'd taken it off for the dancing, and now she tucks my hair in under the edges. 'Sit at the table, Brede, and I'll give you some tomatoes to slice.'

She puts one, two, three in front of me, and I start cutting away, keeping my thumbs clear, as she's taught me. Then, as I listen to the bacon frying in its pan, I hear another sound – the click-click of feet along the passage.

The next moment Missus Thompson is in the room. She has on some boots that are white with a row of black buttons, like currants, running up the sides. Yesterday, her frock had a lovely green skirt, and a bodice with a scratchy kind of pattern that Kate said was called Tar Tan. The frock she has on today is as blue as her eyes, and there's a ribbon the colour of cream in her hair. She looks so gorgeous that I put down my knife, and stare and stare at her.

Missus Mack-Elroy heaves herself off her seat. 'You and Mister Thompson will be wanting your breakfasts now?'

'We will indeed. I can see Kate's made a good start on them.'

Kate drops a curtsey, and Missus Thompson smiles.

'And make sure not to forget the cream for my porridge, Nellie.'

Missus Mack-Elroy wrinkles her forehead. 'I'm afraid Mister Thompson had the last of it yesterday.'

'Oh?'

Kate steps forward. 'But I'm sure I saw a bowl of it in the pantry.'

Missus Thompson gives Missus Mack-Elroy a look. 'Did you now?'

'Would you like me fetch it?' Kate says.

'Please.'

When she returns with the dish, Missus Thompson says, 'Amazing what you can't see when it's under your very nose. Put it on the tray there, would you, Kate?'

I'd have thought Missus Mack-Elroy would be pleased that the cream was found, but the look on her face is enough to sour a bucketful.

The yard door opens. 'Ah, here's Mister Thompson now,' she says.

He pulls off his boots and throws them in the corner. He's in his shirt sleeves, and there's a big patch of mud on

22

his front. He goes over to Missus Thompson, and I wait for him to tell her how well she's looking. Instead, he takes some pieces of paper from his pocket, and waves them in the air. 'We need to speak about these.'

'All in good time,' she says.

He bangs his fist on the table, so the dishes on it go rattle-rattle. *'Now!'*

I slide off my chair, and tuck myself under the table, where it's all dim and dusty. In the corner is a spider, and its legs are very thin and trembly, and I'm thinking how glad it must be to have this place to hide.

Above our heads, Missus Thompson says: 'And a very good day to you too, Alexander!'

'The size of these bills. I can't begin to...' He stops. 'Bring our food through would you, Nellie?'

'Certainly, Mister Thompson.'

The door slams on the two of them, and I scramble out. Kate has a look on her that says if we were on our own, she'd give my legs a good slapping. Instead, she pulls a cobweb from my cap, and points to the table.

'A pity you've not thought to teach the girl manners,' Missus Mack-Elroy says. She points at the two breakfasts that Kate has served up. 'Mister Thompson always has his tomatoes next to his eggs.'

'I'll remember for tomorrow, Missus Mack-Elroy.'

'So I should hope.' She picks up the tray. 'Tomorrow's the day Missus Thompson visits her sister, and she always takes me with her. Though I'm wondering if you can be trusted here on your own.' She goes off down the passage, muttering away to herself.

23

'Well,' Kate says, 'maybe we'll get the place to ourselves then.'

There's still not a smile to be had from her, but I'm hoping she'll be in a better mood soon, so she can help me with my steps.

When Missus Mack-Elroy returns, the three of us sit for our breakfasts. She has the same big fry-up as Mister Thompson, and Kate and I have one rasher, one egg, and one, two pieces of bread.

I'm just tucking in, when Missus Mack-Elroy points to a dish beside her. 'You forgot to put out the Thompsons' butter, Kate.'

'Shall I'll take it through now? It'll save your legs.'

Missus Mack-Elroy has that sour look on her again. 'The girl can do it.'

I'm busy eating my egg, but it's hard to get it to stay in my mouth.

'Let Mister Thompson see what I've to put up with.'

Kate gives my face a wipe. 'You can do this, Brede. Just set the butter on the table, and come straight back.'

Halfway along the passage, I stop. The dish is made of glass, with a curly bit round the edge that winks up at me. The butter is in a big slab in the middle, and is a lovely soft yellow. Kate never said anything about not tasting, so I scoop a piece out, and it goes slip-sliding down my throat.

The parlour door is ajar, and through the gap I can see Mister and Missus Thompson at the table. It has a lovely white cloth, with a jug of flowers in the middle of it. The pair of them are sitting very still, and then I see he has one

24

hand round her wrist. She goes to pull away, but he keeps tight hold of her.

'... a different story when you came courting,' she's saying. And her face has gone all pink. 'Nothing too good for me then.'

He drops his hand, and takes a swallow of tea. 'Enough, woman.' The cup is white with a blue band round the top. 'I'm telling you now fair and square this must never happen again.'

'Or what, Alexander?'

'Or this.' He reaches out again, and gives her arm a twist.

'You're hurting me, you brute!'

'What do you expect?'

'If my father were alive...' She starts to cry, and the sound is soft, and makes me go all sad inside.

'But he's not. I'm the one in charge of things now, and don't you go forgetting it!'

I scoop some more butter into my mouth. A piece of tomato has dropped into the dish, so I push it down with my thumb.

'Do I make myself clear?' He gives her arm another twist.

'Yes,' she whispers.

I'd like nothing better than to run back to the kitchen, but if I do that I'll be in for such a telling-off from Kate and Missus Mack-Elroy, so I draw in my breath, and kick the door open, to let the Thompsons know I'm here.

They swing round.

'What are you doing out there?' His eyes are as black as the range, and they have such a fierce look to them, that I rush forward, and drop the butter onto the table.

'And just look at that dish!' I hear her say, but I'm off down the passage, as fast as my legs will carry me.

'You took your time,' Missus Mack-Elroy says, as I sit myself at the table.

I push my plate away.

'Do you not want the rest of your breakfast?' Kate says.

'Wasting good food. I've a mind to dish it up again for her supper.'

'Shall we clear away then, Missus Mack-Elroy?'

'Yes, you may as well make yourself useful.' She takes off her apron. 'I've a list of jobs that I expect to be finished by the end of the day. So don't think you can put your feet up.'

'I promise that's the last thing I'll—'

'Ah, Nellie.' Missus Thompson is in the doorway, rubbing at her wrist as she talks. 'I came to say how good my porridge was this morning.' She smiles across at Kate. 'That drop of cream made all the difference.'

'I've always done my best to please, Missus Thompson,' Missus Mack-Elroy says.

'I'm glad to hear it, because unfortunately the state of the butter left much to be desired. Half out of the dish, and with tomato and goodness knows what else mixed in with it. Mister Thompson was not pleased.'

'It was perfectly all right when I last saw it.' She looks across at us. 'I'm worried what these two will get up to when they're left here on their own.'

Missus Thompson waves a hand. 'Never mind that. Just see there are no more unfortunate lapses.'

When she's gone out, Missus Mack-Elroy turns to Kate. 'And what have you to say for yourself?'

Her voice has gone all cold, so I go and stand very close to Kate.

'I didn't mean to cause trouble over the cream, Missus Mack-Elroy. It's just that Missus Thompson did ask. And Brede's trying her very best.'

'Well, let me tell you here and now, this sort of thing will get you nowhere.'

I reach up my hand to Kate, but she slaps me away.

'Let's get these dishes washed and dried, Brede, and then we can make a start on the other jobs.'

'Don't think I can't tell what you're up to!' Missus Mack-Elroy points her finger again. 'And just remember this: One word to Mister Thompson, and the pair of you will be out.'

I'm thinking of the cold look in his eyes, and the marks on Missus Thompson's arm, and, if it wasn't for all the lovely food and the room of our very own, I'd be out of here as fast as my legs would carry me.

FOUR

IT'S ANOTHER SOFT DAY, WITH THE WATER RUNNING off the roof, and the chickens clumped together in a corner of the yard. They're very sad-looking altogether, and I'm wondering why they don't go back into their house, where they'd be all nice and dry. But I'm thinking that maybe when Missus Thompson is away out at her sister's along with Missus Mack-Elroy, Kate will let me practise my steps by the range. It'd be easy enough to shift that turf basket, and—

'Stop your day-dreaming, Brede, and pass me that blouse!'

We're busy hanging the washing in the big scullery that has the privy in the corner. Above our heads are those rows of presses, and one rail of clothes that Kate's pulled by up its rope, so now they're going drip-drip onto the floor.

'And those drawers.' They're white, with curly pieces on the ends. Kate hangs them over the rail beside her. 'Did you ever see the like of that lace?'

I never have, but then before we came here, I thought that drawers were for putting things in.

'That skirt,' she says, 'and then the—'

The door swings open, and Missus Mack-Elroy steps into the room. I can't see her shoes, but she has on a black coat and a hat with a grey feather in it. 'Are you not done in here, Kate?'

'This is the last of it now, Missus Mack-Elroy.' She picks up the empty pail that had the wet clothes in.

'Good – I want to go over that list again before I leave.'

We follow her into the kitchen, and there, standing by the range is Missus Thompson, in a gorgeous blue coat that's so soft-looking, I'm longing to give it a stroke.

'Is everything all right, Missus Thompson?' Missus Mack-Elroy asks.

'It couldn't be better, Nellie.' She gives a smile that doesn't reach up to her eyes.

'But I've come to tell you there's been a change of plan.'

'Oh?'

'I've decided to take Kate with me today.'

Two spots of red come into Nellie's cheeks. 'You know I always—'

'You've complained often enough about how that mountain road tires you. And now you're worried about leaving Kate on her own.'

'But—'

29

'So you can enjoy a quiet day at home.' She turns to Kate. 'The boy will bring the trap round in five minutes. So get yourself ready.'

'Yes, Missus Thompson.' Kate draws in her breath. 'Would it be all right if Brede comes with us? You won't know she's there, I promise you.'

'The girl? Well, I suppose so.'

As she turns away, I give a skip, and Kate slaps my arm. 'Behave yourself, Brede!'

'Don't think I'll forget this,' Missus Mack-Elroy hisses, as we go to fetch our shawls.

In the yard, it's still spitting with rain, but I don't pay any heed to it, because there in the middle is the pony and trap. It has two big wheels that are a bit rusty-looking, and a load of leather strips that tie the animal to it. I can see the space for sitting in, and perched in the front of it is a boy, with hair the colour of carrots.

'I'm Kate, and this is Brede.'

'Francis.' He jerks his thumb at the back. 'Hop on. We'll pick Missus Thompson up at the front entrance.'

The pony has a hairy lip that it curls up over its teeth, as if it's having a good laugh. Then I look over at the kitchen window, and see Missus Mack-Elroy staring out at us, and my insides twist about.

We pick up Missus Thompson, and set off along the lane. Carrot Hair is in the front, holding a long, thin whip. 'Get up there, Mary,' he says to the pony.

Kate gives a 'tch', because it's a surprise all right to come across a creature with the same name as the Blessed Virgin. When I picture the pony with a blue frock on her, I drum my feet on the floor, but Kate nudges me to stop.

She and Missus Thompson are sitting side-by-side, and I'm perched on Kate's knee. It gives me a grand view, although there's not a deal to see at present – a big hill ahead of us, and bare hedges on either side. It puts me in mind of the times Kate and I slept under them, with just a bit of sacking to keep off the damp, and I'm wondering what the one word is that Missus Mack-Elroy would say to Mister Thompson that would have us on the road again.

'I meant for us to leave earlier,' Missus Thompson says to Kate, 'but I couldn't decide between my green or my grey frock.' She leans forward. 'Get a move on, would you, Francis.'

The boy flicks his whip, and it goes crack-crack against Mary's side. The animal takes not a blind bit of notice, but just keeps on at the same steady rate, its feet going clop-clop along the lane.

Missus Thompson sighs, and then gives me a sideways look.

'She's such a big lump of a girl, Kate. Are you not squashed to death?'

'I'm managing fine, thank you. But stop that kicking, Brede!'

Francis puts up a hand to give a good scratch under his cap. His fingers are all black, just like mine used to be before I was given that sink to wash in.

We've entered a straight stretch and the pony has decided to make a run for it. It's going at such a lick that the air rushes against my face. When I look up, there on my straw-foot side is the hill, and it's now so tall that I can't see the top of it. The sun has started to shine, and I can see a load of sheep grazing the heather, and above them some big patches of rock where the turf has been eaten away.

Who'd have thought that one day, Kate and I would find ourselves sitting up here beside Missus Thompson? She's wearing that beautiful blue coat, and her hat has a bright green feather sticking out of the top. I'm wondering if it's from one of her hens, though I've not seen any that colour. But then Kate's always telling me I've not seen much of life either.

All of a sudden, the cart gives a jolt, so that I knock against Missus Thompson.

'I'm sorry,' Kate says, 'it's just that neither of us has ridden in a pony trap before.'

Missus Thompson rubs her arm. 'Well, you'd better get used to it. I visit my sister, Missus Henderson, each month, and then there's my mother, and my other sister, Nora – to say nothing of all the errands to run in the town.'

'So you'll not be taking Missus Mack-Elroy with you?'

Missus Thompson leans towards us, and I catch a lovely smell off her, as if she's holding a bunch of summer flowers. 'I'll be honest with you, Kate. It makes a pleasant change to be with someone who doesn't go against my every wish.'

'I certainly hope never to do that, Missus Thompson.'

She points to the hill. 'That's the biggest mountain hereabouts. Knockmarran.'

'There must be a great view from the top.'

'I've only climbed it the once, when I was a girl, and I have to tell you, I've no wish to repeat the experience. It was nothing but potholes and bogs.' She points ahead. 'We follow this lower track and, in just a mile or two, we'll be at the house.'

'And it's your brother-in-law, who lives there?'

'Along with his father, and his youngest son, John.' Missus Thompson gives a sigh. 'But there's little love lost between William and his father, I can tell you.'

'Oh dear.'

'Polly ticks. It makes men act very strange. But we'll not bother our heads with any of that. William – Mister Henderson – is a fine figure of a man. He's married to my eldest sister, Helen, and they've just the one child, Rory. Then there's Poor Nora and her brood, and then there's me.' She gives a laugh. 'Last but not least!' She looks at Kate. 'I take it you've never been married?'

'No, I haven't, Missus Thompson.'

'Well, I couldn't care less about your child being born out of wedlock, as long as your work is good.'

'Brede's not—'

'Anyway, marriage isn't all it's cracked up to be.' Missus Thompson lets out another sigh. 'Indeed, no.'

We've come into a long stretch of lane, with fields filled with black and white cows, all munching away, and I'm hoping it'll be time for our next meal soon.

Francis gives another flick of his whip, and we go bowling ahead at a great rate.

Missus Thompson pokes him between the shoulders.

'Remember to slow up as you go through the gates. You nearly had the posts off the last time.'

We turn off the lane, and go up a drive that's covered in small, black stones. They go crunch-crunch under us, as if the wheels are chewing away at them. Then we drive through an entrance with a big post on either side, and a stone creature stuck on the top. 'Lions!' Kate whispers.

I've never come across one before, but from the way they're showing their teeth, it's no wonder Carrot Hair can't wait to get past.

The trap pulls round the bend, and I draw in my breath. The house is twice the size of the Thompsons' place, and twice as grand. The front door has a length of glass across the top and is painted white, with a big gold knocker in the middle. From the way the sun winks off it, I'd say someone has spent a deal of time with the polish. On either side of the door, there are one, two, three rows of long, shiny windows, and the walls are a cream colour, with bits of garden climbing up them. And over to the side, there's a very tall post with a big flag waving at the top. It's a beautiful orange colour, with a red cross in one corner and a wee purple star in the other. Kate sees it too, and she's so taken with it, she grips my arm.

'Adelina!' a voice calls, and out of the house comes a neat-looking man in a dark jacket and trousers. He's older than Mister Thompson, and has a lovely silver head of hair on him. He swings his arms as he walks. When he reaches her side, I see his eyes are bright blue, but he has a very stern expression on him. 'We were wondering where on earth you'd got to,' he says.

'I'm sorry to be so late, Charles,' Missus Thompson says. 'Francis here has not the first idea about time.' She smiles, and his face goes soft as the butter when it's left on the range.

'Not at all, my dear. It's always a pleasure to have you with us.' He points a finger at Carrot Hair. 'In future, you make sure you get a move on when your mistress tells you, or you'll have me to answer to.' He raises his voice to a shout. 'Do I make myself clear?'

Francis's neck has gone all red, and I'm glad it's not me sitting in that front seat. 'Yes, Mister Henderson.'

'Now, come on inside, Adelina. You must have an appetite after your journey.'

She points to a bag at her feet. 'Bring that, would you, Kate?'

He helps Missus Thompson down, and they walk over to the house.

Kate picks up the bag. When I take a peek inside, I see it's stuffed with bundles of grey wool.

We climb down, and Francis drives the pony and cart round the side of the house. I'd like to be sitting up behind him and riding back to where we've come from, but Kate pulls on my arm, and I follow her across the stones and in through the shiny door.

Inside, there's this great big hall, with a picture of a sailing ship, and another of a man with an orange ribbon across his chest. And there's a table with flowers, and another table with a tall pot on it. But the floor is what I can't take my eyes off. It's very smooth, and is covered in big black and white squares, and I can tell it would be just great for practising my steps on. My feet start to move, and Kate gives me a shake, so I know to stay nice and still.

Missus Thompson is handing her coat to a tall, thin woman, who has a dark dress on her with a white apron over the top. 'And how are you today, Annie?'

'In the best of health, thank you, Missus Thompson. And yourself?'

'Couldn't be better.'

'You certainly look very well, Adelina,' the man says, and they smile at one another.

Another woman comes through a door at the end. She's short and stout, and has on a green frock and a brown hat. When she gets closer and I see the small patches of pink on her face, like the ones on the sow's backside, I don't need anyone to tell me who she is. And right enough, Missus Thompson steps forward and says, 'Oh dear, Nora, how very unfortunate.'

Poor Nora puts a hand up to her cheek. 'Everyone assures me they're barely noticeable.'

'I must let you have some of my face cream,' Missus Thompson says. 'It may help a bit. Now, I brought you some wool, Nora – hand me the bag there, Kate – I thought you could knit it up for the children. It's a good dark colour, so it won't show the dirt.'

Poor Nora says not one word.

'Shall I tell cook to start serving, Mister Henderson?' the Annie person says.

'Please do.'

He turns away, and she says, 'Excuse me, Mister Henderson, but what do you want done with these two?'

36

He comes over to us, and he has such a fierce look on him that I step behind Kate.

'What on earth are you doing here, girl? Did you not think to use the servants' entrance?'

Kate drops a curtsey. 'I'm very sorry, sir.'

'I should think so. Take them on through to the kitchen, Annie. I expect Missus Purdy could do with the help.'

'Yes, Mister Henderson.'

He walks off again, and Annie says to us, 'Well, don't just stand there! We've work to do.'

So we go out of the big hall and along a passage. This one has windows set into it, so it's all bright and sunny, not like at the Thompsons' place. We pass a scullery, with a sink piled with pans, and there's Carrot Hair and another boy with a big, round face, playing catch with a potato. When they see Annie, they stop and put their hands in their pockets.

'Any more of that carry-on, Sam,' she says, 'and no dinner for the pair of you. When you've finished clearing up in here, the yard needs a sweep. Oh, and see if the turf baskets need refilling.'

'Yes, Miss Laverty,' Round Face says.

'Now,' Annie says, pushing open a big door, 'see if you can make yourselves useful.'

FIVE

W E'RE IN A BIG KITCHEN, WITH A GRAND SMELL
of roast that makes my belly growl. A woman with
curly hair is at a long table, tipping apples into a bowl, and
a short woman is by the stove. When she looks round, I
see her face is very pale, as if she's covered it in flour, or
maybe got hold of Missus Thompson's special cream. And
it's the very same colour my mammy was when I last saw
her...

All of a sudden I'm back in the room where she and
my da sleep. It just has their bed in it, and a picture of the
Sacred Heart on the wall. And when I look down, I see my
mammy's hands are all wrinkled, like they get on wash-day,
only worse. And I'm just wishing she'd get up, because it's
been such a while since she's been out of her bed. And now
I'm shaking her for all I'm worth, but she just goes flop-flop
onto the pillow, and my da keeps staring ahead of him...

'Missus Thompson's arrived then?' the short woman is saying.

'Better late than never, Missus Purdy.'

Missus Purdy sinks into a chair. 'I'll just put my feet up for a moment.'

Beside her is a box with a black and white cat in it. It stretches out a paw, and she gives it a stroke. Then she says, 'And who have we here?'

'This is the Thompsons' new maid, Kate.'

'And the child is…?'

I have a chew of my hair.

'My sister's daughter, Brede,' Kate says.

'Well, Kate, you know how to mash a potato?'

'I certainly do – and a deal more besides.'

'I'm very glad to hear it. Margaret here will show you where everything is.'

The curly-haired woman gives a nod. She has a nose that turns up at the end, and very pink cheeks.

'Sit at the table, Brede,' Kate says, 'and keep out of everyone's way.'

Margaret points to a big pot that's boiling away on the stove. 'There's the spuds.'

When Kate's doing the cooking, her movements are like her dancing – quick and neat. She mashes the potatoes, and piles them into a blue and white dish. Then she takes a fork and makes swirling patterns across the top.

'Getting very fancy, aren't we?' Margaret says.

But Missus Purdy says, 'I can see you know what you're about, Kate. Could you make us some custard?'

Kate nods, and as she cracks the eggs, she hums away

to herself, and I'm thinking she's not done that all the time we've been at the Thompsons' place.

Missus Purdy stays in her chair, and after a while, she closes her eyes. I watch to make sure her chest is still going in and out, because the minute it stops, I'll be ready to poke her awake.

It takes a long while for the meal to be carried through to where Missus Thompson and the rest of them are eating, because I've never seen so much food in the whole of my life. Besides a bowl of soup each, they have roast meat and potatoes and gravy, with Kate's mash, and greens and carrots, and an apple tart and custard, and a plate of cheese to follow.

Just when I think they'll be dishing up for the rest of the day, Missus Purdy tells us it's time for our own meal. And what with her, and Francis and Round Face, and Annie and Margaret, and Kate and me, we're a good crowd, just like it used to be when I lived in my home. We always had spuds that Mammy would tip out onto the table, so we could dig our spoons into them. And there'd be butter to go along with them, and cabbage, with sometimes a piece of fish or an egg. And I'm thinking how my big sister would like the taste of this boiled bacon, and even the babby would be eating some of the stewed fruit we have for afters.

When we're done eating, Missus Purdy points at Francis and Round Face. 'You two have plenty to be getting on with. I'll save you some of my baking for later.'

'*If* you've done your work properly,' Annie adds, and they go grinning and scuffling out of the door. And watching them brings to mind my two big brothers,

Colm and Seamus, and how they'd throw punches at one another, though they never meant any harm by it. And I'm just wishing it was them here with me as well. And all of a sudden my belly has this great lump inside it.

'So, how are you getting on at the Thompsons?' Annie asks Kate.

'Just fine.'

'Well, that makes a change,' Margaret says. 'Word is the last three girls only stayed a month. They say he's quite a temper on him, which is no surprise given the way she carries on. You know she's been seen in the town with—'

'That's quite enough, Margaret,' Missus Purdy says. 'I'll not have gossip in my kitchen.'

She turns to Kate again. 'The Hendersons are giving a big lunch next month. Do you think there's any chance of Missus Thompson bringing you across to give a hand?'

'Well, she's said she'll take Brede and myself along with her when she goes out and about.'

'One in the eye for Nellie,' Margaret says. 'I'd watch your step there, Kate.'

Missus Purdy looks across at me. 'The child's very quiet. How old are you, Brede?'

I stare down at my plate.

'Cat got your tongue?' Annie asks.

I look over at the animal, but it's fast asleep in its box.

Kate gives a sigh. 'Since Brede's parents passed away two years back, there's not one word to be had out of her.'

'I'm sorry to hear that.' Missus Purdy leans over and gives my arm a stroke, just like my mammy used to when I sat beside her.

And I take a peep at her face that's still all white-looking, and suddenly there's this screaming noise that starts in my head, and gets louder and louder.

Then Kate is slapping my face – smack-smack. 'Stop that this moment, Brede! What will everyone think of us?'

There's a silence, and I can feel all of them staring at me.

'I'm very sorry,' Kate says.

I'd like to tell them that I'm sorry too, because there's nothing I'd like more than to be talking away like I used. But anytime I try, the only thing to come out of my mouth is a load of spit.

'Was it the Koll Erra took them?' Annie asks.

'It was.'

'Well,' Missus Purdy says, 'why don't we all have a nice piece of my barm brack? Fetch it from the press, would you, Margaret?'

She's just slicing it up, and Margaret has put a dish of butter on the table to go with it, when the door opens, and a woman comes in. She's dressed all in grey, and when she comes closer, I see her eyes are the same colour as her frock, and her hair is a soft brown.

'Don't get up,' she says. 'I just wanted to thank you, Missus Purdy, for an excellent meal. And Margaret too, of course.' She looks over at Kate. 'And I understand you were the extra help today?'

Kate scrapes back her chair and gives a curtsey.

'No need for all that bobbing up and down when it's just ourselves,' the woman says. 'It makes me quite dizzy.' Then she smiles. 'You must be Kate. My sister has been singing your praises.'

42

'I was just thinking, Missus Henderson,' Missus Purdy says, 'that we could do with Kate's help at next month's lunch.'

'Of course.' She turns to Margaret. 'It's time Rory finished his nap, so could you wake him? Oh, and I think my sister's ready to leave, Kate.'

She smiles, and then she goes out again.

'She seems a very nice person,' Kate says.

'A kinder one you wouldn't find in all Knockmarran,' Margaret says. 'Unlike some I could mention.'

'*Margaret!*' Then Missus Purdy gives a smile. 'Well, we'll hope to see you and the child again soon, Kate.'

'Thank you all for making us so welcome.'

'We've heard you're Carth Lick, but it's one and the same to us, isn't it?'

'Though, Mister Charles thinks very differently,' Annie says.

Margaret gives a sniff. 'And who could blame him?'

Annie gets up. 'I'd better show you the servants' entrance, Kate, because if Mister Charles catches you in the hall again, he'll skin you alive.'

I don't like the sound of that at all, and why there's a need for two doors in a house is a puzzle. My mammy and da had just the one, so there was never a need for any skinning.

We go down a passage and into a yard with a big tree in the middle of it. Chickens are scratching about in the dirt, and there's a big, brown dog lying chained to the tree. When he catches sight of us, he leaps up, barking for all he's worth, and Kate clutches onto me.

'Angus is a good guard dog,' Annie says. 'He'll not harm you – once he gets used to you. Now...' she walks us round the side of the house. 'Francis should be along with the trap any minute.'

Ahead of us I see the front door, with its lovely gold knocker, and beyond it, the orange flag waving at us in the breeze.

'Thank you again, Annie,' Kate says. 'We're...'

We can hear voices, and out of the door comes two men. The first is old Mister Henderson, with the silver hair, and beside him is a younger man, who's taller and very thin-looking.

Even from where we're standing, we can hear the old one shouting. 'I tell you again, William. I will not put up this!'

'Oh Lord!' Annie whispers. 'They're at each other's throats again!'

I stare at them, but they're not touching each other at all, and now they're walking towards us.

'Have you no thought at all, William,' the older one goes on, 'of where these half-baked ideas of yours will lead?'

'I tell you where they'll lead – to freedom and justice, that's where!'

'Freedom, my arse!' The old one's shouting even louder now. 'You'd be giving away the freedoms we value the most. You'd be—'

Then he catches sight of us. 'What are you doing out here, Annie? You know I can't stand an eavesdropper.'

Her face goes very red. 'I've just been showing Kate

44

and Brede the side entrance. They're waiting on Missus Thompson's trap.'

'Of course – and I need to fetch her. We'll talk about this again, William.' He turns and walks back towards the front door.

William comes over to us. He has a brown moustache, like a mouse's tail, and a long, thin face. 'As you know, my father's bark is worse than his bite, Annie. But I'm sorry you had to hear that.'

'It's all right,' she says, and gives a smile.

'And this must be…?' He stops speaking, and he's not looking at Annie any more, but is staring across at Kate.

I wait for her to drop a curtsey, or to say her name, but she stays quiet.

Annie says, 'She's the Carth Lick, who's working for Missus Thompson. Her name is Kate.'

'Welcome to Knockmarran House, Kate.' He points at the flag. 'My father had that put up two years ago, but if I had my way, all this Orange Order nonsense would be dumped at the bottom of the nearest lough.'

I'm wondering why he'd want to do that to such a gorgeous flag.

'You'd not think those two men were father and son,' Annie says, as he walks away. 'The dear knows where it'll end.'

But then I hear the clop-clop of the pony's hooves, and there's Francis coming round the corner with the trap. Kate and I climb in, and we drive up to the front door. Missus Thompson comes out of the house, with old Mister Henderson, and another man, who's the spit of him, but younger, with the same blue eyes and way of swinging his arms as he walks.

He helps her up. 'Thank you, John,' she says. 'And you, Charles.' She blows each of them a kiss.

John leans forward. 'Come again soon, Adelina,' he says, and his face has taken on that melted butter look.

'Best get a move on, Francis,' Missus Thompson says. 'It'll be dark soon.'

As we drive away, I look back and see the two men standing in the doorway. 'Like peas in the pod, aren't they?' Missus Thompson says.

Francis cracks his whip, and the pony goes through the gate at a trot.

Missus Thompson sighs. 'Sometimes I fear for William. I really do.'

I lean against Kate, thinking it's no surprise because those lions would be enough to scare anyone.

As for myself, I'm just glad to be safely past them.

SIX

CLICK-CLICK. CLICK-CLICK. THE MINUTE I HEAR them steps coming along the passage, I know it means trouble.

Missus Mack-Elroy is in the yard, giving the hens their morning feed, and Kate has her back to me at the sink. I slip off the chair and creep on all fours under the table. My heart is going knock-knock inside my chest, as if it can't wait to get out. So I look about me, trying not to think of what's to come.

Just above my head is the underside of the table, and it's very rough – not like the top that Kate scrubs away at every morning until it's smooth and pale as butter. The spider is still in its corner. It knows to stay very quiet too, so it's just sitting there in the middle of its web.

From where I'm crouched, I can see the lower bit of both doors – the one leading to the yard, and the one Missus

Thompson will be coming through any moment. I can also see the lower door of the range, with Missus Mack-Elroy's ginger cat curled up beside it. It's a mean creature – when I go to stroke it, it spits at me and turns its back into a hoop. But this is a mean sort of a house altogether.

'Never mind the Thompsons' carry-on,' Kate says, when we hear them doors slamming, and the pair yelling at one another so hard a person can't hear herself think. 'No more ditches, and begging for leftovers – so aren't we the lucky ones?'

I know she's right. It's just for all that Missus Thompson's so lovely looking, she doesn't leave me feeling very lucky. Her steps are right outside now, and I see Kate's legs turn around from the sink as she hears them.

Bang! Missus Thompson flings back the door, and the spider trembles in its web. She's wearing black pointy shoes with a silver buckle on the top of each. Really beautiful, they are, and her feet are very small and thin. You can tell just by looking at them she's not someone who goes bumping into things.

'Kate?' The way Missus Thompson says her name sends a shiver through me.

'Good morning, Missus Thompson.' Kate's skirts dip as she curtseys.

'Where is she?'

'Missus Thompson?'

'Where's that good-for-nothing daughter of yours?'

Silence.

I can tell from the way Kate's feet twist about that she knows full well I'm here under the table.

'Because I'm telling you now fair and square, Kate, that I simply will not tolerate this sort of thing!' There's a clattery sound as she drops the pieces of china onto the table. 'Just take a look!'

I know I'm not allowed in Missus Thompson's parlour, but I wanted just a quick peek. The dish was on the shelf, and had two circles running round the outside – one blue and one yellow. In the middle, set into some leaves, was a gorgeous bunch of berries. They looked so real that I reached out to touch them, and before I knew it, the dish jumped from my hand and was on the floor. So there was nothing for it but to pick up the pieces, and pile them in the corner.

'I'm truly sorry, Missus Thompson.'

'And so you should be. Have you any idea of the cost?'

The shiny buckles come closer.

'It was part of my best set. From across the water, no less.' Then she sighs, a soft shushing sound like the lough back home on a calm day. 'It grieves me to say this, Kate, when your work on the whole is very satisfactory. But I have to think: with the child's way of destroying everything she touches, is it really worth it? You follow me?'

'I do indeed, Missus Thompson, and I can only tell you how very—'

'It's not even as if I can dock the money from your wages.'

'I promise I'll work all the hours God gives to make up for what Brede's done. Just please, please, don't send us away!' Kate's legs are twisting about again. 'Where else is there for us?'

Missus Thompson sniffs. 'Well – I suppose for this once, then.' Kate's legs stop moving. 'Considering your cooking's not at all bad. And that reminds me: are you all set for the morning?'

'Yes, Missus Thompson.'

'Francis will take you and the child over to Knockmarran House first thing, so you can make a start in the kitchen. There's always a good crowd at these lunches, so there'll be more than enough for you to do. Nellie will stay here and help me get ready, and then Francis will bring the pony trap back for Mister Thompson and me. I just hope it stays nice and dry, and—'

In the distance comes the sound of steps. Clump-clump! Clump-clump! The pointy shoes turn towards the door, and one toe goes tap-tap on the ground.

There's another bang as the door opens. Mister Thompson has on his old boots that are caked in dirt, and there's a kind of a farmyard smell about him. And I know right away that Missus Thompson won't be liking it. Not one little bit.

'Ah – there you are, Adelina!' he says. 'I've been looking for you all over.' There's a rustle of paper, like a mouse in a sack of flour. 'No need to play the innocent with me. Explain yourself.'

'Well, you still might have left all that mud outside. There's more than enough to do without clearing up after you!'

'Never mind that. You're coming with me.'

She gives a laugh, but it's not one that would make you smile. Her pointy shoes follow his boots out of the room, and I hear them arguing away as they go down the passage.

'… the size of these bills, Adelina… beyond belief!'

'… the pigsty of a place when I first came here…'

'I'm warning you!'

'… that's right – yell for all you're worth!'

And then a door slams, shutting out the racket.

Everything goes quiet and, a moment later, Kate's face appears under the table. 'Come on out, Brede,' she says.

I know I'm in for a good slapping, like the one she gave me when I broke that other dish, so I move very slowly. But when I'm beside her, she just lets out a sigh. 'What in the world's to be done with you, Brede? Any more broken dishes, and Missus Thompson will have us in the Poor House.'

Although I've never set eyes on it, I feel sorry for the place, and wonder if it's covered in pink spots, like Poor Nora.

Kate reaches for the dustpan and brush. 'I swear to God they're getting worse. When we were first here, they seemed a real pair of love birds! But now…' She lowers her voice. 'Maybe I shouldn't be saying this, even to you, Brede, but her bruises didn't get on her by chance.' She stares out of the window. 'These Prods are not slow to pick a fight, that's for sure. And all I can say is, thank the Lord none of this is to do with us. But here's more trouble!' She throws a dishcloth over the broken china, just as Missus Mack-Elroy comes in from the yard. She stands with her back to the range to give her backside a warm.

'It's perishing out there, but at least that's the hens sorted.' Then she gives me a look. 'I was thinking it's a job the child could take on.'

I give a nod, because I'll enjoy throwing the grain down and watching the chickens come running over to peck it all up.

'She certainly could,' Kate says.

'That's settled then. Now, Missus Thompson has asked me to give a hand upstairs. You know what you're cooking for Mister Thompson's lunch?'

'I do, Missus Mack-Elroy.'

'Well, I'll be down for my tea at eleven to check on things. So make sure to have the pastry and vegetables done. And that big store cupboard needs a good turn-out.'

'Yes, Missus Mack-Elroy.'

When she's gone out, Kate sweeps up the broken china. 'One thing's for sure – if they do get rid of us, they'll miss my cooking.' She wrinkles her forehead. 'But you're to promise me to keep out of Missus Thompson's way, Brede. It's really important. Will you do that?'

I nod again.

'For now, I need to get on, so go outside again. You can go over your steps, but don't use that board because it makes too much noise. I'll bang on the window when Missus Mack-Elroy comes down.'

So I go skipping into the yard.

It's a cold morning, with a coating of frost on the ground, as if someone's put a lick of silver paint over it, and when I blow into the air, I see my breath coming out – huff-huff – like bits of smoke. I take out the board that

Kate's hidden behind the henhouse because how can I do my steps properly without it? The chickens are pecking about, and the sun is shining, as bright as the buckles on Missus Thompson's shoes.

Straw foot: hop 2,3,4,5, over 2,3,4,5,
Other foot: jump hop
Straw foot: jump hop.
Other foot: hop 2,3,4,5 over 2,3,4,5.

It's really grand to be here, with my feet drumming away.

Turn, 1,2,3 and kick back, 2,3.
Other foot, hop, kick back, 2,3.

The chickens have moved to the far end of the yard, but perched on a corner of the stable roof is the old rooster. He flaps his wings at me, and I want to tell him I'm light as a bunch of feathers too. But then I think that maybe he knows, because as I turn in the air, he goes cock-a-doodle-do! Missus Mack-Elroy complains about the racket he makes in the early morning, but I think it's a grand noise, and I'm glad he doesn't pay any heed to her.

'I'm promoting you to my personal maid,' Missus Thompson told her the other day. Missus Mack-Elroy's face took on a look, as if she was sucking on green apples.

'I'm none too sure about that. Who knows all Mister Thompson's little ways, and his favourite dishes, as well as me?'

'At your age, Nellie, I thought you'd be glad enough to leave most of that kitchen work to Kate. It'll mean you can concentrate on the lighter tasks.' Missus Thompson gave one of her smiles. 'I know I can trust you to care for my best china, and then you'll be helping me choose what to wear each day, and what to order for the household.'

'Well, there's no denying a bit of a rest would be welcome.' But she still had that sour look on her.

If I'd been her, I'd have leapt at the chance to be able to touch all them lovely frocks. But some people have no sense.

Straw foot back, 2,3.

Turn, turn. Point other foot,

3,4. Turn, turn.

I stop and take a breath. The sun is warm on my face, and I'm just thinking I could do with a nice drink of milk, when the rooster gives another cock-a-doodle-do, and flies down into the yard. He has a lovely patch of green on his side that puts me in mind of the feather in Missus Thompson's hat. And I'm thinking how much I'd like one for myself.

There's no sign of Kate at the kitchen window, so I creep towards the bird. But he's too quick for me, and goes flapping over the yard gate and away round the side of the house. So I climb over, and go chasing after him.

When we reach the front of the house I stop, because I was only in this part once before, and got a good telling-off for it, so I know how much trouble there'll be if Missus Thompson or Kate find me here. But it's a nice spot, even on a cold day. There's a white fence with a patch of grass in the front of it and one, two, three trees that Kate says will have plums on them, but not until summer's been and gone. The grass has a bush with red berries in the middle of it, and there's a stone bench by the house wall.

Missus Mack-Elroy says the area used to be just rough ground, which was perfectly good enough for the first Missus Thompson, but that some people were altogether too high and mighty. And just as I'm trying to remember the tallest person I've come across hereabouts, I hear the clop-clop of hooves along the lane, and coming towards the house is a man on a brown and white pony. When he reaches the front gate, he swings himself down and ties the creature to it. I can see they're both very stout, and he has on a dark coat and a cap with orange and green squares, and a green scarf around his neck.

I look about me, but the rooster's nowhere to be seen. So I stoop down behind the bench, and watch him walk up the gravel path to the door. He knocks. Rap-rap.

The upstairs window opens, and Missus Mack-Elroy pokes her head out. 'Who is it?' she calls. Then she catches sight of him. 'Oh, it's you, Mister Drummond.'

'Good day to you, Nellie,' he says. 'Is Mister Thompson at home?'

'He'll be where he always is this time in the morning – over in the big field, seeing to the bullocks.'

'Well, never mind. Perhaps while I'm here I might have a quick word with Missus Thompson?'

'I'll tell her you're here, Mister Drummond.'

I should be getting back to the kitchen, but this will be a chance to get a proper look at Missus Thompson's frock, because I was only able to see her feet earlier. So I hide myself by the side of the house, and when I hear her come out, I take a quick peek round the corner. She still has on her pointy shoes, and a red shawl over her shoulders.

Underneath it, she's wearing a dress I've not seen before. It's the colour of cream, with black strips down the sides, and is as gorgeous as all the others.

'Good morning to you, Missus Thompson,' the man says, and when he removes his cap, I see he's bald as an egg. 'I'm sorry to disturb you, but it was your husband I was after.'

'No matter, Mister Drummond,' she says. 'I can take a message.' Then she calls over her shoulder. 'Ask Kate to brew some tea, will you, Nellie? I'll be through shortly.'

'Very good,' Nellie's voice answers.

Missus Thompson shuts the door, and then turns to the man. 'What on earth do you think you're doing?' she whispers.

'Ah now, don't be like that.'

'I thought we'd agreed only to meet in the town?'

'Things change.'

'What sort of things?'

He nods towards the bench. 'Let's you and me have a quiet word.'

'Oh, very well. But make it quick.'

They settle themselves on the seat. 'I must say you're looking very well today, Adelina.'

'Enough of that.'

He leans forward and puts an arm around her.

'Are you mad? Anyone might come along.'

'Not out here, they won't. But I'd remind you that we have an agreement, so I hope very much' – he puts his other hand down and lifts the hem of her skirt – 'that you're not having second thoughts.'

'Of course not!'

'Good. Because I've had an eye for you as long as I can remember.'

'Which I'd remind you is a sight longer than I can recall.'

'What has age to do with it? Besides,' he lowers his voice, so that I creep round the corner to hear. 'I'm not an Ork Shaneer for nothing. I made a bid. You accepted. And now it's pay out time.'

He pushes her back against the wall, and starts to pant – huff-huff! And I'm thinking he could do with a drink of milk to cool him.

There's a silence, and I move closer to see if he'll climb on top of her, like my da used to with my mammy. The two of them always made a deal of noise, but when I asked my brother, Seamus, what they were doing, he whispered, 'They're making babbies, Brede.' But that's not right, because any eejit knows it's the fairies that bring them.

Missus Thompson is speaking again. 'Nellie will be wondering where on earth I've got to. And you know what a trouble-maker she is!' She pushes the man away.

He mops his forehead with a yellow handkerchief. 'If not now, when?'

'We'll think of something.'

'One kiss at least – as a down payment.'

'Oh, very well, but first give me what you promised.'

He reaches into his pocket and pulls out an envelope that goes crackle-crackle as she tucks it under her shawl. Then he leans over her again, and I hear a slurping kind of noise as they press their faces together. And I'm so caught up in what they're doing that I clean forget I'm not meant to be here. And all of a sudden, Missus Thompson opens her eyes, and sees me.

She lets out a scream, and he swings round.

'What do you think you're doing, child?' she shouts. 'Get away from here at once!'

'You know her?'

'She's just some Carth Lick, who's working for us. Nellie assures me she can't speak one word, but I'd still not trust her.'

'You think she's spying on us?' He gives a laugh. 'If I were you, Adelina, I'd be more concerned about…'

But I don't wait to hear more, because I'm running round the side of the house as fast as my legs will take me. I scramble over the gate, and run full-tilt across the yard, and into the kitchen.

Kate is by the stove. 'Ah, there you are, Brede. You can give me a hand with these vegetables. Quickly now!'

So I sit up at the table, and listen for the click-click of them shoes coming along the passage. And if I was scared the last time, now my hand's shaking so bad, I can hardly keep hold of the knife.

SEVEN

'IF SOMEONE DOESN'T REMOVE THAT GIRL, I SWEAR I'll do her an injury!'

Margaret wasn't that friendly when we were last in this big house, but now she's fit to be tied.

'Hot fat spilled everywhere. You could have scalded us all to death!'

Through the window, I can see Kate's arm going up-down, up-down, as she fills buckets from the pump. I'm just glad she's not in here, or I'd be getting a scolding from her too.

'A sorry wouldn't come amiss,' Margaret says.

I have a chew of my hair, and she moves over so she's standing right beside me. She lifts her hand. 'I'd say it's time someone knocked some sense into you.'

Missus Purdy is at the table, pouring milk into a basin. 'Leave the child be, Margaret. And how's the gravy coming along?'

'Well the least she can do is help clear up,' Margaret says.

I can see why she's so put out, because there's a terrible lot of grease all right. I rub away at it, making big circles over the floor.

'You're making it worse, you stupid girl! Molly!' she calls. 'Take over here, would you?'

Molly is the new maid. She's very short, with black hair, and a load of pimples across her forehead.

I go and stand by Missus Purdy, who's pouring creamy-looking stuff into one, two, three rows of tins. 'Stand somewhere else,' she says. 'I don't want my batter spilled.'

There's such a crowd of us helping with this meal, it's hard to know where to put myself. As well as Kate and me, and Missus Purdy and Margaret and Molly, there's Francis and the round-faced boy, Sam.

Margaret is at the stove stirring the pans that are boiling away on it; Molly is still clearing up the grease, and Francis and Sam are in and out with bowls of spuds, and cabbage and carrots. And I wish there was some job for me to do, so I'm not put on the road again.

When Kate comes in from the yard with the buckets of water, I hold my breath, waiting for someone to tell her about the grease. But the only person to speak is Missus Purdy. 'You make all the pies and cakes for the Thompsons, Kate. So could you make a start on the pastry?'

'I could indeed.' She gives a smile, so I know she's pleased to be asked.

Missus Purdy settles into a chair. 'I'll just take the weight off my feet.'

I look to see if there's anything on the ends of her boots. But they're the same as they were earlier – a dull sort of a black, with cracks across the top. Not at all like the ones with the shiny buttons that Missus Thompson wears.

The door beside me swings open. 'Out of the way,' Annie says, as she pushes past. 'How are you doing, Missus Purdy?'

'Still a bit of lightness in the head.' She sinks into the chair, and closes her eyes.

'Times like this, I wonder if she's long for this world,' Annie whispers to Margaret.

'Should we send for the doctor?'

Annie shakes her head. 'Mister Charles wouldn't like it. Best to wait until after the meal.'

'If Kate's doing the pies, Missus Purdy, I'll see to the roast and gravy.'

But Missus Purdy has her eyes closed, and doesn't answer. She's still very white-looking, and I'm just thinking of giving her a poke, when Kate calls, 'Come here, Brede!' So I go and stand beside her.

She's busy mixing flour and butter in a bowl. By her elbow are one, two big dishes filled with apples that Sam brought in from the scullery.

'So, where did you learn to bake like that?' Annie says, as Kate sprinkles flour onto the table.

'The people Brede and I were with before the Thompsons. A lovely couple – Mister and Missus Burk they were called.'

'Would they be related to the Burk's over at Mullymore?' Annie asks.

61

'I don't think so, Annie. They lived outside Donegal town.'

I remember the pair of them because they were so old and trembly. He had a face that was all wrinkled up, and walked with two sticks. She had a very screechy voice, and her eyes were cloudy, as if they'd been dipped in milk. But they were a deal kinder to me than Missus Mack-Elroy.

'So what happened?'

Kate starts rolling out the pastry. 'The fever took them.'

'And you were on the road again?'

'We were, and a sad day it was.' She nudges me not to stand so close. 'I wonder: Is there any small job that Brede could be doing?'

Margaret is lifting a big piece of meat onto the baking tin. 'I'm sorry to be saying this, Kate, but when you were in the yard just now, she spilled hot fat all over the floor. Molly's had a time of it cleaning up, I can tell you.'

'I'm very sorry,' Kate murmurs, and there's a silence.

Missus Purdy opens her eyes. 'How about sending the child along to the scullery? She can give the two boys a hand with the apples.'

I'm so glad she's still able to talk, that I don't mind where I'm sent.

'Well, get along, then, Brede.' From the sharp bit in Kate's voice, I'll be in for another slapping later. 'I'll be out to see how you're doing. So mind and behave.'

When I reach the scullery, there's not a sign of the two lads. By the window, there's a big sink, full of peelings. I pick up a piece of apple skin and twist it round my finger to make a ring like one of the queens of Ireland wore. Kate sometimes tells me stories about them. They lived a long while ago, before even she was born, and they slept in castles, and held feasts where everyone ate loads of meat, and danced all night long if they wanted.

I'm wishing I lived in them days, or that I was still all nice and warm in the kitchen, listening to the talk going on around me. But perhaps if I stay quiet here for long enough, Kate will let me back in, and I can have a go at rolling out some pastry. Because I don't like being in this dark old place one bit. It smells of cabbage, and there's a pile of sacks in the corner, and some basins with spuds that still have the dirt on them. The tap goes drip-drip into the sink, and there, creeping towards me along the draining board, are one, two brown slugs. They're very fat, and when I pick one up, it feels all slippery, like the grease I spilled. So I throw them both down and stamp on them, as hard as I can. It puts me in mind of my steps, and now I'm remembering that big hall we came into when we were first here, and all those lovely black and white squares that would be grand for practising on.

I put my head out of the scullery to check if anyone is about, but there's not a peep from anywhere. So I go on my tiptoes along the passage and into the hall, where the light from one, two, three lamps is shining across the black squares. In one corner there's a clock I'd not noticed before. It reaches nearly to the ceiling, and inside there's an arm going backwards and forwards – tock-tock, tock-tock. And there's the picture of the man with the orange ribbon across his front, and I'm thinking that my mammy would have liked one like that for her hair. Below the man is a cupboard, with a big vase on the top of it, painted with birds that have great long tails on them.

'Annie's sent you along to help out, has she?' It's Missus Henderson, the lady with the soft voice. Last time I saw her, she was dressed in grey, but today she has on a green frock that makes her very tired-looking.

'I thought I recognised you. Your mother works for my sister, Missus Thompson.'

She pauses. 'I'm surprised Annie hasn't sent Molly, but I suppose she couldn't spare her. And I'm afraid I can't remember your name.'

I'd like to tell her, but the word won't come out of me.

'You don't say much, do you? Speak up, girl.'

I have a chew of my hair.

'Well, just follow me, then. There's still a fair bit to do before everyone arrives.'

So we go down another passage, and she pushes open a door. I suck in my breath, because I'm in a room with one, two, three windows along one side, and gorgeous red curtains hanging in the front of them. A big fire is blazing away at one end, and there's lamps shining on the longest table I've ever seen in my life – far bigger than the one the Thompsons have. It's covered in a white cloth that reaches nearly to the ground, and there's a load of glasses on it, and silver knives and forks, all winking up at me. But best of all, in the middle of the table is a silver tree with pointy leaves, and sitting underneath it are two horses with wings. And on top of the leaves is a round dish filled with purple plums. Just looking at them makes my mouth fill with water.

'Now,' Missus Henderson points to a table that's set against the far wall. 'Do you see those silver pots? They're for the salt and pepper. You're to put them on the big table. And be sure to space them out.' She hands me a cloth. 'And then I want you to take this and give a polish to any of the glasses that need it. Do you think you can do that, while I see how things are going in the kitchen?'

She stops in the doorway. 'Oh, goodness, whatever's Annie thinking of? She knows my father-in-law is most particular about servants being properly dressed. Come with me a moment.'

In the passage, she reaches into a press, and lifts out an apron and cap. 'Put these on, and I'll be back in a moment to see how you're doing.'

The apron has a lovely white frill. I tie it round me, and set the cap on my head.

It's grand to be given a proper job, but first I need to see to the slugs. I take off my shoes and, sure enough, they're still sticking to them, and are all brown and slippery-looking. The room has a nice yellow carpet, but I find a corner where no one will notice, and rub my shoes backwards and forwards until they're good and clean. And when I've done that, I carry the small pots from the small table to the big one, like Missus Henderson told me. And then I take a cloth and go round, blowing on each glass – huff-huff. But there's so many of them, it takes a deal of time, and sometimes I blow so hard that bits of spit come out of my mouth, and I wipe them away with the cloth too.

And then who should come in but Molly, carrying a tray with dishes of butter on it. She also has on a white apron and cap, but you can still see the line of pimples underneath it. 'Whatever are you doing here? Kate's been looking for you all over.' She carries the butter to the table. 'The salt and pepper need to go further in. Like this.' And she goes around moving them to the middle. Then she sighs. 'And those glasses still have smears all over them.' When she's finished giving them all a wipe, she turns to me. 'Well, I'm off to the kitchen. I'll tell Kate where you are, shall I?'

I wait a moment to be sure no one else is coming. Then I lift one of the plums from the top of the silver tree. One of the horses has its foot raised, like Mary, when she's about to set out with the trap. I take a bite from the plum, and it's every bit as good as it looks. The juice runs down my chin, so I wipe it away with my sleeve.

When I hear steps outside, I put the plum back, with the bite side underneath, and then the door opens and Missus Henderson comes in again.

She walks up and down, looking at the table. 'Well done, child. You've put a nice shine on those glasses too, so I think we're just about finished in here.'

I'm thinking how glad I am to be getting back to Kate when Missus Henderson says, 'The first of our guests will be here soon. So don't just stand there. You can give Annie a hand with the coats.'

So now there's nothing for it but to follow her into the hall.

EIGHT

THE MAN WITH THE RED FACE IS THERE ALREADY and his name is Mister Charles. And beside him is his son, John, who's Pea-in-the-pod.

'So where's that husband of yours got to, Helen?' Mister Charles says. 'He knows he's to be here to greet everyone.'

Missus Henderson bites her lip. 'William's taken a couple of the boys to help sort out some problem in the stables. He should be along any moment.'

'Always with some excuse up his sleeve!' Pea-in-the-pod says.

I tuck myself in beside the cupboard. On the top of it is the vase that has the birds with the great long tails on them. Some are yellow, and some are blue and green. The only bird I've seen with any colour to him is the rooster at the Thompsons' place – the other ones hereabouts are grey or brown, and very ordinary-looking altogether.

There's a rap-rap on the front door. Mister Charles looks at the clock. 'And here's the first of our guests. Ten minutes early too. Well, go ahead, Annie.'

When she opens the door, a great big woman walks in, shaking the rain off her. Behind her is Poor Nora, still with the pink bits on her face, and behind her is a middling sort of a man, with hunched up shoulders. Annie gives a curtsey, and the big woman hands over her coat. She's dressed all in black, and her bosom is large enough to sit a teacup on. Clipped to it is a gold brooch, with a black eye in the middle.

'Honoria,' Mister Charles says. 'First, as always.'

'You know how I hate being late, Charles,' she says, leaning her face towards him.

He gives a quick kiss to her cheek, like a bird pecking a crumb, and Pea-in-the-pod does the same. Then Poor Nora and the stooped-over man say their good-days, and there's so much pecking and hand-shaking, it's a wonder they're not all tired out.

'You're looking a bit off-colour, Helen,' the Bosom says to Missus Henderson.

'I'm in the best of health, thank you, Mother.'

My mammy always put her arms about me, but from the stiff way the Bosom is carrying on, you'd not know Missus Henderson was her daughter.

'And yourself, Honoria?' Mister Charles asks.

'Much as can be expected for a widow, all alone in the world.'

'Excuse me a moment, would you? I need to check Sam's filled the log baskets.'

The Bosom woman looks about her. Then she catches sight of me and my insides go all cold. 'Servants nowadays. Totally useless!' She raises her voice. 'Get a move on there, girl. Can you not see that Annie needs a hand?'

A man and a woman, both with hair the colour of old straw are standing in the doorway. 'A terrible wet day, Annie,' he says.

'It is indeed, Mister Irvine.'

'Ah, good. There's Charles. I was wanting a word.' And he moves off, just as two more people step inside.

'That green really doesn't look well on you, Helen,' a voice says, and when I look up, I catch my breath, because it's Missus Thompson, in a frock with such a low front to it, it's a wonder her bosoms are not catching the death of cold.

Missus Henderson steps towards her. 'Adelina. You must be soaked through. And Alexander too.'

'Good day to you, Helen.' He's different from how he looks in his own house – his boots have a great shine to them, and his jacket and trousers are very smart. You'd think Missus Thompson would be pleased, but she still scowls away at him. 'I'm jolted to bits in that old trap. I swear those pot-holes get worse every week. And you'd not believe the times I've begged Alexander to replace it.'

'We could always loan you one of our—?' Missus Henderson begins.

Mister Thompson shakes his head. 'Thank you, Helen, but no. Your sister and I live within our means, or not at all.' He turns to Pea-in-the-pod. 'How are those heifers coming along, John?' And the pair of them walk off across the hall.

Missus Thompson watches them a moment. 'Maybe, Helen, you and I could have a word sometime about that offer?'

'Of course.'

'Good, because—' Suddenly she looks over and sees me. 'What in the world's that half-wit doing here?'

I mightn't be a whole-wit, but it doesn't stop me wishing for a pot-hole to sink myself into.

'She's being a great help,' Missus Henderson says.

'Well, just keep her away from me.'

The Bosom moves closer. 'Am I to understand, Adelina,' she whispers, 'that this girl is one of the Carth Licks you've taken into your household? Have I not warned you often enough?'

Missus Thompson tosses her head, like Mary the pony does when she's having to stay still for too long. 'I thought you'd be pleased for me having the extra help. The girl may be a dead loss, but the mother's a good worker. And, as I keep telling Alexander, Nellie's well past it.'

The Bosom's chest gives a heave. 'Nellie's a decent Protestant woman. Would you not agree, Helen?'

But Missus Henderson is welcoming the next visitor, and it's another one I never wish to come across again. 'Bob,' she's saying, 'how are you doing?'

'The best, thank you, Helen,' he says, handing Annie his coat. 'And what a pleasure to see your sister after all this time.'

'How do you do, Mister Drummond,' Missus Thompson says, as if the two of them were never huffing away in the garden that time.

The straw-haired woman moves closer. 'I have to agree with your advice, Honoria. I wouldn't trust Carth Licks further than you can throw them.'

I don't want to be thrown anywhere, so I move back against the wall.

'Mind William doesn't hear you say that, Patricia. Where is he, by the way?'

Straw-hair lowers her voice. 'Maybe it's as well he's not here. You saw the solicitor take Charles off for a private word? He'll be giving John the inheritance for sure.'

'You can't help feeling sorry for William.'

'But who can blame Charles? Especially after those happenings in the south.'

The brooch on the Bosom's chest gives a jump. 'Ruff Yarns. Marching up to the house with their pitchforks. And all because their rents were being raised – in a perfectly proper way, I might add.'

'I heard the family had to lock themselves in until the militia arrived. Like animals they were – the Ten Aunts, I mean. And—'

'Annie!' Mister Charles is shouting across the hall. Everyone turns in his direction. 'Come here this minute!'

She moves over to him, and her eyes look like that cat of Mister Thompson's when he gave it a kick one time.

'Yes, Mister Charles?'

'The state of the dining room – it's really not good enough.'

'The dining room?'

'That's what I said. Are you deaf? Dirty marks on the carpet, and the fire all but out.'

'I'm really sorry Mister Charles.'

I'm sorry too, because I didn't think anyone would notice those bits of slug.

'I swear that dirt wasn't there earlier, Mister Charles.'

'Well, see to it now.'

'And I'll just check how things are going in the kitchen,' Missus Henderson says.

Mister Charles walks over. 'What are you thinking of, John? Letting everyone stand about here? There's a good fire in the front room. We'll eat as soon as everyone has arrived.'

The Bosom is smiling away at him, and with his silvery hair, and the lovely orange badge pinned to his jacket, he does look very well.

'I hope, ladies,' he says, 'I didn't hear any polly-tickle talk just now? You know it's a subject best left to us men. No –' he holds up a hand – 'this is one point, Honoria, on which I'll take no argument.'

'And I totally agree, Charles. I'm just trying to knock some sense into my youngest daughter.'

'Isn't her husband already doing just that?' Poor Nora says. But she speaks so softly, I don't think anyone hears her.

'Well come along then.' Mister Charles points a finger at me. 'You, girl. Stay here, and see to the door.'

When they've all gone off, Molly comes rushing past, carrying a bucket, with Annie following behind, still with that scared look on her. But there's no time to pay them any heed, because more people are arriving, and I'm busy opening the door, and taking their coats, and pointing them to where all the talk and laughs are coming from. There's a great heap of coats on the floor behind me, and I wish Kate were here to see what a grand job I'm doing.

'What a morning!' Annie is back in the hall. 'At least that's those stains gone. But just wait till I get hold of Sam because, as sure as eggs is eggs, he's the cause of them.'

I'm glad it's Sam getting the blame, because I don't want myself and Kate to be turned out.

'Mister Charles says that's everyone arrived,' Annie says, 'so we can start serving the meal.' She looks over at the coats. 'Count yourself lucky he didn't see those dumped on the floor like that. You'll find plenty of hooks in the passage.'

I scoop up a load of coats. The men's ones are all scratchy, and smell of the damp. But the women's are softer. One is made of fur, and is a brown colour, like a rabbit's. I'd spend all day stroking it if I could.

But after I hang the first load, there's no room for any more, so there's nothing for it but to carry the rest into the scullery. I don't want them on the draining board, on account of any slugs, so I tip out the potatoes from the big basins, and lay the coats across them. They spill over the edges, but I push them down until they all fit in.

I hear steps, and then Molly and Margaret come walking past with a big pot of soup, and baskets of bread. They smell really grand, but it makes me think how empty my belly is.

In the kitchen, Missus Purdy is still sitting by the range. She has on some black boots that are like the ones that Missus Mack-Elroy wears, only these have no straps across them and are newer-looking. Kate is lifting a big piece of meat from the oven, and placing it beside a dish of roast spuds. Their skins are all crispy and brown, and there's one, two jugs of gravy, and another dish with carrots in it. She stirs in a spoon of butter, and as I step closer, I see them go all shiny.

I give a smile, but she puts her hands on her hips. 'Molly says you were in the dining room, and you know you're not to go in that part of the house. As if I haven't enough to do without minding you all day.'

I feel my lip go all trembly.

'Well, the child's here now,' Missus Purdy says. 'She missed the scones we had earlier, so no doubt she's hungry.'

'Let her wait. It'll do her good.'

'Here.' Missus Purdy hands me a slice of bread, with a spread of butter on it.

'There's stew for us all later, when Mister Charles and the rest have finished their meal.'

I take a bite out of the bread, and the butter's spread so thick, it escapes down my chin. And as I lick it up, I'm thinking that nothing in my whole life has tasted as grand.

The door opens. 'Ah, good,' Missus Henderson says. 'I see the meat's cooked to perfection as always, Grace.'

Missus Purdy wipes a hand across her forehead. 'I'd not have managed without Kate.'

'I'm glad we got you the help. But you're still very pale, Grace. I think the doctor had better take a look at you.'

'The morning will do fine, Missus Henderson.'

74

'Well, I suppose you're right. Mister Charles wouldn't want any delay in the meal.' She turns to Kate. 'I have to tell you that the child has been a big help also.'

My insides go all warm.

Kate stares at me. 'She has?'

'Setting the table, seeing to the front door. It made a big difference, and—' She swings round. 'Ah, and here at last is my husband.'

He's the tall, thin man with a moustache like a mouse's tail. Sam and Francis are with him. They have their jackets over their shoulders, and bring a powerful smell of the stables with them.

I wait for Missus Henderson to start yelling at Mister Henderson, like Missus Thompson does. But instead, she says, 'You got it sorted then, William?'

'One of the mares chose this moment to drop her foal. But I'm thankful to say that all's now well.'

I'm wondering if the poor animal had a telling-off, like I would get whenever a dish drops out of my hand.

'Jim Irvine has been having quite a talk with your father,' Missus Henderson says.

'Has he indeed?' For a moment, Mister Henderson's face takes on a sad look. 'Well, what will be, will be.' Then his eyes fasten on the piece of meat. 'All I can think this minute is that I'm so hungry, I could eat a stable of horses.'

I wait for someone to tell him that it's beef he's getting, but Missus Henderson laughs.

He puts an arm about her. 'I'll be with you the moment I get washed.'

What with his pale eyes, long face, and that mouse-tail stuck to his lip, he's a plain sort of a man. But when he smiles down at her, I'm wishing it was me there beside him.

When they've gone out, Sam says, 'He's not the only person to be starved around here.'

I'm chewing the last of my bread, and he grins across at me. 'Any chance of some of that, Missus Purdy?'

'You'll be lucky to get another mouthful in this house, Sam Morris!'

He stares at her. 'Why, what have I done?'

'You know perfectly well what. Filth from the yard over that dining-room carpet, and the fire almost out. And Mister Charles blaming it all on Annie! She's beside herself, I can tell you.'

'But I never...'

She shakes her head at him. 'Out in the yard the pair of you!' He and Francis go shuffling off and, although I'm sorry about the slugs, I'm glad it's not me being sent away.

'Now,' Missus Purdy says, as Molly and Margaret return with a load of empty dishes, 'let's get that roast served up.'

And for the next while, I stay quiet as a mouse in the corner. And when the last of the dishes are off the table, Missus Purdy says, 'I'm just going to have a bit of a lie-down, Kate. The other three will be busy in the dining room for a while, so I'll leave the pudding to you. If you want me for anything, my room's opposite the scullery.'

'You take all the rest you need, Missus Purdy. We'll manage just grand.'

So Kate and I are left alone, and it's all gone very quiet, but for the tick-tick of the clock on the dresser. I hold my breath, because I know I'm in a for a slapping, on account of all the things I've got wrong, though I'm not sure which one she'll pick on first.

She turns towards me. 'I'm sorry I was so cross with you earlier, Brede. It's just there was so much to do, I didn't know where to put myself.' She pulls out a chair. 'The others will be a while yet, and I reckon we've earned a bit of a rest.'

I move to the table, and we sit side-by-side in two chairs. And my insides give a jump, because this is just how I used to sit with my mammy, before the sickness took her. And she used always to be talking away, and when she wasn't too busy seeing to the babby, or the cooking, she'd beat the time with a spoon so I could practise my steps.

'You've really surprised me today, Brede,' Kate says. 'Who'd have thought you'd be such a help to Missus Henderson?'

I'd not have thought it either.

'So all I'm asking is that you talk a wee bit. It doesn't have to be anything very much. Maybe just give your name when you're asked. Could you do that for me?'

I reach for her hand, wishing I could tell her that the words are all there, but they're stuck inside my head. And it beats me how I can get them to come out.

'I'm not always in the best of tempers with you, Brede. It's just sometimes from the way you carry on, I'm afraid of us ending up in the Poor House. You'd not like that, would you?'

And I give her hand a squeeze to show how sorry I am for the place.

'There's just the two of us now, and we must stick together.'

And just as I'm feeling gladder than ever that she doesn't know about them slugs, we hear a great shout.

'What in the world—?' Kate says, as steps come running along the passage.

The door flies open, and Molly yells, 'Come quick, the pair of you! Something terrible's happened!'

Kate and I jump up and go running after her, and as we reach the end of the passage, we see a crowd in the far doorway. Closest to us is Missus Thompson, and Missus Henderson, with Poor Nora, and Mister Thompson, and the Drummond man. And kneeling on the floor is Mister Henderson, with Pea-in-the-pod beside him. And they're all staring down at the floor.

It takes me a while to see round all the heads, but then I spot the black boots.

Kate puts a hand to her face. 'Please not Missus Purdy,' she whispers.

And Pea-in-the-pod looks up, and narrows his eyes at her.

Because it's not Missus Purdy we're seeing, but old Mister Charles, with his blue eyes staring up at the ceiling, and all the colour gone from his cheeks.

NINE

Iᴛ'ꜱ ᴀ ᴡᴇᴛ ᴏʟᴅ ᴍᴏʀɴɪɴɢ, ᴀɴᴅ I'ᴍ ɢʟᴀᴅ ᴛᴏ ʙᴇ inside, listening to the rain going splish-splash onto the roof.

The Thompsons are taking their breakfast, and Kate has allowed me to carry the basket of bread, but I've to wait in the passage, while she serves them their food. Bacon, mushrooms and sausages for him, and a hen's egg boiled for one, two, three, four minutes for her.

Kate's been told to stay in the room, in case there's anything they need.

Through the open door, I hear Mister Thompson say, 'Not another trip into the town, Adelina? You were in Knockmarran only a few days ago.' His voice is as cold as the rain, and if I were her, I'd pay more heed to it.

'Surely even you must understand that I can't attend Charles' funeral dressed in anything but black?'

I don't rightly know what a funeral is. I don't think my mammy and da had one. When the people in our village stopped their breathing, they were tipped into a big pit for the saints to collect later.

'What you'd do well to understand is that I'm not putting up with any more of this spending.' He takes a slurp of his tea. 'But no matter. I've told the shops that from now on, they're only to supply you with goods for the house.'

'But I promise it won't happen again.'

'Ah, but can I trust you?' He pauses. 'After the way you've carried on.'

'Carried on?' And now her voice has a tremble to it.

'You know full well what I'm talking about.'

She gives a gasp. 'How did you—?'

'I have eyes, Adelina. All that silk and lace and fancy cups and plates. Money doesn't grow on trees, you know.'

Any eejit knows that.

'I'm truly sorry, Alexander.' She's speaking very softly, but her voice has lost its shake. 'I take your point over not buying a new trap, but surely you'd allow me a frock for the funeral?'

'Well – put like that.'

'Thank you. I'll take a run into the town later.'

They go all quiet and I have a peep through the gap in the door. It's such a dark old morning, the two lamps are lit, and they shine across the table where there's a big dish filled with blackberry jam. I know that just one spoonful would do me a power of good, but there's no getting Kate to see that.

She has her back to me, but I can see past her to where Mister and Missus Thompson are sitting. She has on that gorgeous blue frock, and when she moves her head, her earrings that are cream coloured, each one hanging off a piece of wire, sway from side to side.

Mister Thompson gives a sigh. 'If only—'

'What, Alexander?'

He wipes his mouth on his sleeve. 'I don't suppose there's any sign this month…?'

'No,' she says, and her voice has gone all sad.

Then she turns, and I duck behind the door.

'No need for you to be standing around, Kate. I'm sure you've plenty to be getting on with in the kitchen.'

'Yes, Missus Thompson.'

She hurries out of the room, nodding at me to follow.

'A wet old day for Missus Thompson's trip to the town,' Kate says to Missus Mack-Elroy, who's still finishing her breakfast.

Through the window I see the rain still falling and when I went out to the hens earlier, there was a mist like smoke hanging over the yard.

Missus Mack-Elroy stares. 'She never mentioned anything about that to me.'

'She wants a new frock for Mister Charles's funeral.'

'Well, I can tell you now, Kate, that you have it quite wrong. Because she always has the dressmaker come to the house. You'd not believe the hours they spend while Missus Thompson chooses.'

'I'm only telling you what I heard.'

'Less of the tittle-tattle, and in case you hadn't noticed,

the breakfast dishes need clearing. And then we need to make a start on the laundry.'

For a moment, I recall my mammy laying our clothes over the fewsher bushes to dry, and my insides go all sad.

Missus Mack-Elroy holds out her cup. 'Fill this up, would you?'

The pot is right beside her, but Kate wipes her hands on her apron. 'Certainly, Missus Mack-Elroy.'

She's just poured it, and is back at the sink, when Missus Mack-Elroy holds out her cup again. 'Oh – and some sugar. Two spoons, and be sure to give it a good stir.'

'Brede'll put it in for you.'

When I take the cup, Missus Mack-Elroy says, 'The bowl is on the dresser, and for God's sake, don't go breaking anything!'

The bowl is white with yellow stripes, like ribbons, running round it. I place the cup beside the bowl and put one, two spoons of sugar into it. Missus Mack-Elroy is busy talking to Kate, so I gather a big gob of spit in my mouth and land it right in the middle of the cup. Then I give it a stir, and hand the cup to Missus Mack-Elroy. The gob is there, floating in the middle, but she doesn't give it a look.

'None of it in the saucer. Wonders will never cease!'

'Good girl, Brede,' Kate says.

I give a smile, and go on smiling as I watch Missus Mack-Elroy sitting there, enjoying her tea.

When the breakfast things are cleared, I help Kate lift the big pan onto the stove. The clothes are tipped into it, along with the soap, and they start boiling away, until the kitchen is as misted-up as the yard was earlier.

Then Missus Mack-Elroy hands Kate a bucket. 'These will need to be soaked, and when you have them washed, they're to be hung in the scullery.'

Kate fills the bucket with water, and places it in the corner. It has a lid on it and when she has her back turned, I take a peep. Then I drop the lid with a clash, because the inside is filled with blood. So maybe this is the vessel that Missus Thompson spoke of one time. And my belly gives a heave.

Kate comes over. 'They're just the cloths Missus Thompson uses for her monthlies. I have them too, and you will one day, when you're grown.'

I don't like the sound of them, but wherever all that blood comes from, you'd think someone would take the trouble to stop it.

'Married two years,' Missus Mack-Elroy says, 'and still nothing to show for it.'

'Poor lady,' Kate says.

It's a puzzle why they're talking like that, when Missus Thompson has all of them beautiful clothes.

'I wouldn't waste your breath on that one. Eyeing up all the fellows, and now there's talk of—' She gives a jump, because Missus Thompson is standing in the doorway.

'I've decided to go into the town,' she says. 'I'll need you to come with me, Kate, to help with the parcels.'

'Certainly, Missus Thompson.'

'You're not sending for the dressmaker, then?' Missus Mack-Elroy says.

'I fancy the air. And I wouldn't dream of bringing you

83

out on such a day.' Missus Thompson's voice is as silky as her hair. 'Better that you stay nice and warm by the fire.'

'Well, my bones do suffer terribly in this wet.'

'Tell Francis to have the trap ready, Kate. And we'll need to have the hood up.'

'Of course, Missus Thompson.'

When she's gone out, Missus Mack-Elroy taps her nose. 'I wonder what she's up to this time?'

'What do you mean?'

'No good, I'll be bound.'

Out in the yard, Kate whispers, 'What in the world's the woman on about now?'

I give my head a shake, because I don't know either, and anyway, what does it matter when a while later Francis is driving us off down the lane? I'm perched on Kate's knee, with Missus Thompson beside us. She has on a lovely purple coat, and the hat with the feather sticking out of it. We have the hood up and with a blanket over our knees, we're hardly feeling the wet.

We go along the mountain road, and onto the straight stretch with the fields on either side. We pass the lane that leads to the big house with the green creeping up the walls and that gorgeous flag and, after a while, we see some roofs sticking out above the trees. 'Knockmarran,' Missus Thompson says. 'And over there is the linen factory.' She points to a great big building with a load of windows, and the tallest chimney I've seen in the whole of my life.

'I suppose women as well as men work in it?' Kate asks.

'They do indeed. Though why any girl would choose

to spend her days there, rather than in the comfort of a good home, is beyond me!'

We enter a street, with more buildings on either side, and I lean forward to take a closer look. It's the first town I've been in, and the windows on either side are filled with a load of stuff. We pass a place selling meat that's hung on hooks with patches of blood under them; and another with buckets and brooms outside, and another with boxes of cabbages and spuds.

'What a big place,' Kate says.

Missus Thompson gives a laugh. 'More of a one-horse town, if you ask me.'

She's wrong there, because coming towards us is a carriage pulled by a brown horse, and behind it is another trap with a grey-looking pony, so with Mary that makes one, two, three horses.

And then ahead of us, I see a building propped up on two posts, and it puts me in mind of Mister Burk with his sticks. Above its door is a big sign that I can't make out, because although Kate's tried to learn me my letters, I keep forgetting them.

Missus Thompson pokes Francis with her umbrella. 'Pull into the hotel yard there.'

We go through an arch, and Francis says, 'Whoa there, Mary!' and the pony comes to a stop. The yard has walls on one, two, three sides and is empty, apart from a man in a dirty apron, leaning against a door and smoking a pipe. When he sees us, he knocks his pipe against the wall, and heads into the building at a great rate.

'Good,' Missus Thompson says, 'all nice and quiet.

We don't want everyone knowing our business.' She steps from the trap, and all of a sudden the rain stops, and I feel the sun warm on my face.

She reaches into her pocket, and pats her face with her handkerchief. It's the gorgeous blue one with the flowers across it. 'Wait here, Francis. I'll not be long. Kate, you come with me.'

Kate signs for me to follow, so the two of them go along the street, with me following behind. There's a deal of people going past, all in a tremendous hurry. A man with a neat-looking beard, and a row of badges pinned to his coat, gives a bow. 'I'm sorry for your loss, Missus Thompson. Your father will be sorely missed.'

'Indeed,' she says, but it's as if she's only half listening.

An old woman leads a girl along by the hand. The girl is shorter than me, and has a green shawl over her frock. I'd like a shawl that colour, but all I have is the old brown one that Missus Mack-Elroy found for me. Another man lifts his hat in the air when he sees Missus Thompson, and a fat woman carrying a basket steps aside as she passes.

She stops by a window that's filled with rolls of fabric. They're all different colours – green and yellow and red and orange – like the mat she has at home. I could stare at them all day long, but she pushes open the door and steps inside, and Kate and myself follow.

The shop is empty, so I stand inside the door, and look about me. Straight ahead there's a wooden counter, covered with rolls of material, and there's loads more on the shelves behind. I never knew there could be this much cloth in the one place.

A man steps forward. He has nice brown hair, and a neat-looking beard. 'My deepest sympathy, Missus Thompson, although I have to say this is a pleasant surprise. You don't usually honour us with a visit.' When he smiles, I see a gap where his front tooth should be. 'Now, how can I be of help?'

'I need a dress for the funeral, Jim.'

'Of course. Poor Mister Charles. He's a big loss to the Order. Why, I think he ran the last march single-handed.'

Missus Thompson picks up the nearest roll of fabric. 'How much?'

'Very reasonably priced, for silk. New in this week too, and if I may say so, an excellent choice. Grey is so much less draining than black.'

She bites her lip. 'My husband hasn't sent word to you, then?'

He shakes his head. 'No. What—?'

'I'll take the whole roll, then. And the crimson one beside it. And buttons and ribbons to go with them.'

'Very good. I'll have them parcelled up for you in no time.'

Outside the shop, Missus Thompson stops and bites her lip. 'I've other business in the town, Kate, so wait for me by the trap. The girl here can collect the packages when they're ready.'

'Very good, Missus Thompson,' Kate says and, as she passes me, she mouths:

'Stay inside, Brede!'

But she's not been gone long, when two women come in. With their wide skirts and big hats, there's not a deal of

87

room, and one of them says, 'Can you not see you're in the way, girl? Out of here, this minute!'

So I step into the street, and there, just a little way off, is Missus Thompson, and I'm glad she has her back to me, because I don't want another telling-off. She's standing quite still and has her hands up to her face. And I'm thinking it's no wonder she's so bothered, because Mister Thompson won't like her buying all that cloth.

Then, all of a sudden, she turns and begins walking away up the street. It's all very quiet and is filled with patches of water, and piles of manure that steam away in the sun.

She crosses to the other side of the street, and every so often she stops and stares about her, as if she doesn't know what she's about.

A boy driving a cart goes by, and pools of rain spray up on either side. She smooths down her skirts, and as she moves off again, I see something blue falls from her sleeve.

I open my mouth to shout, 'Stop, Missus Thompson!' but not a word comes out. Kate's not here to tell me what to do, so I kick the ground with my shoe, and then start heading after Missus Thompson.

When I reach the handkerchief, I pick it up. I could keep it safe for later, but I'm thinking that she'll be needing it.

She's stopped in front of a green-coloured building, and as I come running along, she goes up some steps to a big door. I hear a rap-rap, and then the door opens, and in she goes.

I wait a moment, and then I climb the steps to the top. The door isn't closed properly, so I give it a push and step inside. I'm in a small room with an open door in front of me. I walk over and put my head round. There's a lamp in the far corner, but it's all dark and shadowy, and there's not a sign of Missus Thompson. I'm afraid of bumping into things, so I move to the side. After a moment, I make out two big tables and some chairs, and a stand with coats on it, and a pile of paper stacked against the wall. I crouch beside one of the desks. The place smells of dirty washing, and I can hear my heart going bump-bump in my chest, and I'm wishing I'd stayed in that shop like I was told to.

I'm just deciding to make a run for it outside, when a voice says, 'You can finish for the day, Reid. I'll clear up here.'

'Thank you, sir,' and a thin kind of a man comes past me, and goes out of the door.

Then the voice says, 'Step this way, Missus Thompson,' and I see that she's been standing a little way ahead of me all the time. I can make out her coat, and the hat with the feather sticking up. She has her back turned, and is keeping herself very still. Now she moves forward, without speaking.

'I'll just lock up,' the man says, 'so we're not disturbed.'

He comes past me to the door. He's holding a big bunch of keys, and as he walks, he goes huff-huff. And it's then I realise he's the Drummond man, who was with Missus Thompson in the garden that time. They were cross enough when they spotted me then, so what'll they do if they catch me in here?

But it's too late to run back into the street. The next minute he turns the key in the lock, scrape-scrape, and I'm shut in with the pair of them.

TEN

H IS FEET COME TO A STOP, AND I HEAR HIS BREATH going in-out, in-out.

I curl myself behind a desk. *What in the world are you doing now, Brede?* I can hear Kate saying. *Get up this minute!*

Missus Thompson's steps go click-click towards me. 'You've sent Reid off for the day, then?'

'Indeed. We'll be quite alone, I promise you.' I hear a drawer opening. 'Will you take a glass of something?'

'Thank you, no.' There's a silence. 'I hope this won't take long.' She gives one of her pretend laughs. 'If I'm not home within the hour, Alexander will wonder where on earth I've got to.'

'Ah, how's that husband of yours doing?'

'In the best of health, thank you.'

'I'm glad to hear it.'

The floor is all splintery under my knees, and I can see a load of dust in one corner. I could do with a spider for company, but there's only a grey slater crawling towards me. When I give it a poke, it rolls itself into a ball, so here's the two of us curled away together.

I hear a gulp, and then the Drummond man says, 'That's better! But you're shivering, Adelina.'

'It is rather chilly in here.'

My drawers feel all cold and wet and, as I pull my shawl across my chest, I'm wishing I'd never followed Missus Thompson along the street. I'm still holding on to her handkerchief. I put it up to my nose, and it has a lovely smell, as if those flowers have just been picked.

'Let me put a match to the fire,' the Drummond man says.

'Please don't bother.'

'No bother, dear.'

The rain has started again, making a noise, drum-drum, over my head. There's the strike of a match, and he gives a grunt. 'That's catching nicely. It'll soon warm you up.'

'It's very good of you to help out like this,' Missus Thompson says. 'As I explained when you came to the house, there's been more bother over some bills.' Her voice is all soft, like when she asks Mister Thompson for a new frock. 'You know how unreasonable these shop people can be.'

'Indeed.'

'But can you expect Alexander to understand? And he has got such a temper on him.'

'Poor Adelina. All those bruises. But I'm sure that between us we can fix things.'

'Thank you, Bob.' Now there's a smile in her voice. 'I knew you'd see it my way.'

He's begun to huff again, and I risk a peek round the desk. They're standing by the fire, with their backs to me, so now's my chance. I crunch up the handkerchief and crawl forward. Then I throw it as hard as I can and it lands right in the middle of the floor.

I wait for one of them to turn, but all he says is, 'It's just a pity you're having this spot of difficulty.'

'So I wondered,' – her voice goes so soft I have to lean round the desk again to hear – 'if you'd have another think?'

Now it's his turn to laugh. 'Oh no, dear, I think not.'

'It's just I can't imagine how I ever agreed to this. A moment's madness, I suppose.'

'Or sanity, dear – given what you've told me about Alexander.'

'God knows what he'll do if he ever finds out about this visit!'

'Well, we must just make sure that never happens.'

'You'll not change your mind, then?'

'We have a deal. Remember?'

She sighs. 'Anything else doesn't bear thinking about.'

'I knew you'd see reason.'

He moves from the fire, and stoops down. 'Here, you've dropped your hand-kerchief.'

'What was that noise?' she says.

I crouch behind the desk again.

'Just a gust of wind. No need to be so jumpy. I told you no one can get in.'

Their feet move over to the desk. 'Here's the envelope,' he says. 'It's all here, as you can see. Now, let me take your coat and hat.'

'Oh, I'd rather keep them on.'

'Nonsense. I'll put them by the fire. They'll be nice and warm by the time we leave.'

'Very well.'

'Come over here.'

'If I must.'

'Damn it, Adelina, it's a bit late to go all coy on me.'

I hear the rustle of her skirts, and he says, 'Now then, how about a nice kiss, to start things off?'

When I take another peek, they're standing facing one another, and he has his mouth fastened on hers. There's a sound like Mister Thompson makes when he drinks his tea.

Missus Thompson steps back against the wall, and the Drummond man removes his jacket. It's the one with orange and green lines across it – and hangs it over his chair. Then he removes his necktie.

'You'll have to help me with my frock.' She turns her back on him, and he starts to unfasten her. He's taking a deal of time over it, which is no surprise because I remember seeing the buttons. They're a lovely cream colour, and there's a whole row of them, like small teeth. Then I hear something tear, and one flies up into the air, and goes ping-ping across the floor. And I'm thinking there'll be plenty of mending for Missus Mack-Elroy to do.

Missus Thompson's frock drops to the floor, and when she turns round, she's standing in just her underclothes – the pink ones that I remember from washday. If I were her, I'd worry about catching cold, because there's not a deal of heat from the fire.

He backs her against the wall, and I crawl forward to take a closer look. He slips his hand inside her bodice, and she hitches up her petticoats, and lowers her drawers. When he puts his hand between her legs, I go even closer, because if they want a babby, they should be lying down, with him on top, like my mammy and da used.

Then he reaches his other hand into his breeches, and I can't rightly see what he's doing, but after a moment he starts shoving against her for all he's worth. She goes bump-bump, against the wall, and she's all floppy, like the rag doll I once had. I really liked that doll. She was called Deidre, which was the name of a famous queen of Ireland, who fought in battles and did a load of other stuff I can't remember, because it's a while since Kate told me the story.

The Drummond man is huff-huffing even louder. Missus Thompson has her eyes shut, and says not one word, and I'm hoping he's not hurting her. His head is how I remember it from that time when they were on the bench together – bald as a stone, with one, two brown patches in the middle.

Then she lets out a laugh that makes me jump.

'I'm just picturing my mother walking in on us. Can you imagine the face she'd have on her?' And she laughs again.

'You Feck Ing haw,' he whispers.

I don't know rightly know what a haw is, but his voice is none too friendly.

Suddenly he gives a great shout that makes me jump again. When I put my head out, he's stopped shoving against her, and is buttoning his breeches. She takes out her handkerchief. I thought it was only for blowing your nose on, but she wipes it around the inside of her legs before placing it on the desk. After he's helped her with the buttons, he picks up her handkerchief, and presses it against his face. He goes all red, which is no wonder when it stops him breathing.

'If you've quite finished,' she says – and her voice is so cold, my insides turn over – 'I'll take what's owing. And then perhaps you'd unlock the door?'

'Certainly.' He hands her the envelope that she tucks down her front. 'I trust our encounter gave satisfaction?'

'Make no mistake, you horrible old man. This will never happen again.'

Her voice makes me want to run as far and as fast as I can, but he's not one bit put out. 'I like a woman with spirit. And you've certainly got plenty of that, dear.' He clicks off the lamps, and moves to the door.

My chest is heaving up and down, because I need to make a run for it, but suppose he tries to grab hold of me as I go past?

It's gone very quiet – the only sound is the turn of the key in the lock, and then grey light from the street comes creeping in.

He holds open the door. 'Good day to you, then,

Missus Thompson. My best regards to Alexander. Oh, and you know where to find me, if I can be of further help.'

She doesn't answer, and I hear her steps go click-clicking away.

I peer out. The Drummond man is fetching the handkerchief from the far desk. Then he comes towards the door again. He places the handkerchief on a table beside him, and reaches for his coat.

Now's my chance, so I jump up.

'What in the name of God…?' he shouts.

I push past, snatching up the handkerchief as I go. But the step has a raised part that I don't see, so I go arse-over-tip down to the street. And when I pick myself up, who should be standing over me but Missus Thompson.

I feel my heart going thump-thump.

She narrows her eyes. 'What on earth…?'

The Drummond man is beside her, and his face is even more red with the breath coming out of him very fast. 'She must have been shut inside.'

'Oh my God. All the time?'

He nods.

Her voice drops to a whisper. 'Whatever shall we do?'

'Well…' he begins.

I don't wait to hear more, but start running back down the street, going splash-splash through the puddles. I cross the road, and go past a shop, where a dark-haired girl is putting up the shutters for the night; past a place with a load of brown bottles in the window, and past the shop with the rolls of fabric in it. Ahead of me is the hotel, resting on its two sticks, and beyond it, the arch that leads into the yard.

When I take a peek over my shoulder, there's not a sign of Missus Thompson, or of the Drummond man, so I run into the yard, and there facing me is the trap, with Francis and Kate sitting in it. And I'm so glad to be safely back that I put my arms round Mary, and hug her for all I'm worth.

Kate climbs out of the trap. 'Stop that, Brede, or you'll choke her. And where in the world have you been? I've gone up and down that street I don't know how many times looking for you.'

Mary gives me a nudge with her head, so I know she's wondering about it too.

'And the state of you! Mud all over your skirt.' She brushes me down. 'And I can't think where Missus Thompson has got to either.'

I picture her with her drawers down, going bang-bang against the wall with the Drummond man, and I wish I could tell Kate about it, so she can take away the sick feeling I have inside me.

'Keeping us waiting all this time,' Francis says. 'If that's not Feck Ing typical!'

'Language, Francis!' Then she puts a hand to her mouth. 'Those parcels, Brede? What have you done with them?' She looks into my face, and sees I've clean forgotten them. She lets out a sigh. 'I'll fetch them. And I just hope Mister Whelan's not shut up shop for the night.' She turns back to me. 'Get into that trap this minute. Francis, you make sure she stays there.'

I climb into the back, wondering what in the world Missus Thompson will do when she next sees me.

Francis turns in his seat. 'I bet you could say a thing or two, if you chose.'

But I'm too tired to even give him a look.

And the next thing I know Kate is back and Francis is helping Missus Thompson up beside us. 'Get going then, Francis,' she says.

I perch on Kate's knee. She places a lantern at our feet, and we move out of the yard, and into the street.

Missus Thompson keeps looking at me. There's an odd smell that I'm hoping is not from my drawers. But when the trap gives a jolt so that I almost fall to the side, I'm thinking that it's coming off her, and it's like some of the clothes Mister Thompson puts out for the wash.

'I hope you had a good day in the town, Missus Thompson,' Kate says. 'Did you get what you came for?'

'How do you mean?' There's that spike in her voice again.

'Just that you were away quite a while, and have no parcels with you. So I was just wondering if there was anything else that needed collecting?'

'And you think it's your place to question me?'

'I'm sorry, Missus Thompson, I was only trying to—'

When she turns towards us, her face is like a big, black cloud. 'I'll let you know when I want you to speak. Do I make myself clear?'

Kate bites her lip. 'Yes, Missus Thompson.'

She pokes Francis in the back. 'Get a move on, you lazy good-for-nothing. Do you think I want to be stuck out here all night?'

He flicks his whip, and Mary breaks into a trot that makes the trap roll from side to side, and I have to clutch on to Kate to stop myself falling.

We go along the road a good way, past the turning that leads to the lions. Although there's a bit of moon, the mountain beside us is all black and scary, and when an owl goes hoot-hoot, I feel Kate give a shiver.

I'm still holding Missus Thompson's handkerchief, so I put it to my nose, like I saw the Drummond man do. But it doesn't smell of flowers anymore, and even in the lantern light, I can see there's streaks of dirt on it.

I glance up at Kate, but she has her eyes closed. *Nothing a good wash won't fix!* I can hear her saying. And then I'm thinking how glad Missus Thompson will be to have her handkerchief safely back.

I tap her on the knee, and when she turns to me, I hold it out. The next moment, she lets out such a screech that Kate and I give a jump.

'All right back there?' Francis says.

'You pay attention to the road.' Then she whispers, 'Where did you get that?'

'Get what?' Kate says. 'What are you talking about?'

'Make the child tell you how she came by it!' Now Missus Thompson is shouting, and I drum my feet on the boards.

'Came by what?'

'That handkerchief, you stupid girl!'

Kate looks at it a moment. 'I'm sorry, Missus Thompson, but as you know, Brede can't speak.'

'Can't? Or won't?'

I start to cry, and Kate slaps my arm to stop.

'Well,' Missus Thompson says. 'I don't know where she's picked it up from, but it's not mine anyway.' And she leans forward, and throws it into the lane.

Kate stares in surprise.

For the rest of the way, neither of them says a word and I sit with my eyes shut very tight, just wishing I could explain things to her.

The trap pulls up at the front of the house and Missus Thompson steps down. 'You and your daughter are to stay in the kitchen,' she says. 'I don't want to see either of your faces again.' She looks up at Kate. 'And don't think for one minute there's a household in the area that's going to employ you. Not after what's just happened.'

Kate lets out a gasp and we watch Missus Thompson go inside, her feet moving very quick on account of the wet.

Francis drives us round to the yard. There's a light in the kitchen window, and I can see Missus Mack-Elroy sitting at the table.

Kate helps me down. 'What in the name of God has got into Missus Thompson?' she says to Francis. 'Friendly as you please on the way into town, and now she's like a bear with a sore head.'

I remember old Missus Burk showing me a picture of a bear in a book that she had. She told me the creatures like fish best of all, but I don't recall her saying anything about them having bad heads.

Francis leans towards us. 'If I were you, Kate, I'd be moving on.'

'Moving on?' Her voice has a wobble to it, and I squeeze her hand. 'But Missus Thompson will get over it, surely? She has these moods all the time. You've seen the way she is with Mister Thompson and now carrying on about her handkerchief!'

'There's never any knowing with that one. But I can tell you this – it went just this way with the girl that was here before you – and the one before that.' He shakes his head. 'One moment, nice as pie, and the next…' He draws his hand across his throat. 'Once she takes against you, it always ends the same.'

'If only I knew what we're meant to have done.' I can see she's holding in the tears.

'I've a cousin who can fix you up at the mill.'

'The Mill?' Kate looks at him. 'Oh, I'm not sure.'

'It's hard work, but you'd have food and a roof over your heads.'

'I suppose we've no choice.' She thinks for a moment. 'But why would you be doing this for us?'

He taps his nose. 'My ma brought me up a Prod, and that's what everyone thinks I am, because how else can a fellow get any decent work around here? But my da, who took off when I was just a lad, was a Carth Lick. And that's where my loyalties lie.' He turns up the collar of his coat. 'Shall I get a message to my cousin, so?'

'That would be grand.'

'Well, I'd better see to the pony, or Missus Thompson will have the hide off me too.' He clicks his tongue. 'Gee up there, Mary,' and the trap rattles off to the stable.

I move closer to Kate, waiting for her to tell me

everything will be all right. But even when I give her arm a tug, she doesn't move.

The wet has set in again harder than ever, and when I look up, I can't tell if it's rain or tears on her face.

ELEVEN

I'T'S A FINE DAY, WITH JUST A BIT OF A BREEZE
blowing, and a grand smell of gorse in the air. I'm back
in the pony trap, along with Kate and Missus Thompson.
She has on her boots with the buttons up the side. Ahead
of us the mountain is stretched out on its side, as if it's
enjoying a snooze in the warm. On the slope beside us,
patches of yellow sunshine are leaking onto the green, like
when the wrong garment gets added to the wash.

The trap gives a rattle, and Missus Thompson says,
'Easy there, Francis. Do you want us in the ditch?' But her
voice is soft, and she's stopped narrowing her eyes when
she looks at me.

Kate is humming a tune called 'Robin on the Post', and
as my feet go tap-tap in time to it, I feel all warm inside.

'Keep a close watch now, Brede,' Kate says, 'because it
was about here that it was dropped.'

I'm sure we were nearer the house at the time, but I lean forward, and watch Mary's hooves go clop-clop along the road. By the side, the rain has left brown pools of water – the brown is from the turf, Kate says. And there's reeds growing beside them, and one, two, three rabbits sitting up to take a good look at us as we go by.

I'm so busy staring about me that I've clean forgotten what it is I'm searching for. Then Francis flicks his whip, and I let out a cry. The grass on my straw-foot side is covered with pieces of china, and they're the ones from all the dishes and bowls and jugs I've broke. Kate has stopped her humming, so I know she's spotted them too.

Missus Thompson points at the pony, and gives a 'tch', which is a sure sign she's getting cross too. At first I think it's because the pony has on Missus Thompson's blue frock, but then I see it's her best handkerchief – the one with the line of flowers across it – spread over her backside.

Missus Thompson seizes my arm. 'You stupid haw!' she yells. 'This is all your doing!'

And Kate takes hold of me on the other side, and starts shaking me for all she's worth. And now my mammy comes walking down the slope, the broken pieces going crunch-crunch under her shoes. Her head has come loose and her neck has a load of blood running down it. She holds her head in front of her. 'Brede!' she cries. 'I told you to put this out to dry.'

*

105

'Brede!'

Kate is standing over me. It's still very dark, and as I hear the rain falling, drip-drip, onto the roof, I heave a sigh of relief to be safely in my bed.

She gives me a shake. 'Get up!' she whispers. 'We're leaving.'

I pull the blanket closer about me.

The next moment she has it whipped off. *'Now!'* she hisses. 'And not a sound out of you.'

There's no arguing when she's in this mood, so I pull on my clothes as quick as I can. The floor is all cold and damp under my feet, and when I knock into a chair, she gives my arm a slap.

I don't know where we're going, but wherever it is, I wish we weren't.

When we've used the privy, she lights a lamp, and we creep along to the kitchen, hand-in-hand, like the first time we were here, and the place was full of smoke because Missus Mack-Elroy burnt the dinner.

The room is empty, apart from the old cat, who arches its back when it sees us. I stamp my foot at it. 'Quiet!' Kate whispers.

I go to put on the kettle, but 'Not today, Brede,' she says. 'We'll have our breakfast once we're clear of the house.'

'We're only taking what's due to us,' she says, putting some cheese and the end of a loaf into a bag. 'Missus Mack-Elroy's a light sleeper, so we'll have to go round the front.'

She takes a look round the room. 'I can't say I'll miss her – or this house.'

I'm hoping we're not leaving on account of Missus Thompson's handkerchief, but Kate makes no mention of it.

She puts a finger to her lips. 'Not a sound now.'

The rain has eased off and there's just a fine drizzle, like mist, against my face. I drop her hand, and go running over to where the chickens are shut up for the night.

'Brede!' she whispers after me. 'Come back here!'

I stoop down, and lift out my board that I tucked away here for safe-keeping. It's a fair old weight, and when I walk back, Kate whispers, 'As long as you're the one carrying it.'

We creep round the front of the house. There's a bit of a moon peeping from behind the clouds, on its tiptoes, like Kate and me.

I've not been in this patch of garden since the time I came chasing after the cockerel, and saw Missus Thompson and the Drummond man huffing together. I can make out the bench where they sat, and the trees that now have a load of leaves on them.

'The Thompsons' bedroom is just above us,' Kate whispers. 'So quiet as a mouse now.'

The gate gives a big creak, and we hold our breaths, waiting for a light to come on above us, but all stays dark. We step into the lane and she whispers, 'We'll run as far as the bend, Brede, in case the Thompsons wake up and see us.'

She hitches up her skirts and takes off, and I follow after, the board going bump-bump against my chest.

When we reach the bend, we catch our breaths. The drizzle has stopped, and over our heads the sky is a soft grey. In the distance, an owl screeches, and I give a jump, because any eejit knows it means bad luck.

'We can cut across the moor when it gets a bit lighter, but for now we'd better stick to the track.' She looks over her shoulder. 'It'll be a while before we're missed, but I wouldn't put it past Missus Thompson to come after us in the trap, or for him to come galloping up on that white horse of his.'

I start walking as fast as I can. But it's strange how the path that was so short when we were rattling along behind the pony has stretched itself out, like when you pull on a piece of wool.

Although the moon does its best to shine on us, it's still hard to see the way, and there's so many stones and holes that I keep tripping up, and all the time the board is going bump-bump against me.

My steps get slower and slower, and the breath is gasping out of me, until my chest is ready to burst.

'Give it here then.' Kate lifts the board, and we go along together. But every so often she stops and looks over her shoulder, and I feel my belly twist.

Then, just when my legs won't carry me another step, she says, 'Here will do.' She slides down into the ditch, and I follow her. I have a wee in the far end and then we sit and eat our bread, while over our heads the sky turns the colour of Missus Thompson's pink bodice.

But it's still a cold old morning, so I pull my shawl closer round me, and watch the sun move up into the sky. It's going very slow, like my brother peeping round the turf stack whenever someone came visiting. And I just wish he was beside me now.

A bird starts singing, very high up and far away. 'Listen, Brede. A skylark!'

And we hear a lamb going bleat-bleat to its mother, and then the other birds start calling to each other, and there's high notes like a fiddle, and lower ones, like a drum I once heard, until the air all around is filled with the sound of them.

Kate stretches her arms above her. 'I'd forgotten the freedom of it. Like the old days, isn't it?' She pulls me up. 'I just hope Francis is as good as his word, because we'll never make the town without his help.'

As we climb onto the track, I'm remembering our visit and the steps leading up to the Drummond man's office, and the look on his and Missus Thompson's face when they saw me. And I start dragging my feet.

Kate looks at me. 'There'll be plenty of work there, Brede, but you're going to have to do your bit too. No more dropping or tripping over things. And you'll need to say your name when you're asked. Do you understand?'

I give a nod, and then I hitch up my skirts, and she comes after me, but more slowly, on account of the board.

We go along this way for a while, and then in the distance comes the clack-clack of wheels. I clutch Kate's arm, because suppose it's Missus Thompson, shouting and screaming? Or him on that white horse? I daren't take a look, but then she let's out a sigh. 'Thank the Lord, Brede. It's not them.'

When I take a peep over my shoulder, I see a black horse pulling a cart, and we stand and wait for it to come up. Tied to the back of the cart is Mary, and sitting in it is Francis, and an older fellow I've not set eyes on before.

'We're a bit later than we wanted,' Francis says. 'I couldn't get your man here out of his bed.'

'But I swear my head wouldn't have touched the pillow if I'd known there'd be two such gorgeous women waiting for me,' the man says, and he gives a wink.

I can feel the heat rise to my cheeks, because no one's ever called me gorgeous before.

'You must be Francis's cousin, Dermot,' Kate says.

'One and the same,' he says, jumping down.

I can tell he's Francis's cousin, because they have the same carroty hair, but Dermot has a beard with bits of grey in it, and his hair reaches to his shoulders. His eyes look at Kate, and then away, and it puts me in mind of the Thompsons' cat, when it pretends it's not going after a bird.

'And you're Kate,' he says. 'Francis here has told me a deal about you.'

She bites her lip. 'It's very good of you to help us out like this.'

'No problem.' He takes the board from her. 'Brought the Thompsons' front door with you, then?'

Any eejit can see it's too small, but she gives a smile. 'It's what Brede here uses for practising her steps on.'

'Dancers, are you? I'm a fiddle player myself. We must have a hooley sometime.'

He helps her into the wagon, but when she reaches down for me, I'm too heavy for her. 'Here, let me.' He has his sleeves rolled up, and the veins are standing out in his arms. As he hoists me up, there's the same smoky smell from him that I get off Mister Thompson.

The back of the wagon has a load of old sacks in it, and I stretch myself out on them.

Francis turns in his seat. 'If it's all right with you, Dermot, I need to head on back before the Thompsons wake up.'

'Yes, you go. I'll send word when you're next needed.'

Kate gives a smile. 'I don't know what we'd have done without you, Francis.'

His face goes the colour of his hair. 'Dermot'll take you as far as the mill. Good luck to you now!' He unties Mary. 'See you later, Dermot.' And he rides off down the track.

Dermot moves onto the front seat. 'You'll be more comfortable beside me, Kate. And Brede there looks nice and settled.'

'If you're sure?'

'Git up!' Dermot doesn't have a whip, but the horse moves off at a good pace, and I'm not surprised because his voice is like Mister Thompson's – not one you'd want to argue with.

I stretch out, and when I see them glance back at me, I shut my eyes, so they'll think I'm asleep.

'Brede's your daughter?'

'She's my sister's child.'

'Ah, now that doesn't surprise me, because I'd say any girl you have is bound to take after you in the looks department.'

'Get away!' she says, but I can tell from her voice she's pleased.

'The Thompsons treated you like shite, I suppose?'

I know that's a bad word, but all Kate says is, 'I've known worse.'

'You'll be better off at the mill, so. All the girls I've taken there are getting along just fine.'

Her voice drops. 'Oh – you've helped others before us?'

'A few times, but none I've asked to sit beside me like this.'

Kate doesn't reply, and when I open my eyes, she's moved closer to him. If I had Missus Thompson's umbrella, I'd give her a poke.

It's turned into a warm morning, so I remove my shawl and lean back. The cart is bumpier than Missus Thompson's trap, but it's grand watching the mountain and fields go past. There's lambs on either side of us, skipping about the place, and a load of yellow whins. Then we pass a sheep, lying with its legs in the air. It's all swollen-looking, and its eyes stare up, just like old Mister Henderson's, when he was dead on the floor that time.

'Fat bellies aren't just to be found on dead sheep,' Dermot says.

'What do you mean?' Kate says.

'People like the Thompsons and Hendersons. Stealing the land from us – renting out strips you couldn't grow a thistle on.'

'It's just how it is, Dermot. There's the rich, and then there's the rest of us.'

'It doesn't have to be this way, Kate.' He lowers his voice, and I shift myself forward to hear. 'There's plenty of us prepared to do whatever it takes to change things.'

Kate's back has gone very straight. 'Well, I don't know about that.'

'You wait and see. Because when I say, "Whatever it takes," that's just what I mean.' There's a silence, and then he says, 'Well, with the way things are going, you'll be better off in the town, and—'

Kate gives a cry. 'Oh, look. I do believe that's Annie walking ahead. The Hendersons' housekeeper,' she adds.

'I know who she is.'

We've reached the turn in the road, where one part leads to the town, and the other to the gate with the lions. And sure enough, there in the road is Annie, in a brown hat and coat, with a basket over her arm.

'Pull up a moment would you, Dermot?' Kate says. 'I just want to say hello.'

'If you must.' He clicks his tongue, and the horse stops right beside Annie.

She looks up. 'Oh, it's you, Kate, and the child. How are you doing?'

'The best, Annie. And yourself?'

'All good, thanks be to God. I'm just on my way back from taking food to one of the workers – as I do every Sunday morning.' She gives a nod. 'Off to the town, are you?'

'Yes.'

'Has the Thompsons' old trap broken down at last?'

'We need to keep going, Kate,' Dermot says.

She bites her lip. 'I'll be honest with you, Annie. I've decided Brede and I will be better off getting work in the mill. Dermot here is just giving us a lift.'

She frowns. 'The mill?' Then she looks at Dermot. 'I don't recall seeing you in these parts before.'

'No. You won't have.'

There's a silence.

'But you're surely not going to pass us by, Kate, without taking a drink of tea?'

'Well, I—'

'Now I won't take no for an answer. The family are at church, and then they'll be visiting her mother, so we'll have the place to ourselves. And when you're ready to leave, sure Sam will give you a lift into town.'

'The Hendersons go out every Sunday, then?' Dermot asks.

'What's that to you?'

'Just wondering.'

Annie gives Kate a look. 'All these barns torched, and cattle with their throats cut. You never know who you might be talking to.'

'Well, I suppose an hour's stop won't make much difference,' Kate says. 'If it's all the same to you, Dermot?'

'Please yourself. I've plenty to be getting on with.' He hands Kate a piece of paper. 'The people at this address will see you right. Best get to them before nightfall – and tell them I sent you.'

'Thank you again, Dermot,' Kate says, as the two of us climb down. 'You've been very kind.' She takes the board from him. 'And I suppose this is goodbye?'

'Oh, I hardly think so.'

'But you won't know where to find us.'

'Don't you worry about that.' He gives a smile, and her face goes all pink.

Kate and Annie and myself start walking along the straight stretch of lane.

'What an abrupt fellow,' Annie says. 'I wonder where he sprang from?'

Kate doesn't answer, but when we reach the gates with the lions, she turns, and so do I.

Dermot is sitting in the cart, smoking his pipe. And something about the way he's watching us, makes my insides go all shivery

TWELVE

I'M SITTING ALL NICE AND COMFORTABLE, WITH MY shoes off, and my back against the turf basket. Kate and Missus Purdy and Annie and Margaret are in chairs beside me. I've had a drink of tea and a piece of scone, so Missus Thompson can come chasing after us as much as she likes.

Annie takes a sip of tea. The cup is white, with a blue stripe round the top. 'Are you certain, Kate? The vacancy's there and I know Missus Henderson took to you.'

'It's good of you, Annie, but Dermot says the mill always has plenty of work.'

'So how exactly do you know him?'

'He's a cousin of Francis's. And without his help, I hate to think where Brede and I would end up.'

'But are you sure you know what you're letting yourself in for?' Margaret asks.

Her hair is silky-looking with a grand curl to it. I twist a bit of my own in my fingers, but no matter how hard I try, it stays straight as a piece of straw.

'Every Sunday off, and a wage on top?' Kate says. 'It's a sight more than I've been getting at the Thompsons' – or any of the houses I was in.'

'Have you thought of the conditions?'

'I'm not afraid of hard work. And I won't live on charity.' She looks over at me. 'Leave your hair alone, Brede.'

I drum my heels on the floor because the town is the last place I want to be in.

'I'll certainly help out with today's lunch,' Kate says. 'Stop that, Brede. As long as we can be away once the clearing up is done.'

'That's great.' Annie waves a hand at Missus Purdy. 'Because you can see how things are with her.'

The old woman's fast asleep in her chair. Her legs are wide apart, and she has her skirts hitched up, so I have a good view of her bloomers. They reach past her knees, and are the colour of old grass. Every time she draws in a breath, her bosom moves up and down, and an odd kind of noise comes out of her mouth, like a kettle when it's near boiling.

'Has she stopped cooking altogether, then?' Kate asks.

'More or less, God love her,' Margaret says. 'The last fruit tart she made, she used lard instead of butter, and her gravy had more lumps than a tapioca pudding.'

'She's been with the Hendersons these forty years,' Annie says. 'They've fixed up a cottage for her along the lane – she can move there any time she pleases.'

'But I imagine they'll have no trouble finding another cook?'

'That's just it, Kate. Times aren't what they were. There's many a woman these days would rather work in the mill.'

She sighs. 'You always make Brede and me so welcome, but it's just I swore blind I'd never work for the likes of the Thompsons again.'

'But two more different sisters than Missus Thompson and Missus Henderson you wouldn't wish to meet,' Margaret says. 'The one with all those fancy airs and graces, and the other with her feet on the ground.'

I remember Missus Henderson's grey eyes, but I can't for the life of me recall what she had on her feet. But I'm thinking her shoes could never be as gorgeous as Missus Thompson's pointy ones.

'Well, you must do what you think best.' Annie gives Margaret a look. 'I expect Bridget will be coming by later?'

'She will indeed.'

'She's someone who worked here?' Kate asks.

'Not for this long while, the creature.'

Annie gets to her feet. 'Margaret, would you ever check where Sam's got to? And, Kate, could you make a start on the pastry?'

Missus Purdy opens her eyes. 'Did you get the goose stuffing done? And for God's sake don't let that pudding boil dry!'

Annie pats her shoulder. 'Christmas is long gone, Missus Purdy. It'll be Easter in another few weeks.'

'Fancy that.'

'Do you see who's come to help out today? Kate and her daughter.'

The old one looks up. 'It's Brede, isn't it? Come and sit here, child, and tell me what Christmas presents you're hoping for.'

Annie rolls her eyes. 'I'd better get on upstairs.' She points at me. 'You're to sit by Missus Purdy, and don't move one finger until I say so.'

I tuck my hands under me, glad I'm not being sent out to that scullery again.

Missus Purdy has her eyes closed, so I start thinking about what I'd like to have best. Kate and I have not been great ones for the present-giving. I found a lovely round pebble for her once, and a bird's egg the colour of the sky. And when it was my birthday, she gave me a pink ribbon, but I must have dropped it on the road somewhere.

But what would be really grand is to wake up one morning and find myself in the house with my mammy and da and brothers and sisters. We'd be sitting up at table as we used, tucking into a pile of spuds, with a nice bit of butter to go with them.

Kate says that they're all in heaven, along with Jesus and Mary – that's His mother, not the Thompsons' pony – and a whole load of saints. And they're having such a great rest, they won't be coming down in a hurry. And I can't say I blame them.

The other thing I'd really like is another board for my steps, and—

'You're not going to talk to me then?' Missus Purdy has woken and is staring about her, as if she's never seen the place before. 'Ah well,' she says. 'Suit yourself.' And her chin drops back onto her chest.

The cat has been fast asleep in its box, but now it uncurls itself and gives a good stretch. It's the colour of turf with a white bit on its front. I'm just giving it a stroke, when the door bangs open and a small boy with his hair all on end comes running in, roaring for all he's worth. He has nothing on his lower half and I can see his tinkler poking below his shirt.

For a moment I think it's my youngest brother, Colm, come back to me. So up I jump, and go rushing towards him. And then I see that this boy is all wrong. His hair is a pale colour, instead of brown, and his cheeks are pinker and fatter. For a moment, it feels as if someone's turned off a light inside me, but he looks up, and gives a grin. And Kate says, 'I think you've made a friend there, Brede.'

And then a voice calls, 'Rory! Come back here this minute!'

The little fellow runs behind Kate, and peeps out from behind her skirts, just as Colm used with our mammy.

'Rory!' the voice calls again, and who should appear in the doorway but Pimple-face. 'Where on earth has that boy got to this time?' Then she catches sight of him, and drags him out from behind Kate, and gives him a good slap. He opens his mouth and yells for all he's worth, and when I see the tears running down his face, I'm so sorry for him that I start to cry as well.

'Stop that at once!' Kate says. And the child and I go quiet.

'Well, you've certainly got a way with you,' Molly says, 'because he takes not a blind bit of notice of anything I say.'

'You're not working in the kitchen any more, Molly?'

'Missus Henderson promised she'd give me a chance as a nursemaid, but the way things are going, it'll be a wonder if I last the week.'

Kate stoops down, so that she's on a level with Rory. Then she takes out her handkerchief and wipes the snotty bits from his face. He wriggles around, but she holds him firm. And when she's done, she says, 'Now, you're to go with Molly, and do what she says. And if you put your clothes on like a good boy, maybe there'll be a slice of fruit pie for you. Would you like that?'

He gives a nod.

'Are you replacing Missus Purdy then, Kate?'

'I'm just here for the day.'

'That's a pity.' She starts hauling Rory to the door. 'By the way, I saw your daughter in the town.'

'Missus Thompson had some errands to do, so she asked the two of us to go with her.'

'That's as may be, but I was helping my father shut up shop when the child came running along the street, as if all the devils in hell were after her. And behind her was my Uncle Bob, with a face on him like thunder. He's very thick with Missus Thompson, so you may have come across him?'

Kate shook her head.

'He's an ork-shaneer and owns the mill – some say he owns the town – though you'd never know it from the tight way he carries on.'

Kate looks over at me. 'Whatever were you up to this time?'

I chew my lip.

Molly gives a laugh. 'Mind you, I'd rather have the devil after me than Uncle Bob in one of his tempers! Anyway, he couldn't keep pace with her, so she was safe enough.'

Kate shakes her head and I know I'll be in for a telling-off later. Now she says, 'I'd better check on that roast.'

Margaret is back in the room. 'There's not the big crowd we had when you were last here,' she says. 'Just Mister and Missus Henderson, and Mister John, the brother.'

That's Pea-in-the-pod.

'He's not married then?' Kate asks.

'He is not, poor fellow. He courted a city girl, but she went and jilted him. Mind you,' – Margaret lowers her voice – 'that's not the only setback he's had.'

'Oh?' Kate points to a basin of apples. 'Do those need peeling?'

'I'll make a start on them,' Margaret says. 'Mister John will create if he doesn't get his apple sauce.'

'He eats here often, then?'

'He has a place of his own not five miles away, but he's up to the house every Sunday, just as he did when his father was alive, God rest him. But here's the thing.' She starts taking the peel off an apple. 'There was talk about Mister Charles changing his will in favour of Mister John. But then what happens?' She starts cutting up the apple, her knife going chop-chop on the board. 'The old man drops stone dead, so now Mister William gets to keep the house and land. And Mister John is none too pleased about it, I can tell you.'

'But Mister William is the eldest brother?'

'Yes, but him and his father never saw eye-to-eye. Terrible arguments they used to have. About the Order.'

'The Orange Order?'

'Don't look like that, Kate. The marches are really good *craic*. Getting all the food ready keeps us busy for days beforehand. You should see the spread – baked hams and sausages and pies and cakes and trifle.'

Just hearing about it makes my belly grumble.

'And all the men get dressed up,' Margaret says, 'and they look really grand in their sashes and hats – even the bog-ugly ones. And you should hear the bands. All that drumming and piping fair stirs the blood. The march finishes in one of the fields, and there's a big picnic, and a lot of speech-making, though you don't have to take much notice of *that*.'

Kate gives the gravy a stir, and some of it spills onto the stove. 'I'm glad you enjoy it.'

I know I'd like dancing to one of those bands if I'm given the chance.

Margaret sighs. 'But what will happen now Mister William's in charge of things, the dear knows. And—'

Annie puts her head round the door. 'They're back from church and will be ready for their meal at the usual time.'

A while later, Margaret and Annie carry the food through to where the Hendersons and Pea-in-the-pod are eating. And when all that's done, Kate and Margaret and Annie and Sam and myself sit up at the table, and have our stew. Missus Purdy has some too, but she takes hers by the range.

And Kate looks across at Annie and says, 'If it's all right with you, when Brede and I have finished our tea, we'll head for the town.'

'Of course. Sam here will take you.'

Outside, it's a rainy old afternoon, with the water going splash-splash against the window. And I'm just wishing I could stay here in the warmth, when there's a rap on the yard door. 'That'll be Bridget,' Annie says. 'Let her in, would you, Sam?'

When he opens it, in steps a very thin woman, with stooped shoulders, with a girl beside her. The rain's fairly dripping off them, and Margaret says, 'That week's gone quick. Come and warm yourselves by the stove.'

When they remove their shawls, I see that the woman is old-looking, with grey hair. And the girl is so small she doesn't come up to my chin, and the minute she gets by the fire, she starts to go cough-cough.

'Deirdre's chest hasn't eased, then, with the medicine Mister Henderson got for her?' Annie says.

The woman shakes her head. 'Nothing seems to fix it, but sure everyone's got a cough in that place.'

'Where's that then?' Kate asks.

'The mill.'

'Oh. But surely something can be done?'

The woman doesn't answer.

'Well, who's for more tea then?' Annie says.

I hold out my cup, but she doesn't fill it up for me like she did before. Instead she looks at me and says, 'Where are your manners? You should be pouring for the rest of us.'

Kate gives a nod, so I pick up the pot, feeling all of a glow to be doing something on my very own. But it's a fair old weight, and when I start to fill the cups, it's hard to keep the tea from running over, and some of it spills onto Margaret's front. She jumps back. 'For God's sake!'

Kate stands up. 'It's all right, Brede. I'll take over now.' She moves round the table and offers a cup to the Bridget woman, who's sitting all hunched up.

Suddenly, Kate lets out a cry and I draw in my breath. Because the woman has her arms on the table, and where one of her hands should be, there's just a stump, like a sausage or the end of a log you'd put on the fire. I've never seen anything like it in the whole of my life, so I give it a poke.

Kate slaps my hand away. 'Stop that!' Then she turns to the woman. 'I'm sorry, Bridget.'

'It's all right.'

'But what in the world happened to you?'

Sausage Arm looks at her. 'Did the others not tell you?'

Kate shakes her head.

'The mill,' the woman says. 'It does this to a lot of us. All them hackling and carding machines grinding away for hours at a time, and the heat and the noise. Easy enough to forget what you're doing.' She presses the stump to her forehead. 'A moment is all it takes.'

There's a silence. Then Kate says, 'So what about Deirdre? Did she have to work those machines?'

The woman shook her head. 'She was a doffer, like the other children.'

'A what?'

'When the bobbins run out of thread, they've to fit new ones to the spinning frames. You'd think it would be easy enough.' The woman sighs. 'But you'd not believe the dust, and the damp. Most of the children go down with mill fever after a week or two.'

'But that's terrible,' Kate murmurs. 'Did Dermot not know any of this?'

Annie makes a snorting kind of a noise. 'Everyone around here knows.'

'But I can tell you now,' Margaret says, 'that Bridget here is not the only one to have lost a hand, or worse.'

'Indeed I am not. Most months there's someone killed or maimed.'

'Mother of God!' says Kate.

'And now look at me,' Sausage Woman says. 'I used to be a housemaid before I took it into my head to try my luck in the town. And I'm telling you now, fair and square, that it was a bad day when I did.'

Everyone seems to have run out of words, and soon the only sound in the kitchen is Deirdre, who starts up her coughing again, so loud that Missus Purdy jerks awake.

'Is it time to get up?' she asks.

'No, you're all right where you are,' Annie says. She turns to Kate. 'So, you're still for the town, then?'

And I bang my feet on the floor because if the Drummond man's at the mill, isn't he likely to have all our arms chopped off?

THIRTEEN

KATE IS BITING HER LIP, BUT BEFORE SHE CAN answer, Sausage Arm says, 'Well, I'd best be off. We've a fair old walk ahead of us.'

'You're still at your brother's place?' Margaret says.

'And I thank God for it. Without him, heaven knows where we'd be.'

The woman reaches out her good hand for her shawl. 'You've all done more than enough.' Then she turns. 'Come along, Deirdre.'

The girl is still warming herself by the fire. Her feet are bare, like mine used to be before I was given my shoes, and there's patches of mud on her legs. Missus Purdy has woken again, and now she leans over, and gives the girl's hair a stroke. Mine sits on my head in a dark sort of a clump, but hers is the colour of sunshine, with a soft curl to it. Missus Purdy smiles down at her. 'Come and see me again, dear.'

'I've wrapped you some bread and cheese,' Margaret says, and the woman tucks the food into her pocket.

Annie and Kate have their backs turned, so I walk over and give the girl's cheek a sharp pinch. She looks at me in a startled kind of a way before running to the door.

'Well, someone's happy enough to be going,' Annie says.

Sausage Arm gives the girl a slap. 'Where are your manners, Deirdre?'

The rain is fairly beating down, and the woman shivers, pulling her shawl closer to her. The pair of them go out into the wet, and I hear the girl going cough-cough as they cross the yard. Kate closes the door, and I sit myself next to Missus Purdy, glad to be the one beside her in the warmth.

'Poor souls,' Kate says. 'On the road in this weather.' She looks across at Annie. 'I was thinking that maybe I'll not start that mill job straightaway.'

'Would you like me to put in a word for you with Mister Henderson?'

'Would you, Annie? I know it's a big chance you're giving me.' Kate hesitates. 'But suppose the Hendersons don't want me?'

'No need to worry on that account. They usually leave things like this to me, and I can tell you now—'

She doesn't get to finish her sentence, because Mister Henderson comes in. 'There you all are!' He has on a brown waistcoat and trousers, and with his long face and that mouse's tail stuck to his lip, he's still very plain-looking. But still the sight of him warms my insides.

'Missus Henderson asked me to pass on her thanks for the meal. She's having a lie-down, or she'd be here to tell you herself.' He looks across at Missus Purdy. Her mouth is open, and there's a terrible racket coming out of it. 'Still no change with Grace, then? I meant to say earlier, Annie, that I've had little luck so far in finding a new cook.'

'Ah,' Annie says. 'You remember Kate?'

He frowns. 'Kate?'

She steps forward, keeping her eyes on the floor.

He looks her up and down, just as he did the first time we saw him outside the house arguing with old red cheeks. 'Of course I remember.'

'Kate's an excellent cook,' Annie says. 'She managed fine again today, and given all the meetings and lunches you're planning, she wondered if you'd consider her for the post?'

'It would certainly save a lot of bother. And that lunch was certainly excellent.'

'The thing is, Mister Henderson,' Kate says, still with her eyes on the floor. 'There's also Brede here to consider.'

'Your niece,' he says, with a nod in my direction. 'That shouldn't be a problem. My wife said what a big help she was, so I'm sure we'd find plenty for her to do.'

My insides go all warm again and, before I know it, I'm out of my chair, and standing right beside him. He smells of rain and turf. If he were sitting down, I'd want to be on his knee, but now I'd like nothing better than to lay my head against his chest.

'Brede,' Kate says. 'Come over here this minute!'

'It's all right. Margaret will fix you up with a bed and I'll have a word with Missus Henderson. But I'm sure she'll have no objections.'

'Thank you,' Kate says, but still she doesn't look at him.

He clears his throat. 'Well, that just about wraps things up. If you could take Missus Henderson some tea, Margaret? And see if there's anything else she needs.'

'Certainly, Mister Henderson.'

When he goes out again, Annie says, 'That's all settled, then.'

'How can you be so sure?' Kate asks.

Annie smiles. 'Trust me.'

'When the Hendersons take you on,' Margaret says, 'you won't know you're born.'

It's a puzzle why that would make things any better, but Kate puts her hand to her forehead. 'Oh, Lord!'

'What?'

'Missus Thompson. I forgot that she visits here.'

'Don't you worry about that,' Margaret says. 'The likes of her have no call to be in the kitchen and, anyway, Mister Henderson will soon see her off.'

Kate wrinkles her forehead. 'I hope you're right.'

I'm hoping so too, because the thought of Missus Thompson in a mood, is enough to put the fear of God into anyone. And then I recall the Drummond man, and how the pair of them shouted at me when I fell down the steps that time. And I wish there was some far-off place where Kate and I could go and never clap eyes on them again.

'I must see to Missus Henderson's tea,' Margaret says. She holds out a big dish piled with meat and spuds and greens and gravy, the same as the Hendersons had for their meal. 'Perhaps this once you'd give the dog his feed, Kate?'

She presses her lips together, and I can tell what she's thinking.

A while back, before we were at the Thompsons, we were passing a farm, with a great black and white dog by the gate. Before we rightly knew what was happening, it ran out and sank its teeth into Kate's leg. She screamed at it until a fat man with whiskers came from the house, and began shouting at us: 'That'll teach you to keep off decent folk's land. If I had my way, I'd shove all Carth Licks over the nearest cliff.' He was yelling so hard that bits of spit got stuck to his beard.

Kate limped off, with me beside her, crying for all I was worth, because the blood was fairly pouring from her leg. We found a quiet place to sit while she tied her handkerchief round the sore place. 'I'm almost good as new, Brede,' she said, so I knew to stop my worrying. But ever since then, she hasn't cared much for dogs.

I step forward and she gives a smile. 'Thank you, Brede.'

'He'll be in his kennel in this weather,' Margaret says, 'but he'll come out quick enough when he smells his dinner.'

'The kennel is the house he sleeps in to keep him out of the wet,' Kate says. 'Just place the food down, and come straight back in.'

The courtyard is bigger than the one at the Thompsons' place, with a big tree in the middle, and some chickens sitting under it. Behind the tree is a row of stalls with one, two, three horses poking their heads out, and off to one side a pump with a shiny handle.

It's a dark old afternoon, but the rain has eased off. The kennel is over to the side, and I can see the gap where the dog comes out. I creep towards it on my tiptoes, because I don't want him taking a bite out of me. Then I hear a kind of a whining noise, and out he comes. He's dark all over, except the ends of his paws that are white. He looks up at me, and I stop where I am, and hold my breath. Then his tail gives a wag, so I know we're going to get on together.

As I go to put down the dish there, sitting on the top of it is a piece of crackling, all nice and crispy, with a load of yellow fat round it. I look about me to make sure there's no one watching. Then I stuff the crackling into my mouth. The dog gives another whine, but he doesn't jump up, and, after I've taken a good few mouthfuls, I place the dish in front of him. He starts to eat, with his tail still wagging away, so I give him a pat, and walk back into the kitchen.

'Well done, Brede,' Kate says. Then she stares. 'What on earth's that round your mouth?' She glances about her, but there's only Missus Purdy still sleeping and Margaret is busy stirring something on the range. 'Here' – Kate hands me a cloth. 'Wipe your face.' She points to the table. 'Sit up there,' she whispers, 'and for heaven's sake behave yourself. Do you want us on the road again?'

I have a chew of my hair.

Margaret comes over. 'It might be an idea if I reminded

you where everything is, Kate. We get drinking water from the pump in the yard, but there's all the store cupboards to go through.'

'And what about the milk and butter?'

Margaret heaves a sigh. 'The dairy's in a separate building, under the lee of the mountain. It's a bit of a walk, but Sam goes up first thing, and again in the evening.' She stoops down. 'What in the world is this?' She's got hold of my board, and in a moment, I'm down from the table, and seizing it from her.

'Gently, Brede,' Kate says. 'It's for practising her dance steps on.'

Margaret gives a sniff. 'Well, put it somewhere safe, or it'll get chopped up for firewood.'

My chin gives a wobble, and Kate lifts the board off me. 'We'll tidy it behind the dresser for now, out of harm's way.'

'So let me show you this far cupboard, Kate. It's where most of the stores are kept.'

The talk of dancing has put me in mind of the floor with the black and white squares on it. The two of them are still talking away, so there's time to take just a quick peep.

I walk past the scullery. Sam is at the sink with his back to me, so I go past the other doors, until I come to the hall. It's very quiet, but for the big clock tick-tocking away to itself. And there's the vase with birds on it, and the picture of the sailing ship, and the one of the man with the gorgeous orange sash across his chest.

I'm just wondering how many of the squares I can count up to, when there's a knock on the front door.

Before I can make a move back to the kitchen, the handle turns, and in walks a tall man in boots and a long coat. He gives himself a shake, so that the wet sprays everywhere.

'Oh Lord,' he says, unbuttoning his coat and handing it to me. 'What a night!'

He gives a smile, and I see he has nice dark eyes, and his hair and beard are so neat they look as if they've been painted on. 'I've not come across you before. You must be the new maid?'

I give a nod.

'Well, I'm Mister Johnson, and we'll be seeing plenty of one another, because I'm at this house a great deal. So, is Mister Henderson in the front room?'

I have a chew of my hair.

'Never mind. I'll go on through.'

I should be getting back to the kitchen, but while I'm here, I just want to see what Mister Henderson's doing. So I follow the man down another passage towards the room with the long table, where all the people ate their lunch that time.

But the man doesn't go in there. Instead he pushes open the door on his straw-foot side.

'James,' I hear Mister Henderson call, 'how good to see you! I wondered if you'd be out in this weather.'

'And miss our Sunday evening talk? What do you take me for? Besides, we've important matters to discuss.'

'First things first,' Mister Henderson is saying. 'You'll take a drop of whisky?'

I hear the chink-chink of glass, and then he says

something else I can't catch. So I step inside, and the door closes quietly behind me.

The room has green curtains at the windows, and there's a line of shelves with books on them. A fire is burning away at the far end, and the two of them seat themselves in front of it. Beside them is a table with a lamp, but the part of the room I'm standing in is all dark and shadowy.

After what happened at the Drummond man's office, I'm careful to stay near the door. Beside me is a big chair covered in a soft kind of fabric that looks a deal more comfortable than the wooden ones in the kitchen. So I tuck myself behind it.

'No Helen?' the James man is saying.

'She sends her apologies. She has a bit of a chill, but I'm sure she'll have shaken it off by the morning.'

I hope when she does, it won't go flying all over the place, like the wet from the man's coat.

'So – your brother's still taking things badly?'

Mister Henderson gives a sigh, and starts talking away about how Pea-in-the-pod is thinking he should have the house and land.

'Done out of it by a whisker,' the James man says. 'But I can't say I'm sorry, William. It was yours by rights, and he's well set up in his own place.'

'True enough.' I hear them gulp their drinks.

'And the news from across the water?'

'Continues promising. Glad Stone looks set to push Home Rule through. Just think what that will mean for Ireland, James!'

I don't care about Ireland – I'm just pleased Mister Henderson sounds so happy.

'The likes of your brother won't take it lying down, surely?'

'Oh, they'll come round in the end. They'll have to.' Mister Henderson gets to his feet, and his shadow dances along the wall beside him. 'More whisky?'

'Please.'

'As you know, the meeting is only three weeks away. We'll hold it in the big barn. It'll seat a couple of hundred, no bother.'

'And what of this fellow, Chivers?' the James man is saying.

'I have it on good authority that he's no longer the Prime Minister's man.'

'And you trust him?'

'His letters are certainly convincing. But I'm sure we can handle it, James, if he tries to cause trouble.'

'So, do you want us to go over some of the points?'

'Good idea. But what a poor host I am.' He walks over and pulls at a length of cord hanging from the wall. 'Let me get us some supper.'

I could do with something to eat too, especially if it was another piece of that crackling.

I wait for the food to come down from the ceiling, but the door opens behind me.

'Oh, Mister Johnson,' Annie says, 'I didn't realise you were here.'

'The new maid let me in.'

'New maid?'

'We could do with some supper, Annie,' Mister Henderson says. 'Ham will suit nicely, and perhaps some of that excellent fruit pie?'

'Of course.'

'And how's Missus Henderson doing, Annie?'

'The last I looked on her, she was fast asleep. And Molly's just putting Master Rory to bed.'

'Excellent.'

'I'll bring your meal to you straight away.' Then she turns, and lets out a cry. 'Brede – what are you doing in here?'

'Who is it?'

'I'm so sorry, Mister Henderson. It's the new cook's daughter. I don't know how she got in the room.'

The three of them are staring at me, until I don't know where to put myself.

'She's the girl who took my coat,' the James man says. 'I expect she came to ask about our food.'

'Well, I can't see how—'

'Never mind,' Mister Henderson says. 'Why don't you go on back to the kitchen, Brede?'

So I jump up and, as I run out into the passage, I hear him say, 'It's for the likes of her that we're fighting.'

I saw a fight once, when two of my cousins set about a man who'd come to collect the rent. 'What do you expect us to pay you with?' my cousin Liam said. 'Donegal air?' And he pulled out his jacket pocket to show how empty it was. But the man wouldn't listen, and they ended up punching one another until his front teeth flew onto the ground. 'If you don't cross the water tonight, the pair of you'll be strung up,' my da told them.

So I hope there'll be no more fighting, because I don't like to think of Mister Henderson all covered in bruises, and having to go across the sea where I'd never set eyes on him again.

I wouldn't like that one bit.

FOURTEEN

I OPEN MY EYES, AND FOR A MOMENT, I CAN'T FOR the life of me think where I am. Facing me is a smooth kind of a rock, with a patch of sun peeping from behind. But there's no birds calling, and no wind going whoosh-whoosh in the trees.

I sit myself up, and then I see that I'm in the big bed, and the rock isn't a rock at all, but a chest with drawers to put things in. And behind it, set up high in the wall, is the window that's letting in all the light.

Kate and I have been here for one, two nights. Our room is beside the scullery, with the privy just along the passage. Kate has given me the middle drawer of the chest for my very own, and into it I've placed one of Rory's socks that I found in the passage, a piece of twine, and a spare scone in case I get hungry.

I never heard her get out of bed, but I know she'll be

seeing to the breakfasts. I pull on my clothes, and then take a look at my board to be sure it's still against the wall, where I put it for safe-keeping. When we're settled in a bit more, Kate will ask Mister Henderson if I can have a corner of the yard for practising my steps in.

When I walk through to the kitchen, Kate's at the range, stirring the porridge.

'I was just coming to fetch you, Brede. Did you have a good sleep?'

Annie's at the table, putting things on a tray. She's been none too friendly since she found me in the room with Mister Henderson and the James man. Now she says, 'Someone needs to learn she's not here to loll about the place like Lady Muck.'

I'm remembering the Bosom woman who came to the big lunch. She was the one with the gold brooch pinned to her chest, but I don't recall her other name.

'Brede tries her best,' Kate says.

'Well, let's leave it for now,' Annie says. 'Goodness knows, we've enough to be getting on with.' She picks up the tray. 'I'll just take this on up to Missus Henderson. From the look of her, she won't be out of her bed today. Margaret, you're to go into the town for those groceries. Sam can take you in the trap.'

'I'll be glad of the run,' Margaret says, but I'm thinking that the way she rushes about the place, she could do with slowing down a bit.

'That leaves you in charge of the kitchen, Kate,' Annie says.

'No worries. I'll have the lunch underway in no time.

But what about Missus Purdy?'

'Missus Henderson says we're to let her rest for now.' Annie gives me a look. 'The child can make herself useful, and take her a drink.'

'You'll do that, won't you, Brede?' Kate pours tea into a cup, and hands it to me, along with a saucer. 'Her room is three doors up from ours,' Kate says, 'so be sure to count. And when you've done that, you're to give the chickens their feed, and then it'll be time for our breakfast.'

All the while she's speaking, the rashers she's frying are giving off a grand smell that makes me want to skip. But I remember to go carefully because of Missus Purdy's drink. So I walk along the passage, with the cup in one hand and the saucer in the other, and when I'm past our room, I count one, two, three doors, before pushing the next one open.

Missus Purdy's room is bigger than ours, and there's a red mat on the floor, and a chest like the one Kate and I have, with a jar of white flowers on it. When I walk over to the bed, her bosom is going up and down. Not like the time I shouted at my mammy and she stayed still as a stone.

I'd like Missus Purdy to wake up and give my hair a stroke, but her eyes stay tight shut. When I put the cup down beside her, some of the tea escapes onto her sheet, so I give it a wipe with my sleeve, and tiptoe out again.

I've still the chickens to feed, so I put on my shawl on account of the drizzle that's falling. The hens don't mind the wet, but go pecking about the place, just as the ones at the Thompsons used. I wish I'd managed to catch the

141

rooster I chased, because I'd like one of his lovely green feathers to put in my special drawer.

The dog comes out of his house, with his tail wagging away, so I give him a pat, and then go in for my breakfast.

We sit at the table – myself and Kate, and Annie and Margaret, and Sam and another older fellow called Brian, who's brought the groceries from the town. Brian is very thin and eats so fast he's finished his bacon and eggs before I'm halfway through mine. He has a fine beard on him, but when I give him a smile, he's too busy staring at Kate to notice. Her hair's so wavy, some of it has escaped from under her cap, and I'm thinking he'd like her to tidy herself up a bit.

'Off with you then, Margaret,' Annie says when we've finished eating. 'Kate will do the clearing up. Sam, you have the trap ready at the back entrance.' She gets to her feet. 'Well, I'd better see to Missus Henderson.'

Kate and I are just finishing the dishes, when the yard door opens and in comes Mister Henderson.

'I hope you're settling in all right, Kate? If there's anything you need, you've only to let Missus Henderson or myself know.'

'Brede and I are doing just grand, thank you.' She begins to dip her knees, and he says, 'No need for any of that.' So she straightens up again.

'A fine morning,' he says.

When I look through the window, I see the rain has stopped, and the sun is shining down for all it's worth.

'I've been thinking,' he says, 'how would it be if Brede took over the dairy work from Sam? It would free him up to help in the stable.'

It would be grand to have work that's my very own, so I give Kate a look.

'What exactly would she have to do?'

'Oh, nothing too difficult. Collecting the milk, butter and cheese each morning and evening. It's a bit of a walk, but she's young and fit.'

Kate nods. 'She'd probably manage that.'

'I tell you what. Why don't I show you, so you can see for yourself what's involved?'

I drop the tea towel I'm holding and as I go skipping over to the door, my elbow catches a tray that goes flying.

'For heaven's sake, Brede!' Kate shouts, as it goes clatter-clatter on the floor. 'What will Mister Henderson think of us?'

'Only that it's a grand day for skipping. And if I were twenty years younger, I'd be doing the very same.' I wish she'd smile back at him, but when she doesn't, he says, 'Well, let's get going, then.'

The three of us set off across the yard, and I stay as close as I can to Mister Henderson. Then he calls, 'Angus!' and the dog comes running up, and starts barking away. I can tell he's pleased to hear his name, just like I am. Kate moves so that Mister Henderson is in between her and the animal. 'He has been known to bite,' Mister Henderson says, 'but only with strangers. And I can see that he's taken to Brede.'

I give a grin, and one of the horses pokes his nose out at us, and goes snicker-snicker as we walk past. And it's not the only one watching, because when I look up, who should be standing in the window but Missus Henderson?

Kate says you can tell the mood of a person from the way they hold their bodies.

Which is why she makes me keep upright when I'm dancing, to show that I take pride in my steps.

Even from this distance, I can see that Missus Henderson is all stooped over, and altogether very sad-looking. But maybe when she's in her bed again, she'll feel more cheery.

We go out of a gate at the far end. It has posts on either side, and each one has a round ball on the top, cut into a kind of curly shape. Mister Henderson points at them and says: 'The pineapples were my father's idea, as so much in this place is.'

I'd have thought only an eejit would put apples on top of a gate, but at least they don't have teeth, like those lions.

We go along a track, with trees on either side. The birds are singing for all they're worth, and there's a load of yellow flowers spread out on the ground. Angus runs ahead, but I stay right beside Mister Henderson.

'Building the dairy away from the house was another of my father's ideas.' His voice has a nice kind of a rumble to it.

'Other folk round here don't do the same?' Kate asks.

'They do not. "Crackpot" a lot of them called it, but I have to admit it makes sense.' He points ahead. 'We keep the cows in those fields, so they can be driven straight up to the dairy to be milked. That way, the manure doesn't get trampled into the yard. The old dairy was where the scullery is now, and the milk didn't stay nearly as fresh.'

Kate is usually a great one for conversation, but today she's very quiet, so I think she's just enjoying being out in the air.

Mister Henderson doesn't mind, but carries right on talking. 'We follow the track over this first field. We'll be crossing four fields in all, and then there's just a short climb – a bit of a steep one, I admit – until we reach the dairy.' He stops for a moment, and I bump right into him.

'Steady,' Kate says.

'Why not see where Angus has got to, Brede?' Mister Henderson says.

So I draw in my breath and take off up the path as fast as my legs will carry me. It's grand to smell the air, and to feel the turf soft under my feet. The dog's enjoying himself too, chasing after the rabbits, who go running across the hillside when he gets near to them.

I head up the path, and there's one, two stiles to climb over. On either side of me are fields with cows, munching away on the turf. Then Angus comes running back to me, and I give him a pat and we go on together, with him just a little way in front.

When I was just a wee girl, my mammy and da had a brown dog, but it went and died, and we never had another. My da said there wasn't enough food for humans, let alone an animal. But I missed that dog, and I'm glad now to have Angus as my friend.

I come to another stile, and a very steep stretch of path that Mister Henderson spoke of. And then I'm on a long piece of ground, with two buildings, and a big tree. One of the buildings has no walls, but the other one is white, with a grey roof, and a door.

I'm all out of breath, so I sit myself with my back against the tree. And Angus must be tired also, and lies beside me, panting away.

From where I'm sitting, I can see right across the valley where the fields are all spread out like green and brown mats, with the cows moving across them very slowly. Below me is the roof of the house, and the track that winds its way up here. Kate and Mister Henderson are coming along it. He's waving his arm in the air and after a moment, I hear him talking away to her.

They climb over the last stile, and when they come towards me, he calls, 'I see you're enjoying the view, Brede.'

Kate looks about her. 'I do believe we're on the top of the world!'

He gives a laugh. 'The view certainly takes some beating. Missus Henderson thinks me very fanciful when I tell her that treading up that track is like walking on the backbone of the mountain!'

'I wonder which direction Donegal is?' Kate says.

'Is that where you're from, Kate?'

'Yes – a small place in Fanad – you won't have heard of it.'

'Was it very hard to leave?'

'It was home,' she says, and her face takes on a sad look.

'I've been in Knockmarran all my life, and can't imagine living anywhere else.' He gives a laugh. 'No doubt they'll be carrying me out in a box.'

I can't see why anyone would do that to him, when there's the trap and a carriage, and all the horses.

'But I hope you'll soon feel settled in here, Kate,' he says. 'You and Brede both.'

I give him a smile, because it's grand to be up here in the sunshine with the pair of them, and to know we've a bed of our own to sleep in, and as much food as my belly will hold.

'It's very good of you and Missus Henderson to take us in,' Kate says. 'Though one day, God willing, we'll be back in Donegal.'

'Of course.'

I'm thinking that going back to our village would be even nicer than being here, especially if my mammy and da were waiting for me. But then I remember the powerful stink of their room, worse than pig-shite, when I went to wake them that morning, and the cold feel of their skin. And although the sun is shining, I give a shiver.

'There's a wind getting up,' Mister Henderson says, watching a piece of straw blow across the ground, 'so let's take a look at the dairy.'

I scramble up, and Kate and I follow him over to the building.

'Over there are the stalls, where the cows come to be milked.' He reaches into his pocket, and draws out a big key. 'The fellow of this is on a hook behind the kitchen door, so Brede will have to remember to bring it with her. Not so long ago, we didn't have to keep everything locked up, but nowadays there's plenty of people about who'd be only too glad to help themselves.'

He pushes open the door that gives a kind of a creak, and we step into a long room with a window at the far end and shelves either side of a passage that runs up the middle. The place smells like wet earth. On the shelf nearest me is a big plate of butter, all yellow and shiny, and opposite are rows of basins, filled with milk. I've never seen so much in my life – the Thompsons kept just a small bowl of it, on the pantry shelf, along with the butter.

'The bowls nearest us are from this morning's milking,' Mister Henderson says. 'So when you come up here, Brede, you'll need to fill your pail from the one at the back. The dipper is beside it. The buttermilk is on the other side, and the cheeses are hanging on that rack there. You'll have a bag to put the cheese in, and of course a bucket for the milk.'

Just as I'm wondering how I'll remember it all, Kate says, 'I'll come up with Brede the first couple of times, to show her what to do.'

'Splendid,' Mister Henderson looks across at her, and then away. It's strange how neither of them looks at the other. 'She can bring Angus for company. The run will do him good.'

It'll be grand to come up here with him every morning and evening, so I give another smile.

'Well, we'd best be getting back. I've plenty to see to, as doubtless you have too, Kate.'

Angus goes off down the path, with me behind him. And when I get past the steep bit of track, I put my hands out, as if I'm a bird with wings. And I go flying down that path, feeling the air lovely and cool against my face, with Angus barking away beside me.

When we reach the trees, we stop and wait for Kate and Mister Henderson. And when they come up, he says, 'You can find your way back from here, Kate? I've to check on one of the calves.'

'Certainly, Mister Henderson,' she says.

'Oh, by the way. I'll need to go over the arrangements for the meeting I'm holding at the end of the month. There'll be a big crowd to feed, but I'm sure you'll handle it.'

'No problem,' she says, and we watch him turn and head off along the track, past the gate with the apples on either side.

'It's good of him to give you that job,' Kate says, as we cross the yard. 'But we must make sure you get it right.'

When we walk into the kitchen, Annie is standing there, looking none too pleased. 'Where on earth did you get to, Kate?'

Her face goes all pink. 'Mister Henderson has been showing us the dairy. He needs Sam's help on the farm, so he's asked Brede to take over the work.'

'I'd have thought Sam or Brian could have taken you up there?'

'Mister Henderson wanted to. Now, I'd better get my pastry made.' She reaches for the flour. 'He mentioned some big meeting. Do you know much about it?'

'Oh, *that*,' Annie's mouth turns down again. 'Only that it'll bring nothing but trouble.'

'How do you mean?'

'Well, for a start he and Missus Henderson are at loggerheads over it.' She lowers her voice, although there's no one about to hear. 'Mind you, it's no surprise, given her support for the Order.'

Kate draws in her breath. 'I thought it was only the father he disagreed with.'

Annie fetches three cups from the dresser. 'She's not Frank Curran's daughter for nothing.'

'I don't understand – she and Mister Henderson seem to get on really well.'

'You're not alone in that thought, Kate. And maybe the less we know about it all, the better. But I will say this: for all his kind ways, Mister Henderson has some very odd ideas.' She watches Kate pour the tea. 'It'll turn out badly,' she says, 'you mark my words.'

FIFTEEN

THE SUN IS A CIRCLE OF BUTTER OVER OUR HEADS, and the birds are singing for all they're worth, as Kate and myself and Angus set out. This is the biggest job I've ever had, and Kate wants to see how I'm managing. I know I'll get on really well, and as we go out of the yard, I give a skip.

The lambs are bleating on the other side of the wall, and a small, green frog goes hop-hopping in front of us. I stoop to pick it up, and Kate says, 'Leave it be, Brede. You'll only squash it.'

So the dog and I run on ahead, with Kate following more slowly on account of the pail she's carrying.

It's a steep old climb to the top of the world, and by the time I get there, I'm all puffed out. So I sit myself under the big tree, stretch out my legs, and watch the cows ambling about in the field below.

Kate comes up the path, and settles beside me, and I lean against her, with Angus panting away on the other side. She gives my hair a stroke, and suddenly I'm recalling my mammy's voice. 'You're a great wee girl, Brede, do you know that?' I touch Kate's cheek, and feel it all warm against my hand.

'We must get going in a moment. But isn't it a grand view?' She points ahead. 'Look – the roof of the Hendersons' place. It must be the biggest farm in the district. His brother's house is closer than I thought. And there's the town beyond it.'

From up here, it's just a heap of small boxes. I picture the Drummond man, huff-huffing away in one of them, and I'm glad to be somewhere he'll never come to, because I'd say a stout fellow like him would never get up that steep path.

The fields are all spread out around the town, and each one is a different colour, with a line of grey around it.

Kate sees where I'm looking, and gives a laugh. 'It's just like the patchwork cover Missus Thompson has on her bed. Do you understand the colours, Brede? The grey is from the stone walls. The light green is the new summer barley, the blue is the flax, and the pink and white is the potato flowers.'

I'm not sure I'll remember them all, but Kate is pointing above our heads. 'Look, a pair of curl Ewes!'

I jump up, because just the sight of them swooping around makes me want to go running back down the path, with my arms spread out on either side of me, and the air rushing against my face.

'You're right.' Kate brushes the grass off her skirt. 'There's work to be done.'

She goes over to the dairy, and I drag myself after her, because there'll be no running for me now, not with the full pail to carry down to the house. And for a moment, I think how grand it would be if we were back on the road, free to do whatever we pleased.

'Here's the key.'

It takes both hands to turn it in the lock, but at last the door creaks open.

She puts down the pail. 'Now, what have you to do first?'

I look across at the basins of milk. Each has a layer of yellow cream on the top, as if the sunshine has melted into them. But the floor is made of stone and the place has that damp smell to it. So even though it's a warm day, I give a shiver.

She gives me a shove. 'Brede! Are you listening?'

I think for a moment, and then I pick up the dipper. It's cold and heavy in my hand. I start filling the pail from the far bowl. Some of the milk spills onto the floor, and it takes more scoops than I can count, but at last it's full almost to the top.

Kate stands with her arms folded across her chest, watching. 'Now what?'

I reach for the cheese. There's such a big round of it, and it smells so gorgeous, that I press it to my nose.

'Just place it in the bag, like I showed you.'

When I've done that, I carry the pail outside, and lock the door after me.

'Good,' she says, and my insides give a smile.

She calls to Angus and the three of us set off along the path. It's much slower on the way down, because the bag of cheese is going bump-bump against my chest, and the milk keeps jumping out of the pail whenever it gets a chance. So I'm glad when at last we're back in the kitchen.

Annie is polishing knives on a cloth. 'So, how did the child get on?'

'Just fine, Annie.'

Margaret turns from the sink. 'There's a wonder.'

'Put the milk in the corner there, Brede,' Kate says, 'and I'll get the kettle on. I could do with a drink of tea after that climb, and—'

Someone is whistling 'On a Fine Summer Morning'. It's a tune that Kate sometimes sings, and just the sound of it makes my feet go tap-tap.

A moment later, Mister Henderson comes in from the yard. He has his boots on, and a grey shirt with the sleeves rolled up. He gives a big smile. 'Good morning to you all. Another grand day.'

'It certainly is,' Annie says.

'The doctor was here earlier, and it's fine for Missus Henderson to come down for her lunch.'

'We're very glad to hear it, Mister Henderson,' Annie says, with a look at Margaret.

'And I came to tell you that my brother will be arriving shortly, along with Missus Henderson's mother and sister. So that'll be five of us for lunch, Kate.'

I count them off in my head: Mister and Missus Henderson, Pea-in-the-pod, the Bosom woman, and Poor Nora.

154

'Very good,' Kate says. 'Did you want to go over the menu, Mister Henderson?'

'Missus Henderson usually sees to that side of things, so I'm sure she'll be discussing them with you in her own good time. Meanwhile, she's taken a great fancy to your chicken broth. So if you could be sure to have plenty made?'

'Certainly, Mister Henderson.'

He gives another smile, before leaving by the yard door, whistling as he goes.

Annie goes back to her polishing. 'There goes a happy man!'

'Although he must be the last one in the household to know,' Margaret says. 'Since February it's been.'

'Without her monthlies?' Kate says.

'Yes, and let's just hope it works out better for her this time.'

'How do you mean?'

'One stillborn girl, and a boy lost at a week old.'

'Poor lady,' Kate says.

When she and I were on the road one time, I ran on ahead, and when I stopped and looked about me, she was nowhere to be seen. I was only lost for a short while, but it's a terrible feeling all right.

Annie pushes back her chair. 'Margaret, have you cleared that parlour grate yet?'

'I'll do it right away, Annie.'

Kate looks up at the clock. 'Oh, goodness, that can't be the time! I've not yet started on the steak and kidney. Fetch the baking dish from the shelf, Brede, while I cut up the beef.'

I put it on the table, and watch her slice up a big piece of meat. The blood runs off its board onto the table, and I put out my finger to have a taste. 'Stop that!'

Her voice is so sharp, my chin starts to wobble.

She gives a sigh. 'You did well at the dairy. And from tomorrow, it'll be just yourself going up there. With Angus, of course.'

I give a skip, and she shouts, 'How can I get anything done, with you under my feet all the time?'

I'm nowhere near her feet, so there's no call for her to be so cross.

'You can make a start on the potatoes,' Kate says. 'There's a dish of them on the scullery draining-board, but we'll only need to use half.'

I move along the passage slowly, and I'm glad when I reach the scullery and there's no sign of any slugs. But I'm thinking that Kate has it wrong, because my knife has a way of taking off most of the potato along with the skin, so I'm going to have to do the lot.

I've just peeled the first one, when I hear steps. Then Margaret says, 'Mister Henderson and his brother are at it again. Arguing so loud, it's given Missus Henderson a bad head.'

'Her mother's taken her for a walk,' Annie says, 'so maybe things will have calmed down by the time they return.'

'Pigs might fly!'

Sam showed me the litter that one of the sows had, and as I picture them, all wrinkled up and pink-looking, taking off over the yard, I give a grin.

'Mister Henderson's still dead set on it,' Annie says, 'and he's the one in charge now.'

'More's the pity. Any more talk of Home Rule, and I swear I'll go crazy!'

'Well, if I had my way, Margaret, I'd…'

They carry on into the kitchen, and all goes quiet.

The tune Mister Henderson was whistling is still going round and round in my head. So I check that no one's about, and then I go on my tiptoes along the passage and into the hall.

I'm standing beside the picture of the man with the gorgeous sash, when a door opens, and I hear Mister Henderson's voice. 'I'm telling you, John, that's how it's going to be!'

He comes out, followed by the brother. So I turn my back, and give a chair a wipe with my apron.

'And what gives you the right to order me around?'

'You're a fine one to be talking of rights!'

'Don't think you'll succeed in this, William – not if we loyal Ulstermen have anything to do with it.'

'Do you understand nothing? It will be out of your hands.'

And Pea-in-the-pod yells: 'You can stick your Home Rule up your arse!'

I draw in my breath, because Kate says that's a very bad word, along with Fek and Boll-ox, and some others that I can't recall. I'm just trying to remember them all, when Pea-in-the-pod turns on his heel and the front door slams shut behind him.

'Heaven preserve us!' Mister Henderson says.

I give him a smile to show that I want him to be kept nice and safe too, but he doesn't see me, and back he goes into the front room.

So I'm left by myself in the hall, wondering what all the fuss is about over this Home Rule, because there's at least three other rules that I know of, and not even Kate in one of her moods gets this worked up over them.

Rule 1: When you're dancing, shoulders back, and point your toes.

Rule 2: Keep your thumbs clear when you're chopping vegetables.

Rule 3: Don't go wandering through the house, because the Hendersons won't like it.

I'm not really wandering – it's my legs have carried me into Missus Henderson's parlour for a quick peek around.

There's a hearth at the far end, but the fire's not lit, and the windows have curtains with bunches of flowers over them. There's one, two, three chairs with frocks on, and a table with pictures, like Missus Thompson had. One picture is of Mister and Missus Henderson, and the little fellow, Rory. They're dressed in brown, and they stare out at me, with their faces all solemn. I like it better when Mister Henderson is smiling, but I lift up the picture, and give him a kiss.

By the window is a table with something that's all bright and shining. It's on this piece of sewing that's spread over the table, and is as beautiful as any of the trimmings on Missus Thompson's frocks. In the middle of the cloth is a man on a horse. The gold is at the top of his hat, but where his face should be hasn't been stitched

158

yet. The horse is white, and the man is dressed in a red coat. I put out my hand and give the gold a stroke. It's soft under my fingers, but a bit of dirt from the kitchen comes off on it.

I'm just giving it a rub with my sleeve, when the door behind me opens, and a voice says, 'What in heaven's name do you think you're doing, girl?'

It's the Bosom woman, in her black frock and hat, and behind her is Missus Henderson, still very tired-looking, and Poor Nora, with those pink patches over her face.

'Nothing to be concerned about, Mother,' Missus Henderson says. 'It's only the new cook's daughter.'

'Well, if it was down to me, I would *not* be permitting a kitchen servant to roam the house.' She gives a sniff. 'Especially a papist one. I take it that was another of your husband's ideas?'

Missus Henderson's voice goes all tight. 'William and I always discuss these matters together.'

'Well, I think Mother has a point,' Poor Nora says. 'Surely it's a bit odd, Helen, for a Carth Lick servant to be taking an interest in one of our banners?'

'I'm glad that at least you can see the danger, Nora,' the mother says.

Poor Nora goes all pink, but it makes not a bit of difference to the patches, which only show up the more.

'The only sense we need to make of it,' Missus Henderson says, 'is that our new cook is a hard worker, and her food is excellent.'

I move closer to her.

'How is Grace Purdy doing?' Poor Nora asks.

'Still in her bed most of the day, but as soon as she's feeling stronger, we'll move her into her own place. William has had one of the cottages done up. She's earned some peace and quiet in her last years.'

She looks across at me. 'Run on back to the kitchen now, Brede. I'll be along in a while to check how the lunch is doing.'

The Bosom woman has such a fierce face on her that I don't need to be told twice.

I duck past her, and go along the passage as fast as my legs will take me.

As I reach the scullery door, there's a shriek that makes me jump out of my skin. The next moment a shape comes rushing out at me.

'I've caught you!' young Rory says, flinging his arms about me.

I put back my head and laugh, and then he lets go of me, and I go chasing after him into the scullery, and we're having a great game of jumping out at each other, when Pimple-face comes in.

Rory tries to hide behind me, but she drags him out, and smacks him across the legs, one, two, three times. He lets out a roar, and just at that moment, in comes Kate. 'What on earth's going on here?' Then she turns to me. 'I'm waiting on those potatoes, Brede.'

She goes over to the sink, and my insides give a jump. Because there's only the one peeled spud at the bottom of the bowl. The rest are still in a pile beside it.

'So what have you been doing all this time?'

'I can tell you what she's been doing,' Pimple-face says.

'Chasing Rory around the place, and making a tremendous racket into the bargain.'

'For two pins I'd turn you out this minute, Brede!' And Kate smacks my arm so hard that now I'm the one crying.

'You're to peel the rest of those potatoes. *Now!*'

She goes out again, and Pimple-face seizes Rory's ear, and drags him off. I can hear him sobbing away as they go down the passage.

And I'm crying so hard that water from my nose drips all over the spuds. I wipe my face with my sleeve, wishing the morning had not turned out so bad. Because what in the world will happen if Kate stops looking out for me?

Home Rule 4: If you don't want to be put in the Poor House, finish the spuds like she tells you.

SIXTEEN

I'M UNDER THE BIG TREE IN THE YARD, FASTENING the piece of straw round my foot. It's a Sunday afternoon, so there's just Kate and myself here.

Straw foot – lift heel, down.

Other foot – slide, step.

She's busy baking, and the minute she has her sponge cake and scones finished, she'll be out to see how I'm getting on with my steps.

Other foot – lift heel, down.

Straw foot – slide, step, step.

The Hendersons are away out to her mother's, taking Pimple-face and young Rory with them. Margaret is visiting her sister, and Annie has gone to take tea with Missus Purdy, who moved into her cottage a week past. She says I must call in for another chat about Christmas, but I've not yet had the chance.

It's a fine afternoon, with the chickens pecking about the place, and the rooster perched above them on the fence. With his red and black feathers, he's every bit as handsome as the Thompsons' bird. I thought about chasing this one, but I got into such a load of trouble the last time, I'll wait till one of his feathers comes loose.

It's as well for the creature that Kate has Angus tied up, because he likes nothing better than to give it a chase. He also likes to join in the dancing, and the last time he did that, the two of us got all tangled together, and ended up falling in a heap. I didn't mind one bit, and by the way his tail kept wagging, he didn't either. But Kate said better safe than sorry. Which makes no sense, because I'd rather have him fall over me, however sore it makes me afterwards.

Straw foot, lift heel up, down—

Clap-clap. Clap-clap.

I stop what I'm doing and look to see where the sound is coming from. Clap-clap, it goes again. When I look over at the gate, who should be leaning against it, with his arms folded across his chest, but a man with red hair and a beard with white bits in it. He walks towards me, and I see it's the Dermot fellow. I've not set eyes on him since the time he dropped us off in the lane, and I can't say I've missed him.

He has a bag slung over his shoulder, and a pipe that he takes a big puff on.

'Hello there, Brede! You're a sight to behold!' The smoke rises around him in a grey cloud.

It's nice to hear my name, so I give him a smile.

He jerks his head towards the house. 'Kate's inside, is she?'

When I nod, he moves to the kitchen door. 'Well, let's see what she's up to.'

I follow him in, and Kate looks up from the table, where she's beating sugar and butter in a brown bowl. 'Dermot Friel! What on earth brings you here?'

'Is that any way to greet a fellow who's travelled miles just for a glimpse of your pretty face?'

'Get away with you!'

But he doesn't get away. Instead, he goes over, and stands right beside her.

She carries on with her mixing. 'The family wouldn't care for you calling in like this.'

'But they're not here, are they? They're away out visiting the widow mother, and won't be back until evening.'

'How in the world do you know that?'

'How about some fresh soda bread?' He dips his finger into the bowl and scoops up a piece of mixture. 'Or a nice piece of pie?'

Kate always tells me off if I put my hand in the food, but now she gives a laugh. 'You're a bold one!'

'I'll take that as a "yes",' he says, pulling out a chair.

'Lift the kettle onto the stove, would you, Brede?' she says. 'We may as well have our tea now.'

'Tea? I think not.' He draws a brown bottle from his bag. 'I thought a drop of the hard stuff might go down well.'

'Not for me,' Kate says.

'Brede?' I go to take the bottle, and she hits his arm.

'You should know better than to offer her that!'

He gives a shrug, then pulls at the stopper with his

teeth. They're very white and strong-looking, and the cork comes out with a pop. I watch his throat tighten and loosen as the drink goes right down inside him. Then he wipes his mouth with his hand. 'That's hit the spot!'

I'm just thinking that it might do Pimple-face a power of good too, when Kate moves to the door. 'You should be going.'

He pushes his chair back. 'Only codding.' He jerks his thumb towards me. 'What do you take me for? I'd never waste the good stuff on her. Besides, I enjoyed seeing her dance just now. And' – he reaches into his bag again – 'I've brought my fiddle.'

Kate's face lights up. 'I've not heard one since – since…' Her voice trails away.

'You'll enjoy hearing it all the more now. So let's not waste any more time.'

'The baking?'

'Forget the bloody bread, woman! This is your afternoon off. If you'd taken that job at the mill, you wouldn't be thinking twice about it!'

She hesitates a moment, and then wipes her hands on her apron, and walks out into the yard. Dermot follows, and I come along behind.

He stops, and takes a look around him. The dog gets up and gives his tail a wag but, apart from him, there's nothing to be seen but the rooster and one, two, three chickens.

Dermot walks over, and leans against the big tree. He puts the bottle down beside him, and takes the fiddle out of his bag. It's brown and shiny-looking, like the one my da used to play. There were plenty of others in the village who had a fiddle, or a drum or a pipe. And on a summer's evening, everyone would gather at the crossroads, and have a bit of a dance. The old ones were there, as well as us children, and altogether it was great *craic*. Just thinking of it now makes me happy and sad all at once.

I look across at Kate, wondering if she recalls those times too, but she's busy watching Dermot, who tucks the fiddle under his chin, and starts to play.

The music starts slow and soft, like something heard a long way off. Then it gets louder, as if a flock of birds is circling around and coming to land on our heads. And all the time, his arm is going backwards and forwards, backwards and forwards, as if he's cutting a bunch of twigs in the air.

Kate nods at me, and I step out, shooing the chickens away. I put my arms down by my sides the way she's taught me, and start to move. But it's so long since I've heard a fiddle, it's hard to make my feet behave as they should.

'You missed a half-turn there, Brede,' she says. 'Go back and start it again.' And when I've done that, she says, 'Good. But that straw-foot leg isn't near high enough. And remember to count, like I told you!'

She's moved over, so that she's standing next to Dermot, who lowers his fiddle.

'You're terrible hard on her.'

I give a smile, so Kate will know I don't mind.

'It's the only way she'll learn.' But she's not looking at me. It's him she can't take her eyes off.

'True enough.' He raises his fiddle again. 'But what I'd like now, girl, is to see you dance.'

'Other than showing Brede her steps, I've not done any since I was with my family. Quite a while back now.'

'Time to give it another try, so.'

She takes off her apron, and steps into the middle of the yard. At first, when he begins to play, her feet stumble, but then she picks up the beat of it, turning quick and neat as she keeps time to the music. Up and down the yard she goes, moving so fast that the horse puts out his head from the stall to watch her.

I'd like to join in, but already Dermot's playing is too quick for me. And it gets faster and faster, and Kate's hair comes loose, and blows over her face, and her shoes go click-click-click across the yard, as if they've a life of their own.

Then Angus starts to bark, rushing up and down on the end of his rope, and twisting himself into knots around it. And his noise sets off the pigs and chickens, so there's a deal of squealing and squawking and flapping around – altogether a great carry-on. But through it all Dermot never once stops his playing, and Kate never misses a step.

When he's done, he lowers his fiddle, and she stands there, panting away.

'By God,' he says. 'What a wonder you are, Kate O'Hagan! When did I last see the likes of that?'

They stand there, looking at one another, and then he picks up his bag, and walks over to her. He wipes a line of sweat from her forehead. 'Stay out here,' he says to me, taking her hand in his own, and they walk into the house.

Angus has lain down, panting away, with his head resting on his paws. So I go over and sit beside him. The kitchen door is open, and I hear them laughing together. And I wish I wasn't left here, with the pair of them having a great old time without me.

Then she comes to the door, and calls: 'Are you not ready for your tea, Brede?'

So I go running into the kitchen, and sit myself at the table. She pours the tea, and puts out a plate of scones that are all warm from the oven. Dermot is sitting on the chair Missus Purdy used to have, with his feet up on the range.

Kate puts butter on the scones and some red-coloured jam, and when I take a bite from mine, some of the jam escapes down my front. So I scoop it off with my finger, and it tastes so good, I put in another big piece.

'Remember to close your mouth when you eat,' Kate says to me.

Dermot reaches for another scone. 'She's a good appetite, all right!'

Kate gives a laugh. 'You're not doing so badly yourself!'

'You're not worried the Hendersons will miss these?'

'They've always said Brede and I are welcome to eat our fill of them.'

'Well, wonders will never cease!'

'You shouldn't talk like that. They've been very good to us.'

'I was hoping you'd be very good to me too.'

I wait for her to pass him another scone, but instead she says, 'Get away with you!'

The cat gets up from its box, puts its back into a hoop, and then settles again, and the three of us keep eating, and sipping away at our tea.

Then Dermot says, 'Isn't it time Brede went up to that dairy?'

Kate gives him a surprised look. 'It's too early.'

He holds out his cup for her to fill again. 'Never too early.'

She turns to me. 'Well, it's such a lovely afternoon, Brede, and we could do with some more cheese. So why don't you take Angus, and fetch us another round? You won't have the pail to carry.'

I'm thinking how I'll be free to run about as much as I like, so I pick up the cheese bag and the key, and walk into the yard. Angus is so pleased to be untied, he goes yelp-yelp, and then he's away through the gate like the wind. When I reach it, I turn around. Dermot and Kate are at the window, and I give a wave.

It's lovely being out in the open, feeling the sun on my face. When I reach the first field, I spread my arms, and go swooping about, as if I'm a bird or a butterfly. Then I go running up the slope, and over the stile. Ahead of me, the white arses of the rabbits disappear into the hillside. There's a load of sheep lying by the track. One is right across my path, but it's a lazy old thing and doesn't move an inch. So I reach down and dig my fingers into its coat, which is all soft, with a greasy feel, as if it's had butter melted through it. It gets up then all right, and goes wandering off, and I head up to the next stile.

I've just climbed over it, when I spot someone coming down the track towards me.

When he gets nearer, I see that it's the man who's in charge of the cows. His name is Barney, and he lives along the lane from Missus Purdy. He's very fat, and always in a good humour. The last time I saw him, he gave me an apple, which was all nice and crisp. I didn't eat the inside bit because Margaret says if I swallow the pips, I'll end up with a tree growing inside me. So I gave that part to Angus, who crunched them all up.

Today Barney just says, 'Hello there, Brede! A fine evening!' And we go on past each other.

I'm not usually at the top of the world at this time of day, and the place has a quiet feel to it. There's no birds singing, so maybe it's too warm for them, and in the field below I can see the cows lying with their feet tucked under them, taking a nap.

I open the door of the dairy, and breathe in its cold, earth smell. There are the shelves on either side of me with all the basins of milk on them. The nearest one has a gorgeous yellow skin of cream on it, so I dip my finger in and put a scoop into my mouth. It has a lovely taste to it, but I'm still so full of Kate's scones, I've no room for more.

And as I collect up the cheese, I'm trying to think when the last time was that I had this amount of food around me, let alone a fiddle to dance to, and a proper bed. And if my voice would just come back into my mouth, where it used to be, then everything would be really grand. And I know Kate feels the same way because I heard her tell Annie that she couldn't wait for the day when I had something to say for myself.

I put the lids on the milk and lock the door behind me. Then I set off down the track, with Angus running ahead, and before I know it, I'm going along the straight bit of track under the trees, and turning in through the gate. I tie the dog up in the yard, and walk into the kitchen.

Kate and Dermot are sitting in front of the range. When they see me, they jump up. They're both very sweaty-looking, and Kate says, 'Ah. You're back already!' Her blouse has come undone, and there's a smell of onions, although she's not been making any stew. 'Did you have a great time up there?'

I hand her the cheese.

'Good girl.'

'Well, I'd best be off.' Dermot stands, and gives his trousers a hitch. 'Same time next week?'

I'd like him to play his fiddle again while I go over my steps, so I look across at Kate.

She bites her lip. 'I'm not sure. Mister Henderson has this big meeting arranged, so there'll be plenty to do for it.'

'I hear your man, Chivers, will be over from London shortly.'

'And who might he be?'

'Someone well in with the Prime Minister.'

'You always have something new to tell me.' She lifts the kettle onto the hob. 'But I have to say that I don't care about any of it.'

He moves over, and grips her arm. 'Well, you should. Because Home Rule is the best hope we have.'

She pulls away from him. 'It's quite enough to be worrying if I have enough pies made.'

I'm glad she says that, because I don't like these rules either.

He brushes some hair off her face.

'Maybe if you came round for just a short while?'

'See you then, darlin'.' He gives a grin. 'And maybe you'll have something to tell *me* about what Henderson's planning.'

SEVENTEEN

It's the day of Mister Henderson's meeting, and there's been a deal of coming and going between the house and the barn.

First thing, Sam and some of the Ten Aunts carried up a load of chairs and tables. Then Sam and Annie took plates, along with knives and spoons and glasses and cups and saucers, and those silver pots for the salt and pepper, and dear knows what else.

Kate has been baking all the morning, but we just had bread and cheese for our lunch because all the cakes and pies and scones are to go up to the barn.

She wipes her face with her apron. 'Thank heavens this is the last of them. Pass me that dish, would you Molly?'

It's a lovely green colour, and is the one that's used for putting the slices of fruit loaf on.

Molly is helping in the kitchen, because Missus

Henderson and young Rory are away to the Bosom woman for the night.

'Who could blame Missus Henderson?' Annie says, when she comes in from seeing to things in the house. 'Not the way she and Mister Henderson keep arguing.'

Kate tips flour into a bowl. 'I thought they were getting along better?'

Annie sighs. 'On everything but this. One mention of Home Rule from him, and she's fit to be tied.' She looks across at Kate. 'Though no doubt you'll be in favour?'

'To be honest with you, Annie, I don't pay much heed to any of it. It's enough to have work, and a roof over my head.'

'The best way to be.' Annie shakes her head. 'I wish Missus Henderson felt the same, because she shouldn't be getting so worked up – not in her condition. And—'

The door opens, and in comes Margaret. 'Would you look at that rain! I'm telling you now that I'd like this evening over and done with.'

I want to have a peep inside the barn, to see what's going on, but as I creep towards the door, Annie spots me.

'You're to stay right here, child. You'll only go knocking things over.'

'Come and help me stir this mixture, Brede,' Kate says. 'Goodness knows, it seems a deal of fuss over one meeting.'

I'm thinking that maybe it'll be a bit like the old days in our village, with everyone coming round to have a bit of a song and a dance.

'There'll be a good turn-out,' Annie says, 'because the men will want to hear every word this English fellow says.'

'And the man is Robin Chivers?' Kate asks.

Margaret gives her a look. 'How in the world do you know that?'

'My goodness, is that the time?' Kate says. 'I need to make a start on the custard.'

'And I must see to the fire in the front room,' Annie says. 'Mister James is already in there, drying himself off after his journey.'

'It's setting in all right,' Annie says. 'Molly, you come with me. I'm all behind-hand, so you can let the English fellow in, because he'll be on the doorstep before we know it. And Margaret, could you go up and check on those barn heaters?'

'And I need the privy,' Kate says, turning to me. 'So be a good girl, Brede, and give the table a wipe.'

But I don't want to do that – I want to have a look at an Englishman, because I've never set eyes on one before. So I go tiptoeing along the passage, and into the hall. The place is empty – not a sign of Annie or Molly – although the big clock is still tick-tocking away to itself. I'm just heading back to the kitchen, when there's a knock on the front door.

Mister Henderson and the James man are coming along the far passage, with Molly following. She dodges round them, and as she opens the door, I press myself into the corner.

'Mister Robin Chivers – at your service, sir.'

The wet is fairly running off the man, and when he removes his coat, I see he has on a blue waistcoat, with a gold chain across it. His trousers have lines running up them, like one of Missus Purdy's tablecloths.

Mister Henderson steps forward. 'Come in, Mister Chivers. Let me get you a drink to warm you.'

'What a dreadful night.' The man hands his coat and hat to Molly. 'Does it ever stop raining in Ireland, do you think?'

He may be a robin, but when he sticks out his chest, he puts me in mind of the rooster. He doesn't look much different from an Irish fellow. Only when he speaks, it's as if he's chewing on a mouthful of scone.

I tuck myself further into the shadows.

'Let me introduce, Mister Johnson,' Mister Henderson is saying. 'A keen supporter of ours.'

'Indeed,' the Robin says, as they shake hands. 'There's a good turn-out, I take it?'

'Well over a hundred,' Mister Henderson says. 'We were going to have the meeting in the town, but decided the barn here would be better.'

'I see.'

Mister Henderson waves his arm. 'Come on through to the fire. There's one or two points we need to go over.'

'That won't be necessary,' the Robin says, and his voice is very cold-sounding.

The James man strokes his beard. 'Perhaps you're not aware of just how high feelings are running, Mister Chivers? Things could get a little rough.'

'If there's one lesson I've learned in life, gentlemen,' the Robin says, patting his waistcoat, 'it is this: There is seldom any need for panic.'

I'm thinking if he had all the baking and setting up of the tables to do, he wouldn't be talking that way. Mister

176

Henderson and the James man are giving each other a look too.

'If I might have a wash?' the Robin says.

I'd have thought he was wet enough already, but Mister Henderson beckons to Molly. 'Show our guest the way, would you, Molly?'

When they've gone out, the James man whispers: 'His letter said that Salisbury's come round to our way of thinking. But can we can trust him?'

Mister Henderson shakes his head. 'It's in the bag, James. Even this government can hardly go back on its word.'

'But we only have a handful of supporters. Suppose the rest of them turn on us? They're not likely to take the news lying down.'

'But no doubt Robin Chivers has been picked precisely for his ability to smooth things over.'

'Well, let's just hope you're right.'

The only smoothing over I know is when Margaret or Kate are at the ironing-board, and I'm not such an eejit as to think the English fellow will be doing any of *that*.

After a bit of a wait, the Robin man is back. 'Let's get started, gentlemen,' he says, and Molly hands the three of them their coats.

When she opens the door, I can see the rain fairly bucketing down. They make a run for it, stooping very low, and holding their hats on for all they're worth.

I step forward, and Molly catches sight of me. 'Aren't you meant to be in the kitchen?' She's a bit taller than myself, with the line of spots showing below her cap.

'Well, never mind. We'd better see what we're wanted for next.' As we walk along the passage together, she says, 'My uncle's cousin lives in Salisbury.'

I wish I could tell her that I can't make head nor tail of any of it.

'Oh, there you are, Molly.' Kate points to trays that are set out on the table with covers over them to keep out the wet. 'I don't know why the other two haven't been back to collect these, but you'd better take them up to the barn now. You can carry something, too, Brede. Through the gate on your straw-foot side, and along the path. And come straight back.'

Although I have my shawl round me, I'm soon soaked through, but I don't mind one bit, because now I'll get to see inside the barn.

It's easy enough to spot because it's a great big building, with lamps set all around it. There's a load of pony traps at the entrance, and Francis, with no shoes on him and his legs splashed with mud, has a hold of Mary. He has his head turned away, and doesn't see me. From inside the open door comes a buzzing of voices, as if someone's poked a stick into a nest of wasps.

Then I hear Mister Henderson's voice. 'Francis, you can't stay out here on such a night. No – never mind what Mister Thompson's told you – the pony will look after itself. Get yourself into the warm, and tell Annie to give you something to eat.'

They go in through the door, and Molly and I follow. Then I stop, and stare about me, because this isn't like any barn I've ever been in. There's no creatures, for a

178

start, and no bits of machinery in the corners, or clumps of hay hanging from the walls. Instead, there's rows and rows of men, sitting with their backs to me. They're all wearing black hats, which make them look like a line of mushrooms, and there's a powerful smell of wet coats. Facing them is a raised ledge, with a table and chairs on it, and who should be sitting in the middle seat but the Robin, talking away to a stout man with a bald head.

It's the Drummond man. I push myself against the wall because I'm remembering him huff-huffing away with Missus Thompson, and how I took her handkerchief off him, and fell arse-over-tip down his steps. So the last thing I want is for him to set eyes on me.

Annie is beckoning me forward. She and Margaret and two other women are behind the table that has a great spread of food on it. But I can't move, because Mister Henderson and another fellow are blocking our path.

'I'll never understand why you mollycoddle these people,' the man is saying, nodding his head at Francis, who's munching on a piece of cake. 'A feckless lot!'

I'm glad Kate isn't with me to hear the bad word.

The man is so bundled up against the wet, it's only when he turns his head that I see it's Pea-in-the-pod. 'They need to stand on their own feet,' he says.

'But isn't that just what the lad was doing, John? And in a night not fit for a beast to stand in!'

'Why don't you get it into your thick skull, William Henderson, that you don't speak for me, or for anyone else here?'

I don't care for his tone of voice one bit, and I don't think Mister Henderson does either, because he says, 'Let's see what our English guest has to say about it, shall we? Come along, James, we—' He breaks off. 'Who in God's name put *that* up?'

I look to where he's pointing. Across the room from us, on the far wall, is the piece of cloth that was in Missus Henderson's room the time I shut myself in. There's the man on the horse, with his face all filled in. He has that lovely patch of gold on his hat, and down at the bottom is a row of letters.

'Helen and the other women have done us proud,' Pea-in-the pod says.

I think the stitching looks very well too, but Mister Henderson has gone all red in the face. '"The Loyal Sons of Knockmarran". Self-indulgent clap-trap! I want it down from there this minute!'

The James man tugs on his sleeve. 'It's only put up to annoy, William. Maybe better to leave it for now?'

Mister Henderson draws in his breath. 'You're right. We need to get this meeting started.'

The two of them start walking towards the front, and Pea-in-the-pod follows, with a big grin on his face. As they climb onto the ledge, everything goes quiet, so the only sound is their steps, and the rain on the roof.

Molly places our trays on the table, and Annie leans towards her, and whispers, 'Bring the rest of the food up here, Molly, quick as you can. But leave the child back at the house.'

There's quite a crowd just inside the door, and as we

move towards it, Molly whispers, 'Let's wait a wee moment and see the *craic*.'

So we stand, along with Francis, who's munching away. My belly feels all empty, but I daren't put out my hand to the food, in case Annie sees me.

Mister Henderson has stepped to the middle of the ledge, and now he clears his throat. 'I have pleasure in introducing Mister Robin Chivers. As you all know, he comes to outline the Prime Minister's latest proposals regarding Home Rule for Ireland, and—'

A voice from the back shouts, 'No Sir Enda!' But they must still have a great liking for the fellow, because a slow clap-clap begins, like the time Dermot admired my dancing in the yard.

Mister Henderson has a very angry look about him, but when he raises his hand, no one takes a blind bit of notice. Some of the men are stamping their feet, and others are making hissing sounds. I can tell you now that if I carried on this way, I'd be in for a good slapping.

Then the Robin man gets off his seat. He moves very slowly, with his toes turned out, as if he's going for an afternoon stroll.

'Gentlemen! Gentlemen!' His voice is so pleasant-sounding, that the racket dies away. 'Your concern is justifiable. Indeed it is. For everyone here knows what the Irish problem is. It is the Carth Lick problem.'

'Here! Here!' someone shouts.

I'm wondering why he's calling attention to himself, because if I've learned one thing, it is that it's always best to tuck yourself in a corner until the problem goes away.

The Robin holds up his hand. 'The season of goodwill may still be a long way off, gentlemen but, nonetheless, the words I bring you now are ones of comfort and joy.'

Mister Henderson starts to say something, but the man carries right on speaking. 'Would you give away your land and birthright to the papists?' The Robin moves his arm up and down, as if he's drawing water from the pump. 'I say, as well give them to the pigs. Would you have our queen turned from her throne? I say as well put a crown on one of the murdering Feen Yuns! Would you come under the rule of Rome? I say, as well be ruled by a pack of heathens!' His voice has such a grand ring to it that it's no wonder the feet begin drumming again. The Robin moves to the edge of the shelf, and the drumming stops. He lowers his voice, and the men stretch their necks forward to have a listen. 'Tonight, gentlemen, I bring you an assurance. And it is this: Salisbury will *never* support Home Rule for Ireland!'

There's a moment's silence.

Mister Henderson has his hands over his face, and the James man has a shocked look to him, and I don't know why they can't be as pleased as everyone else. Because all the men are leaping from their seats, shouting and cheering, and throwing their hats in the air. It's such a grand sight, that I start jumping up and down for all I'm worth.

'Stop that, Brede!' Annie has come round, and she pinches my arm so hard that I let out a cry; but no one hears it above the din.

When things quieten down, Pea-in-the-pod steps forward, and he starts going on about a difficult time that's now over. 'Three cheers for Salisbury!' he calls. 'Three cheers for Mister Robin Chivers!'

I wish I could shout along with everyone else, but now Annie has me by the shoulders, and is pushing me to the door. 'For God's sake,' she says. 'This is no place for the likes of you.' She turns to Molly. 'Back to the house, the pair of you. And don't let me catch you up here again!'

I can't work out if she's talking to us that way because Molly is a Prod, or because I'm a Carth Lick.

Outside, the rain has stopped, but there's great pools of water everywhere. The face of the moon shines up at me from the nearest one. I stoop down, trying to see myself in it, but Molly pulls me back. 'Are you not wet enough already?'

Then there's a great pounding of boots, as three men in coats and black hats come running past. 'See you at the march, boys!' one of them shouts.

And I'm wishing I could be there too to do more of that jumping up and down.

In the kitchen, Kate's sitting, having a drink of tea. I'm hoping for a cup, but she says, 'You've both taken your time. There's more food for the barn. You'd better take it on up now.'

There's one, two, three trays of cake sliced up and arranged in rows. Some are pink, some are yellow and some are brown with currants in them, and they smell really gorgeous.

'Brede mustn't go,' Molly says.

'Whatever do you mean, Molly?'

'It's because of the way she's been carrying on – stamping her feet, and leaping about.'

'For heaven's sake, Brede!' Kate turns all cross again. 'Can I not trust you with anything?'

My chin starts to wobble, but before she can say anything more, the door opens, and in walks Mister Henderson. And behind him is the James man, and behind him is Mister Thompson.

The minute I see him, I tuck myself into the corner.

Mister Henderson has such a long face on him, that I long to tell him if he wants to speak, I won't do any more jumping.

'I've left Margaret and Annie clearing up in the barn.' He's speaking very soft so it's hard to hear him. 'Could you bring us some tea in the front room, Kate?'

'Certainly, Mister Henderson.'

Mister Thompson gives a laugh. 'Tea? By the looks of you, Henderson, you're in need of something much stronger.'

'I know you're not in sympathy, Alexander, but can't even you see what a disaster this evening's been – not just for all of us in the region, but for the whole of Ireland?'

'Oh, I never let any of this polly tickle stuff trouble me, and no doubt you and I will remain friends. But you do realise that you've upset a good many here tonight?'

'That our neighbours cannot listen to reasoned argument is beyond me,' Mister James says. 'And many of our friends across the water will be saddened by what has taken place.'

'Ah, England – a foreign country! Have a care. The differences between us widen by the hour.'

Mister Henderson shakes his head. 'I'll not believe that a mere handful of men can block progress. They just need time to get used to the idea. I'll check with London as to how we should proceed.' He moves to the door. 'But come on through, the pair of you. I'm sure our excellent cook here can find us some ham and cheese.'

Mister Thompson looks across at Kate. 'Small world, isn't it? I wondered where you'd got to.'

His voice makes me want to hide myself under the table, but he's standing in front of it, so I stay right where I am.

'And now we know. Missus Thompson said she'd come across your daughter, but I'd no idea you were in the household as well.' He turns back to Mister Henderson. 'Thank you for the offer of a meal, William, but I'm away to my bed.'

'Of course, Alexander. You've quite a journey in front of you. Give my best to Adelina.'

With a nod, Mister Thompson is out of the door, and I'm not sorry to see him go.

The James man gives a yawn. 'And I'm done in, too. If you'll forgive me, William.'

'Did you see the look that Thompson man gave you, Kate?' Molly says, when the three of us are alone. 'I'd not want to be working for *him*.'

Kate bites her lip. 'I doubt they'll be wanting the rest of this food, Molly, so you can make a start on the clearing up.' She turns to me. 'Time for your bed, Brede.'

As I go off down the passage, I hear her say, 'Can they not see that all these goings-on only make it worse for us Carth Licks?'

EIGHTEEN

MARGARET AND MYSELF ARE HAVING A TRIAL run, though there's no chance of any running on account of all we're carrying. I have a dish with a cover, and inside are one, two, three slices of lamb, a spoonful of mash, and some greens. Margaret's basket has in it a bowl of stewed apple and some of the day's baking. If she weren't beside me, I'd be biting into a slice of that fruit cake, because the smell of it is really grand.

'It doesn't mean you're a trial,' Kate said earlier, when she saw me pulling a face. 'We just want to be sure you know where to go.'

Margaret and myself walk past the barn, where those men in their black hats did all that jumping up and down at Mister Henderson's meeting. That was a while back, so there's not a sign of them today, and no chance of taking a peek inside either, because the doors are tight shut.

The sun over our heads is as bright as a buttercup and I wish the Robin man could see how different the place looks with all the pools of water gone. The birds are chirping their heads off, and the sky is the same blue as that gorgeous frock of Missus Thompson's. I'd rather Mister Thompson hadn't seen Kate and myself in the kitchen that time, but she says we're to pay no heed, as Mister Henderson will see them off. So I'll not fret about them, because right now I'm so excited over being on my way to somewhere new, that I give a skip.

Margaret pulls at my arm. 'Careful – we don't want that food spilled!' She points to a row of cottages. 'That's where the Ten Aunts live. They're the ones who work on the farm.'

It's a puzzle where the Ten Uncles have got to, but I soon forget about them because we stop beside a hedge filled with those red and purple bells that grow all around. 'Isn't that fewsher lovely?' Margaret says.

If only young Rory was here, we'd have a grand time popping them flowers.

Behind the hedge is a white house, with a roof that has a load of turf on the top of it. We walk up a path to a brown door, and Margaret goes rap-rap on it. Then she pushes it open. 'Hello!' she calls. 'I've your dinner for you, and a visitor!'

I follow Margaret in. On my straw-foot side is a shelf with cups and saucers, and a dish with some old tea leaves in it. We go through another door into a room that has a black range with a kettle boiling away on the top. There's a table in the corner, and one, two chairs pushed against the wall and sitting in another chair by the range is Missus Purdy.

She looks up when she sees us. Her skin is still kind of floury, but her eyes have that nice soft look to them. 'Ah, Margaret. I was wondering when you'd be coming. And who have we here?'

I step forward.

'Good heavens! If it isn't Kate's daughter, Brede! Come and sit by me, child, so I can hear you properly.'

Margaret gives a laugh. 'You won't be doing much listening with this one.' She points to the table. 'Put your dish down there,' she says to me.

Missus Purdy pushes back her chair. 'I'll just make us some tea.'

'Not for me, thank you. Missus Henderson wants me to take a run into town. But the child will keep you company.' She turns to me. 'Sam will collect you when it's time for you to return for your dinner. And from tomorrow, God willing, you'll be doing this on your own.'

She goes out, and Missus Purdy and I give each other a smile.

She makes us both tea, and then she lifts two scones out of the basket, and spreads butter on them. We sit by the range eating and drinking and, after a while, she starts talking away. 'I'll tell you something, Brede. I miss the company of the big house more than I'd have thought. Do you know that I first went to the Hendersons when I was about the age you are now?'

I shake my head.

'My mammy was the cook for Mister Henderson's

father, and she taught me everything I know. As I expect Kate is doing for you?'

I think of all the steps she's shown me, and give another smile.

'Old Mister Charles had some odd ideas, but not as strange as some of Mister William's. Though a decenter couple than him and Missus Henderson you wouldn't wish to meet. Fixing me up with this place is more than I could've hoped for.' She sips her tea. 'But how's Annie getting along? And that new nursemaid – Molly, isn't it?'

I take another bite of my scone.

'Young Rory's quite a handful. And what about Missus Henderson? She must be far gone by now.'

I'm just wondering where Missus Henderson has gone to, when Missus Purdy sucks in her breath. 'You mustn't mind me carrying on like this. It's just grand to have some company. But I forgot how quiet you are. So' – she passes me another scone – 'your turn. Tell me something about yourself.'

I feel the spit in my mouth, but it's no good – the words won't come. So I give the table a kick, and move to the corner, where there's a good clear space. Then I put my hands down by my sides, and keeping my back nice and straight, I start on the Beginner's Reel.

First foot: forward 2,3
Straw foot: forward 2,3
First foot: point, hop, back
Straw foot: point, hop, back.

Maybe it's because Dermot comes round each

Sunday, and I'm getting more practice in, but my feet stay where I want them, and I only knock into the wall the one time.

When I'm done, I stand with the sweat fairly trickling off me, because with the stove lit, the room is very warm.

'My goodness gracious!' Missus Purdy says. 'That was something to see. Now, why don't we go outside, so you can cool off a bit?'

The two of us stand by the fewsher hedge, and she tucks her arm through mine. I give it a squeeze because, although she's fatter and has that white face on her, she puts me in mind of my granny, who lived in the next village and used to come visiting my mammy and da and us children before she was took. I always liked sitting up on her knee.

'There's a grand view of the moor from here,' Missus Purdy says.

Sure enough, there's the fields with the cows in them, and the white dots that are the sheep grazing away, and above it all is the mountain that's a lovely pink from all the summer heather.

'Do you see in the distance, Brede, the roof of the dairy, and the track leading up to it? My eyesight isn't what it used to be, but some clear days I can make out you and the dog running along together.'

It makes me smile to think of her watching Angus and me enjoying ourselves in the sunshine.

'So,' she says, 'what's all this nonsense about your not talking? Because I think you could if you really wanted.'

I have a chew of my hair.

'It's just the two of us here, child, so come along with you. Spit those words out!'

I can hear them in my head all right, but although I shape my tongue around them, they still stay stuck fast inside me.

She gives my arm a shake. 'Try harder.'

I wish I could tell her how hard I am trying.

'Come on now, child,' she says again. 'If you'd just—'

Suddenly we can hear voices and, when I look along the lane, I see one, two, three people walking towards us.

'Who have we coming here?' Missus Purdy says.

As they get nearer, I see that one of them is Barney, the fat cowman, talking away to a couple of young fellows. 'Good day to you, Missus Purdy,' he calls, and the fellows touch their caps. One of them has lovely wide shoulders, and the other has a great head of hair on him. I smile away at them, but they just walk on past.

'Them's the new Ten Aunts,' Missus Purdy says. 'Mister Henderson has had two of the cottages done up special.' She gives a sigh. 'It's a pity there's not more around here like him. But I'll tell you this much, Brede, he's fighting a losing battle.'

I don't like to hear talk of Mister Henderson in a fight, so I turn on my heel, and walk back inside the house. Missus Purdy follows. 'You're right, Brede. No point dwelling on what we can't change.'

She lifts the lid off the dish I brought. 'You must be hungry after all that dancing. There's too much here for me, so why don't the two of us sit here and eat it together?'

It sounds a grand idea. I watch her fetch two plates from the press. She puts a small piece of meat on her own, along with some greens and potato, and on the other plate she puts one, two slices of lamb and the rest of the vegetables.

'I'd always hoped to have a daughter or a son. And although there's nothing to beat one's own flesh and blood, I have to tell you, that you come pretty near.'

I'm just thinking that I don't want to be anyone's piece of meat, not even Missus Purdy's, when there's a rap-rap, and Sam puts his head round the door. He gives a nod towards me. 'Time for your dinner,' he says.

'Goodness. That morning has passed quick. Take the basket back with you, Brede, and be sure to come and see me again tomorrow.' She gives my arm a pat. 'You can dance some more for me then.'

So I go out the door and along the path, with the basket going bump-bump against my knees. Sam is running ahead of me down the path, but I'm not in so much of a hurry myself, because I still have the grand taste of meat and potato in my mouth.

As I go past the big barn, the doors are open, and I hear talk from inside. When I take a peek, all the chairs and tables have gone, and so has the ledge that the Robin and Mister Henderson were speaking from, and so has the gorgeous picture of the man on the horse. Instead, there are piles of straw everywhere, like in a proper barn, and on one of the bundles, a man and a woman are sitting with their backs to me.

'I'll be fine in a moment, William,' Missus Henderson is saying. 'I just needed the rest.'

He puts his arm about her. 'You're looking a better colour already.'

'Thank you. But to return to what we were speaking of earlier – please say you'll at least think about it.'

'We're not going over all that again, are we?' Mister Henderson has begun to speak very loud. 'Sometimes I think you're as bad as my brother.'

'People are talking, William! Bob Drummond says some of the shops may stop supplying us, and—'

'Foolish gossip!'

'At least allow the march to start from the house, as it's always done. It would go a long way towards—'

'As I thought I'd made perfectly clear, Helen, my father's ways are not my own.' His voice has gone all scratchy, and I press myself against the door.

'So you're determined to bring ruin on us all?'

Kate once showed me a ruin. It was just a pile of stones that she said was all that was left of a great house. The stones were black, with bits of green, as if a slug had walked over them. I don't care to think of the Hendersons' place in the same state, because then where would she and I sleep at night?

'Can you not see?' Mister Henderson is saying. 'Every thread stitched, and every drum beaten just adds to the problem.'

'It's impossible to make you see sense.'

'I could say the same of you.'

She gets to her feet. 'It's simply not to be borne!'

I can see from her belly that the babby is still there inside, and I'm just sorry that it's not going to come out of her after all.

I run round the side of the barn, and watch her start off down the path. Then he comes to the door, and calls: 'Helen!' She doesn't answer, and I wonder if he'll go running after her. Instead he lets out a sigh, and follows more slowly.

I wait until they've disappeared round the bend, and then I run down the track and in through the back gate.

When I go into the kitchen, Kate and Annie and Molly and Sam are already at the table eating. They look up as I slide into my seat.

'Margaret should have been back from the town by now,' Annie says. 'But we'll not wait for her.'

There's a plateful of stew in each place, and just the sight of it brings water into my mouth. I put a big spoonful in, and start to chew.

'I wonder how the child enjoyed herself at Missus Purdy's,' Annie says.

I want to tell her what a grand morning I've had – almost as good as the time Kate and I were on the top of the world. I open my mouth and give a blow, trying to shape my words, but before I know it, pieces of meat and a whole load of gravy come flying out.

'For God's sake!' Molly says, wiping the splashes from her cheeks. 'Do I have to sit with her?'

'How many times must I tell you, Brede, to close your mouth when you eat?' Kate is all cross, though how was I to know the stew would rush out like that? She reaches for a cloth. 'I'm very sorry, Molly.'

'No real harm done,' Annie says. 'Ah, and here's Margaret at last.'

'I'm sorry to be so late, though the dear knows it isn't my fault.' She takes her seat beside Annie. 'Wherever I went, I was kept standing about. Even when I was the only one in the shop.'

'Well, never mind.' Annie hands her a plate of stew. 'You're here now.'

'But it was the same for me when I was last in the town,' Molly says. 'My Uncle Bob told me it's because people have taken against Mister Henderson, and—'

I don't like to think of people taking against Mister Henderson, so I'm glad when Annie says, 'Eat your meal, and let's have no more such talk.'

We wait for Margaret to finish, and then Kate fetches the pudding: semolina the colour of cream, and a jar of plum jam to go with it.

'But did you hear the latest *craic*?' Sam says, as we start eating again. 'A farmer across the valley has had the throats of his cattle cut.'

'Sam!' Annie says. 'Have you not listened to a word I've been saying?'

I'm thinking what a deal of blood there must have been. I swirl the jam round and round my plate, and the semolina goes a lovely red colour.

'Must she do that?' Margaret says, and Sam gives a laugh.

'These Feen Yuns,' Molly says. 'It'll be our own throats next.'

'Oh, I'm sure these rebels would not harm any of us,' Kate says.

'Maybe not you or your daughter,' Margaret says.

'Enough!' Annie says. 'I'm just going to see if Missus Henderson needs anything. And I warn you all, there's to be no mention of this to her – not in her condition.' She pushes back her chair. 'Sam, there's plenty of work for you outside. Molly, you need to see to young Rory, and, Margaret, there's still both front rooms to clean.'

When the two of us are left, Kate says, 'You can give me a hand with the dishes, Brede, and—' She doesn't get to finish because the door opens and in walks Mister Henderson.

I wish he didn't have such a sad look on him.

'I just came to ask how you're doing Kate.'

'The best, thank you, Mister Henderson.'

'Any chance of some tea?'

She reaches for the pot. 'Certainly.'

'If it's all right with you, I'll sit and drink it in here.'

She looks at him in a surprised sort of a way. But all she says is, 'Of course, Mister Henderson.'

He seats himself in the chair that Annie uses. 'I never thanked you properly, Kate, for all the extra cooking you did for the meeting.' He gives a cough. 'I expect you heard how it went?'

She looks across at him. 'I'm sorry things didn't turn out as you hoped.'

'You and me both.'

I'm glad to have him settle with us for a while, so I move over until I'm nice and close. He has on a brown jacket and smells of the outdoors. He looks up at me. 'I do believe you've grown, Brede.'

I give a smile, and Kate says, 'It's all the good food

we're getting. We've a great deal to thank you and Missus Henderson for.'

He runs his fingers through his hair. 'No need for any of that. To be honest with you, Kate, it's just a comfort to know there's one person in this house who's not opposed to my aims.'

I like the way his moustache moves up and down as he talks.

'It must be a difficult time for Missus Henderson. With the baby not far off, and all.'

I wait for him to tell her it's not to be born, but instead he says, 'You're right, Kate. She has a lot on her plate at the moment.'

I don't know why she'd mind because most people would be happy enough to have a plateful in front of them.

'For my neighbours to be so set against these reforms is a bitter disappointment. Surely you can see the sense of them?'

'I don't know that I understand much of it, Mister Henderson.'

He pulls out a chair. 'Well, come over here, and I'll do my best to explain.'

She waits a moment, and then she moves over very slowly, and seats herself beside him. So I move next to her.

Mister Henderson looks up at me. 'Perhaps, Brede, you could take Angus for a run?'

Kate turns to me. 'Don't go too far, Brede. There's still plenty to be getting on with.'

'I promise I'll not keep you long, Kate.' He moves his

chair nearer hers. 'Now, you know that the driving force behind Home Rule is Glad Stone?'

I didn't know pieces of rock could be happy, but if there's going to be more talk about those old rules, I just want to be well away from it.

So I go out into the yard, and Angus jumps up, his tail wagging away at the sight of me. I untie his rope, and when I look up I see through the open door Kate and Mister Henderson sitting side-by-side. Every so often she glances over at the door, but he keeps talking away, for all he's worth.

And the thought comes to me that if Dermot were to jump over the wall this very minute, he'd be none too pleased at what he sees.

NINETEEN

Young Rory and myself are in the yard busy building a tower. Yesterday's rain is drying nicely, though there's still a deal of mud about the place. The rooster is up on the gate, giving his wings a stretch in the sunshine. Angus sits watching him, and if he wasn't tied up, I'd say he'd be wanting to have a bit of a chase.

Molly has asked Kate for a drink of tea, so I'm left out here, minding young Rory. The kitchen door is open, and I hear her saying, 'Told me he wanted just a quick feel. I've heard that before, I said, but did he take a blind bit of notice?'

'No stopping some fellows!' Kate answers, and they both start laughing away, though I can't for the life of me see what the joke is.

I pick up a stone. It's flat and pale-looking – a Sad Stone altogether. I place it on the ground and he puts the next one, which is a dark grey, on the top and so we go on, until we have more stones than I can count, all heaped one above the other.

From the kitchen, comes the clash-clash of pans. The Hendersons have a whole crowd coming to lunch, and I'm just hoping it won't be like the last time, when I had to be in the hall with the Drummond man and Mister and Missus Thompson coming through the door.

I give Rory a nudge, and put the next stone into my mouth. He gives a laugh, and then he does the same. My one tastes like shite, so I spit it out, and Rory copies me.

We've made a deal of towers before this one, but this will be our tallest and best ever. The hardest part is to keep it from falling over, so I place my next stone very carefully on the top.

Rory reaches out his hand. 'Boom!' he shouts, and with one thwack has the whole lot on the ground.

All our work's gone in a flash, and I raise my hand to give him a good slap, when someone says, 'What in the world are you doing out here, Rory?'

I look up, and there's Missus Henderson standing over us. She has on a green skirt and a white blouse with a frill round the neck. She still has her big belly, and there's dark patches under her eyes.

'Is Molly not with you?'

'She's having her tea, Mammy.'

'Well we'd better fetch her, hadn't we?'

He stands up and takes her hand.

'Would you look at the state of you!'

Right enough, there's a big smear of mud on his face, and more of it all down his front.

She looks at me. 'And I'm surprised Kate hasn't any work for you, Brede. Our guests will be here in less than three hours.'

I wipe my fingers on my skirt, and follow Missus Henderson and Rory inside.

Kate is cracking eggs into a basin, Margaret is at the sink, and Molly is sitting drinking her tea.

'Molly, I thought I asked you to go over Rory's letters with him?'

She bites her lip. 'I'm sorry, Missus Henderson.'

'I'm disappointed in you. Maybe you're more suited to the kitchen after all.'

Her eyes fill with water. 'Oh, no. I'd far rather be minding him.'

Kate steps forward. 'I'm afraid this is my doing, Missus Henderson. I asked Molly to help out.'

'You have the child, Kate, as well as Margaret here, so I don't see any call to take Molly away from her duties.'

'I promise it won't happen again, Missus Henderson.'

'Well, let's say no more about it then.' She puts a hand to her back. 'I think I'll rest for a while before everyone arrives. Take Rory on up to the nursery, would you, Molly?'

'Thank you,' Molly mouths to Kate, as she leads young Rory out.

'Missus Henderson's looking so pale,' Margaret says. 'I just hope it's not going to be like two years ago.'

'She lost it?' Kate says, and Margaret nods.

They both have sad faces on them, and I'm thinking it's a pity someone couldn't have looked that bit harder for the babby.

'You know Mister Henderson's sent word for the midwife?' Margaret says. 'So from next week, there'll be an extra mouth to feed.'

Kate looks up from stirring the gravy. 'Just as well she's coming, from the sound of it. Now, I must give that joint another basting.'

Annie comes hurrying in. 'Are the jugs of water filled, Margaret?'

'They are.'

I'm at the table, kicking the tune of 'Bird on a Branch' against the leg.

Margaret points at me in a way I don't care for at all. 'I'm not having that girl anywhere near the dining room, or those parlours. Not after the last time.'

Kate looks up from her stirring. 'Whatever do you mean, Margaret?'

'Only that Missus Henderson's mother had a great deal to say about the interest your daughter took in the Lodge banner. Not that I'd care to repeat any of it.'

'Well, never mind that now,' Annie says. 'Have you the mustard mixed?'

When the two of them go out, Kate says, 'I wish I knew what in the world Margaret's on about, Brede, because Missus Henderson was full of praise for the help you gave at the last lunch. Though, mind you, I've heard she and her mother don't see eye-to-eye.'

That's the Bosom woman, and from the way she carries on, I'd not want to have her as my mammy.

Kate is busy at the range, and Sam's in and out carrying logs and turf for the front room. So I just sit quiet, with my belly rumbling away at the smell of all the lovely food. And then Margaret rushes in to say the first ones are arriving. So she and Kate lift out the piece of beef. It's turned a gorgeous brown, and just the sight of it brings water into my mouth.

Sam carries the meat through to the dining room for Mister Henderson to cut up. While Sam's doing that, Margaret and Kate put the vegetables into dishes, and the gravy into one, two, three jugs, and Margaret takes them on through.

'Phew!' Kate wipes her face with her apron. 'That's the biggest part over. But I need the privy, Brede. I won't be more than a couple of minutes.'

There's a piece of York Sheer pudding on the edge of the range, and I've just put it into my mouth, when Sam comes running in, holding an empty bowl.

'Where's Kate got to? There's more cabbage needed.' He lifts the lids off some pans. 'Plenty here.' He starts tipping cabbage into the bowl, so that bits of it go spilling onto the table.

I'm busy chewing on a piece of spud when he hands me the bowl. 'I've to see to something in the stable. Just take these on through, would you?'

As I go into the hall with the big squares, there's a deal of laughter and talk from the room where they're having their meal. I start to count all the people I don't want to come across again in the whole of my life. One: Missus Thompson; two: Mister Thompson; three: Pea-in-the-pod; four: the Honoria woman with the bosom. I slow my steps, and it's as well that I do, because coming towards me is the Drummond man. He's number five. He has his head down and turns into the privy without spotting me.

When I reach the dining room, I can see Mister Henderson at one end of the long table, with Missus Henderson at the other, and all the ones sitting between them. I'm hoping for a quick peek at Missus Thompson's frock, but there's no sign of her. Facing me is Pea-in-the-pod, talking away with the James man, and beside him is Poor Nora, and I'm glad none of them gives me a second look.

Margaret comes forward. 'You were told to stay in the kitchen,' she hisses. 'Get on back there this minute!'

So I hand her the dish, and start off down the passage.

As I go past the room where Missus Henderson does her stitching, who should be coming back towards me but the Drummond man, looking about him as if he's searching for something. Quiet as a mouse, I go into the room, and close the door behind me, holding my breath until his steps go past. Then I hear a sound, like a sigh. There's a good light from the window, and I can see the table, where the man in his gold hat was spread out. Only now the table has nothing on it and I'm wondering what they've done with him.

Then, in the chair by the hearth I spot a flash of blue that I'd know anywhere. It's Missus Thompson's gorgeous frock, and underneath it are her boots with the buttons like currants up the sides.

In her hand is a picture that she lifts up before giving it a kiss. It's the one of Mister and Missus Henderson and young Rory, and Mister Henderson's dressed all in brown and his face is very serious-looking. But I don't care one bit for the way Missus Thompson's slobbering over it.

'Oh, William, William,' she whispers. You chose the wrong sister.' Which makes me wonder what he was choosing them for, and whether Poor Nora wishes he'd picked her.

I go to slip out of the room, but the door opens and I've just time to tuck myself behind it. Then there's a rustle of skirts, and Missus Henderson says, 'Adelina? What in the world are you doing?'

Missus Thompson jumps to her feet, and the picture falls to the floor, clatter-clatter.

'At least it's not broken,' Missus Henderson says as she picks it up.

Missus Thompson takes it from her. 'I was thinking how much you've changed, Helen, since these pictures were taken. But you were so much younger then.'

'Just put it on the table there, and go on back to the meal.'

'Of course.' Missus Thompson gets to her feet. 'You know my only concern is for you, Helen. So many lost babies. It must be a worry to think this one could go the same way.'

'God willing, that won't happen. Now, shall we join the others?'

I press myself against the wall as Missus Henderson moves past. Missus Thompson looks around the room before following more slowly. She's almost out of the door when I hear a voice I know only too well.

'I wondered where you'd got to, Adelina.' The Drummond man pushes her back into the room, and I'm thinking that maybe he's going to put her against the wall again and start going huff-huff. 'I assume that now is a convenient moment to resume our conversation?'

'What conversation?' she says, and her voice has that spike in it.

He gives a laugh. 'Yes – we could both think of better ways to describe it.'

And he's right there, because the pair of them did far more than talk that time.

'For God's sake, Bob! This is neither the time nor the place.'

'You're right, dear. So how about my office on Wednesday afternoon?'

'Oh, very well. But I warn you – stop giving me the eye. Alexander is difficult enough as it is.'

'Whatever you say, dear.'

The two of them go out, and all stays quiet.

I go into the passage, and as I start walking along, I give a jump, because there's a shadow in the opposite doorway. I go on past, but it just keeps standing there, still as a stone.

And then I see that the shadow is a big man with shiny boots – the last person Missus Thompson and the Drummond man would want to have listening to their every word.

TWENTY

'For God's sake, Brede! Times like this, I don't know how I put up with you.'

There's no call for Kate to be talking that way when we're having such a grand time – Dermot visiting, and the house to ourselves.

'And take that look off your face. I don't know what's got into you lately.'

Dermot puts down his fiddle. 'One dish less. Why the fuss?'

Kate starts sweeping up the pieces. 'That's beside the point.'

'Plenty more where that came from.' He winks across at me. 'Am I right, or am I right, Brede?'

I tug open the door of the big press to show him the load of plates with a row of green and yellow leaves round the edges. They're piled near as high as the towers young

Rory and I build.

Dermot pushes back his chair. 'How about we take a look at the rest?'

I grin back at him, and open the next cupboard, and the one after that, and the one after that. Some are filled with cups and saucers and dishes, and others have jam and sugar and flour in them. The lower presses have pans and lids and baking dishes, and goodness knows what else besides.

Dermot stands beside me, puffing away on his pipe, the smoke rising like curls of sheep wool about our heads. 'And the one in the corner?'

'Whatever's got into you today?' Kate says. 'It's just the turf store. Come and sit here, and I'll make the tea.'

But from the way he's looking at me, I know he wants a peek at that one too.

'I'd say there's room enough for you to fit in, Brede,' he says, as I pull open the door. 'So how about giving it a try?'

I drop onto my knees. Ahead of me is the turf, in a pile so big, it seems to me there's no getting past it, and I just hope he's not going to make me have a go.

He crouches beside me. 'As I thought, there's a fair amount of space at the back. But maybe if you once got in, there'd be no getting you out again, and we'd not want that, would we?' He tickles me under my arms, and I give a squeal, and then we both stand, laughing and shaking the dust from our clothes.

'Would you look at the pair of you?' Kate says. 'Carrying on like a couple of two-year-olds.' But she's smiling away too.

We settle around the range. Kate has made a load of small tarts with lovely red jam in the middle of them. As I bite into mine, I'm thinking that although I miss my mammy and da, it's still grand to be living here, and best of all is these times when Dermot comes shinning over the yard wall, and the three of us have all this *craic*.

He takes a pull on his bottle. 'Have you anything else for a starving man to get his teeth into? I don't care for all this sweet stuff myself.' He doesn't wait for her reply, but gets up, and lifts a dish off the table.

'Hey!' Kate says, 'that chicken pie's for Missus Henderson.'

He scoops out a piece and shoves it into his mouth. 'Says who?'

She goes to take the dish from him.

'I wouldn't fekkin' do that,' he says, very quietly.

She stares at him a moment, and I wait for her to tell him off for using a bad word. So it's a surprise when she just goes back to her seat.

She watches him eating, but there's no more jokes or laughing.

When he's finished, he wipes his mouth on his sleeve. 'That's better!' He picks up his pipe. 'The Hendersons will be out for a while yet. Maybe it's time Brede went to the dairy?'

'Do as he says, Brede.' Her voice is very tight-sounding. 'You can have some of those tarts later.'

I lift the cheese bag and the key off the hook, and go into the yard. The moment the dog sees me, he starts jumping around. But I don't untie him straight away.

Instead, I stoop down, and take a peek through the kitchen window.

Dermot is still in his chair, but now Kate's sitting on top of him, with a leg on either side, so they're facing each other, and when she takes off her blouse, I can see one of her titties bobbing around. Dermot pulls off his shirt, and puts a hand down to his breeches. I'd like to tell them they're still not doing it right.

On account of the way they're sitting I can't see Dermot's long thing, but I know he'll take it out and push it into her, and jiggle it around inside her. And they'll both be groaning and laughing away, and it seems to me they've no call to be telling me off, when they carry on every bit as bad as Missus Thompson.

Suddenly, the dog gives a growl, and a voice calls: 'You there, girl! Help me unlatch this gate, would you?'

On the other side of it is a tall woman in a black hat.

'Well, come on. I'm not waiting here all evening.'

I unfasten the gate, and she lifts up a big bag, and goes past me without so much as a nod.

Angus is still growling away, and I'm hoping Kate will come out to ask why the carry-on, because I don't think she'll be any too happy to have a stranger looking at her titties. But the woman's heading straight for the kitchen so, quick as a flash, I go running past and fling open the door.

Kate and Dermot are still on the chair, and the room has an onion smell in it. When she sees me, she jumps up, pulling her blouse around her. 'Brede – why aren't you –?' Then she spots the woman standing behind me. 'Who in the world are you? Don't you know better than to come barging into someone's home?'

Dermot is on his feet, buttoning his shirt.

'I'd hoped for a better welcome than this! I've been knocking at that front door for I don't how long.'

'Oh,' Kate says. 'You must be—'

'Missus Maureen Mooney.' She puts down her bag. 'The midwife, come to attend on a Missus Henderson.'

'But we weren't expecting you till next week.'

'Well, I'm here now.'

Dermot picks up his bottle and the fiddle. 'I'll leave you two women to sort things out.'

He goes past me at a great rate, keeping his head down. I look through the window, hoping he'll give a wave, like he usually does. But the next moment, he's vanished over the wall.

'I'm sorry if I interrupted your husband's – er – visit,' the Mooney woman says.

Kate turns all pink. 'No matter.' She tucks her blouse into her skirt. 'I'm sure you could do with a drink of tea after your journey.'

The woman sits herself at the table. Her face is very thin, with a load of lines across it, and her hair is as black as a piece of coal.

'I wouldn't say no to one of those tarts.'

Kate pushes the plate towards her. 'Help yourself while I put the kettle on. Oh, and I'm Kate O'Hagan, and the child is my niece, Brede.' She's moving about in a hurried sort of a way, like the hens do when the dog gets too close.

The woman takes a bite of tart. She has a long chin on her, with a spot on each cheek that's the same colour as the jam. 'I must say these are surprisingly tasty.'

'You've come from far?'

'The city.' She helps herself to another tart. There's only one left on the plate, and I'm holding my breath in case she goes for it too.

'The Hendersons usually visit their family on a Sunday.' Kate hands the woman her tea. 'They'll not be back for a while yet.'

'In that case, I think I'll have a bit of a rest before they arrive. It was a long old journey.'

'Of course. Brede here will show you where to go. Missus Purdy's old room,' she says to me. 'And you can carry Missus Mooney's bag for her.'

It's a fair old weight, and as I go along the passage, I can hear this clink-clink coming from inside it.

'The medicine is for my chest. I get this terrible cough.' She's carrying her tea, but her hand's none too steady, because the cup is rattling away in its saucer.

I've not been in Missus Purdy's room since she moved into her own house, but there's the mat she had, with the green and red colours on it. And her bed's all made up with a white cover. I wish she was still sleeping in it.

She looks about her. 'It's a bit on the small side, but I've seen worse. Just put the bag down there.'

I'm hoping she'll open it, so I can have a peek inside, but instead she looks across at me. 'You seem a nice quiet girl. It makes a change from all the screaming babies, I can tell you.'

212

My young brother used to yell fit to burst when our mammy had no milk to give him, and I'm wondering if all these babbies are going hungry too.

The woman stretches herself out on the bed. Her shoes have mud all over them. I'd get a good telling-off if I did the same. 'Your father works on the farm, then?'

My insides go all cold, because for a moment I can see him, lying beside my mammy, with his eyes staring up at me, and his mouth all twisted round.

I have a chew of my hair.

'Well, never mind. I'm just going to have a bit of a sleep. You can come and fetch me when the family return.'

When I'm back in the kitchen, Kate turns to me, with her forehead very wrinkled-looking. 'Why did the woman have to come in at just that moment?'

I don't know why either, so I collect the pail and the cheese bag and the next minute Angus and myself are heading up the path in the evening sun.

Other than the cows mooing in their field, and a speckled-looking bird cheeping away to itself, it's terribly quiet at the top of the world, so I'm glad to have the dog for company.

It's as we're going back down the path that, far below me, I catch sight of the Hendersons' carriage. It's going at a great lick along the lane and, as it turns in through the lions, I'm thinking maybe I'll get a game with young Rory, before he goes to his bed. But there's no running with this heavy pail, and the bag with the cheese going bump-bump against my chest.

I put the milk down for a bit of a rest, and Angus comes up to take a look. His tongue's hanging out, and he's panting away. I check over my shoulder to make sure no one's watching. Then I take the lid off the pail, and he dips his head in and has a good long drink.

In the yard, I tie him up, and tiptoe over to the pump. When I look through the window, I see Kate busy at the range, and the Mooney woman with her back to me at the table. So I give the pump handle one, two pulls, and top the pail up with water.

But when I go into the kitchen, my insides give a skip, because Mister Henderson is standing in the far doorway. He nods at me, and then carries on talking.

'… a great relief to have you with us, Missus Mooney. My wife and I don't want to take any chances. Not after what's gone before.'

She sips her tea. 'Hardly a child within fifty miles of here, Mister Henderson, that I haven't seen safely into this world. You can rely on me.'

I'd like to tell her this babby of Missus Henderson's is not to be born, so she's wasting her time.

'Well, I'm sure that Kate here – and indeed all the household – will see you're well looked after.' He gives one of his smiles that makes his moustache twitch.

I'm just moving over to stand nice and close to him, when he says, 'I must get on. Missus Henderson is resting, but she's looking forward to meeting you in the morning, Missus Mooney.' And with that, he's away out the door.

'He seems a reasonable sort of a man,' Missus Mooney says. 'You'd be surprised at the carry-on of some husbands when their wives are in the family way. Why, the household before last, there was this young maid who—'

'Put the milk in the pantry, Brede,' Kate says. 'And some more tea for you, Missus Mooney?'

'One cup is sufficient, thank you, though I wouldn't say no to that last tart.'

Kate gives me a look. 'Of course.'

The woman swallows it down in one, two bites, and I'm just hoping it chokes her.

'Give me a hand carrying this pan through to the scullery, Brede,' Kate says. As we go down the passage, she whispers, 'There'll be plenty for you from the next lot I bake.'

I'm thinking that's no fekkin' good, but then she says, 'And I've a surprise for you in the morning. Can you guess what it is?'

I'm hoping I'll like it, because some surprises aren't the good sort – like the dog that took a bite out of her leg, or the time I got shut in the office with Missus Thompson and the Drummond man.

I'm still thinking of them a while later, when Kate tucks me into our bed. 'Go to sleep now, Brede. I'll not be much longer myself.'

In the yard, one of the horses gives a snort, and I can hear doors opening and closing, and steps above my head. But even though my eyes are squeezed shut, I'm too busy thinking of Dermot and Kate's carrying on, and the way the Mooney woman ate my jam tart to get any sleep.

I wish Kate were beside me, so I get up off the bed, and putting my shawl around my shoulders, I head for the kitchen to find out how much longer she'll be.

When I peek round the edge of the door, I get a surprise, because sitting beside her at the table, with his sleeves rolled up, is Mister Henderson.

He takes a bite of sponge that's on the plate in front of him, and I just wish I could have a piece. 'I have to say, Kate, your cooking is really excellent. I don't know how we ever managed without you!'

'I'm glad you and Missus Henderson are satisfied.'

'More pleased than I could ever say.'

He bites into his cake again, and she says, 'Will there be anything else you're wanting, Mister Henderson?'

'Just a quick word about our supplies. No doubt you'll have heard that most of the shops are refusing to serve us?'

'Margaret did mention something.'

'I don't know what's got into this town. The Whelans are the only ones who'll even give her the time of day – and we can't live on ribbons and lace.'

Any eejit knows that, but now I'm remembering the time I was told to wait in their shop so I could carry Missus Thompson's packages. And if only I'd done that, I'd not have seen her drop her handkerchief, and got myself shut in with her and the Drummond man. Because it makes me sick to my stomach to think what he'll do if he ever gets a hold of me.

'So it seems,' Mister Henderson is saying, 'we'll have to get most of our groceries from the city. But this is a setback only. Once Home Rule's finally here, my brother and the rest of them will come to their senses.' He leans towards her. 'There'll be decent work for all Carth Licks then, Kate, and—'

'So this is where you've got to, William!' Missus Henderson is in the far doorway. She has on a nightgown, with a cream shawl around her shoulders, and I see from her belly that her babby has grown even bigger.

Kate jumps up.

'I was just explaining the latest situation to Kate,' Mister Henderson says. 'God knows, it's hard enough for the likes of us to understand.'

'I'm sure Kate's plenty to be getting on with, without having to listen to this foolishness.'

I shuffle my feet, and the floor gives a squeak. I hold my breath, but they just carry on talking.

'Shouldn't you be resting?' Mister Henderson says.

Kate seems all in a fluster again. 'Can I get you a drink, Missus Henderson? Some hot milk, perhaps?'

She shakes her head.

Mister Henderson goes over to her, and when she looks up at him, her face has a hard kind of a look. 'I trust you'll not be much longer?'

'I'll be up in just a few minutes.'

When she goes out, he says, 'I know it's late, but there's never a good time, Kate. I want you to know what it is myself and Mister Johnson are trying to do…'

She looks up at the clock, but already he's going on about how Carth Licks must have their own homes and decent jobs, and there must be no more marching and banners, but that the Glad Stone will see us right.

On and on he goes, so I tiptoe back to my bed. And as I pull my blanket over me, I'm puzzling over why Missus Henderson doesn't want the same things as Mister

Henderson, and why she sounded so cross when she spoke just now.

But what puzzles me even more is how Mister Henderson can think that some old stone, no matter how happy it is, will make things right between the Drummond man and Missus Thompson, and between her and Mister Thompson.

I've always felt nice and safe in this house, but now with all this talk and arguing, I'm not so sure.

TWENTY-ONE

SOMEONE'S SHAKING ME. 'IT'S THE MORNING, BREDE. And do you remember what day it is?'

I know that what's just gone by is yesterday, and that what's not yet gone by is tomorrow, but I'm not sure what this day is, other than being today.

'It's your birthday!' she says.

I remember my mammy telling me that the day she had me was a great one for her altogether, but my da always said there were so many of us, we'd no call to be thinking of such things, or the whole year would be nothing but birthdays. But now I'm recalling the last one I had, when Kate gave me a gorgeous piece of ribbon.

'I wish I knew your age,' she says now. 'I keep telling people you're eleven.' She gives a smile. 'But I don't suppose it matters.'

It's no worry to me either, and as I go along the passage, I give a skip, because maybe I'll be getting another ribbon.

Annie, Margaret and Sam are at the table, along with the Mooney woman. She's very severe-looking, and there's none of the usual talk and laughs going on.

'A very happy birthday to you!' Annie says.

'On the Glorious Twelfth too!' Sam gives a wink. 'Pity you're not a Prod.'

'No polly ticks in this kitchen,' Annie says, but she's smiling too.

'Well, it's not going to be so glorious for any of us either.' Margaret takes a bite of her breakfast. 'To think that Mister Henderson won't allow us to watch the parade, or join in the Pick Nick.'

'You know the answer to that, Margaret,' Annie says. 'Find yourself a better household to work in. If one exists in the whole of Ireland, that is.'

Margaret gives a scowl.

'Let's just help the child enjoy her day.' Annie hands me a parcel wrapped in brown paper. 'And here's something from Margaret and me.'

I rip the cover off, and there inside is a square of cheese. I go to put it to my mouth, but Kate says, 'Oh, a lovely bar of soap. Isn't that kind, Brede?'

It smells of lemons, and I'd still like just one lick, but she gives me a look, so I slip it into my pocket for later.

She puts a big plateful in front of me. My usual breakfast is an egg and one, two strips of bacon, but today I'm also having sausages and tomatoes and mushrooms, and I can't wait to get my teeth into it all.

I've just taken my first bite, when Molly comes in. 'Could I get that boy to put on his clothes? I swear to you he gets worse. If I had my way, he'd be locked in his room for the rest of the summer!'

I'd not want that to happen, because then who would I have to build towers with?

'Never mind all that,' Annie says. 'Come and have your breakfast.'

'Oh, I clean forgot,' Molly says. 'Missus Henderson says you're to have this.'

It's a smaller package than Annie and Margaret's, and it's wrapped in white paper that makes a rustling noise when I touch it.

'She's still in her bed,' Molly says, 'or she'd have brought it herself, and of course there'll be no getting any sense out of *him* – not until after today's march.'

I wipe my hands on my apron to get rid of the bits of egg, and then I open Missus Henderson's package.

Inside is a handkerchief with a pink edge to it, and a pink flower in each corner, and I draw in my breath, because it's every bit as gorgeous as any that Missus Thompson has. Though I'm glad it's not the same as her blue one, on account of all the trouble that caused.

Then Sam gives me a mouse that he's made out of straw. It has one ear bigger than the other, but there's a lovely long tail to it. I run it up and down the table, until Margaret nudges me to stop.

'And now,' Kate says, 'here's my present to you, Brede.' And she goes over to the press, and lifts down a round cake, sprinkled all over the top with sugar. 'It has your favourite jam in the middle.'

I've never had a cake of my very own before, but as I put out my hand to take it, she says, 'We'll save it for later. For now, you're to finish your breakfast, and take Angus up to the dairy. Mister Henderson says you can spend the rest of the day with Missus Purdy. You'll like that, won't you?'

I give a grin.

Margaret winks across at Sam. '*Mister Henderson* says!'

Kate goes all pink. 'He's always had a soft spot for Brede.'

'And for someone else I could name,' Sam mutters.

The Mooney woman helps herself to the last of Kate's marmalade. 'No doubt the child's father will be calling by to wish her well.'

In the silence, I hear the clock going tick-tick, and the cat stretches out a foot, and then settles back into his basket.

'Hush, would you,' Margaret whispers. 'We try not to talk about the child's family – it only sets her off.'

'Well, she seemed happy enough when she was with him yesterday,' the Mooney woman says.

'What in the world are you on about?'

'Kate here will tell you.'

I wait for her to say that Dermot is not my da. But her face has gone even redder, and all she says is, 'I've no time for any of this. I need to be getting on.'

'Suit yourself.'

There's another silence.

'Oh, Missus Mooney,' Molly says. 'If you've finished your breakfast, Missus Henderson wants to see you. And I'm to take you to her.'

The two of them go out, and Kate starts clearing the table.

'Do you think that Mooney one is quite right in the head?' Margaret says.

Annie turns to Kate. 'Do you have any notion of what she was on about?'

I draw in my breath because, even though it's bad to tell a lie, I'm thinking it'll be even worse if she tells them of Dermot's visit, and what they get up to together.

But it's me she speaks to. 'Time for the dairy, Brede. You don't want to keep Missus Purdy waiting.'

It's a lovely warm morning, with the grass all shiny-looking, and one, two pairs of birds swooping about over the mountain. I stop to take a proper look at them, and Angus comes running up to see what I'm doing. I'd like to know when his birthday is, so I can get him an extra load of food, but for now I give him a pat, and we head on up to the top of the world. I stand beside the dairy, listening to the cows mooing away, and watching one, two, three Ten Aunts working in the field below me.

*

When I'm back in the kitchen, there's another nice surprise, because Kate hands me the basket that's filled with the dinner for myself and Missus Purdy. And it's such a fair old weight, I need both my hands to lift it. 'Go carefully with this, Brede. It has special things inside. But no peeking, mind!'

When I go along the path to the big barn, the doors are shut, but there's some bales of hay outside, so I put the basket on one of them, and lift the cover. Inside, there's some shiny eggs with no shells on them, and red tomatoes and soft-looking bread, and a piece of cheese the colour of my new soap. But best of all, in the middle is a pie with lovely brown pastry across the top of it. I go to poke my finger through, but then I stop, because if I'm eleven years of age, then I'm nearly grown up, and besides, my belly's still full of breakfast. So I put the cover back, and carry on up to Missus Purdy's.

She's in her usual place by the range, and when she sees me, she gives a big smile. 'We're going to have a really grand day together.'

We lay the food out on the table, and she puts the pie in the oven to warm. And we're just having a cup of tea and barm brack with butter and black-coloured jam, when she says, 'And this is for you, child.'

Her surprise is a long box, and when I open it, there inside is a lovely looking-glass, with a silver frame around it.

When Kate and I were walking about the country, we used to look at ourselves in the pools of water, and the only other glass I recall seeing is the one with the gold edges that Missus Thompson has on her wall.

I lift up Missus Purdy's glass. There's such a shine off it, it takes my breath away. But the face that looks back at me is all wrong, because I know my cheeks aren't this fat, nor my hair as frizzy. So I drop the glass back into its box.

'Go careful with it,' Missus Purdy says. 'Because we don't want it breaking on us. And you know what they say?'

I shake my head.

'Seven years' bad luck.'

I give a smile, because any eejit knows bad things can't last that length of time.

'It was given me by my mother, God rest her,' Missus Purdy says, 'and seeing I've no daughter of my own to pass it to, I wanted you to have it.'

I miss my mammy, but when I open my mouth to tell Missus Purdy, not a sound comes out. So, I give the box a pat and go over to the corner. I put my arms by my sides, and start on some new steps that Dermot has taught me, taking special care not to knock into the table.

Missus Purdy watches me, smiling away, and after a while she starts talking about growing up with her mammy and da, and the *craic* she and her sisters used to have.

I'm busy with my dancing, so I don't heed the half of what she's saying. But when I'm all puffed out, and we're sitting at the table again, she gives a sigh. 'All that's a while ago now, child – so what good it does thinking about it, I don't know. But it's a comfort to have you here for company.'

She carries on talking away to herself for a while, and when at last she's done, we eat our dinner. The pie tastes every bit as good as it looks, and for afters there's rice pudding the colour of Missus Henderson's blouse, with more of the black jam in the middle of it. And I'm just finishing, when I hear these noises in the distance. One is as high-sounding as a bird, and one is like the growl Angus makes when he meets someone he doesn't care for. And then there's another sound, and that one's going thump-thump, thump-thump.

Missus Purdy seizes my arm. 'We mustn't miss this – come along now!'

We stand by the fewsher hedge, with the sun beating down on us, and the noises getting louder and louder. And soon I'm thinking they're not birds or animals, but drums and pipes, like the ones we used to have in our village.

'Let's go into the road to get a proper view,' Missus Purdy says, 'but not too fast now, as I'm puffed enough as it is.'

We walk along the lane a little way, where there's a gate that leads into the big field. She leans against it, catching her breath, and I peer forward. It's hard to see what on earth it is that's coming toward us, on account of the hedges, and the lane having so many turns to it, but the noise is now so loud, there's no room in my head for anything else. Boom-boom-boom! Boom-boom-boom!

'Here they come!' she says.

At first, all I see is some posts sticking up above the hedge, and then round the corner comes one, two, three men, all in a row. And there's more rows behind them. As they come nearer, I see they're dressed all in black, with boots and those mushroom hats on their heads, and white gloves on their hands. Their faces look very hot, and I'm thinking how they'll be sweating away under all those clothes.

The fellow nearest me is carrying a picture, like the one that was in the barn at Mister Henderson's big meeting.

But this one isn't of a man on a horse – it's of a man with a crown on his head, so maybe he's one of the kings of Ireland that Kate's told me about. And another has a flag that's a lovely purple and gold colour, with writing around the edges. And there's more men marching than I can count, so by the time the front ones are passing, there's a load more coming along.

And they all have strips of ribbon across their chests, and some are beating on drums, and some are blowing away on pipes, and all the while, their feet are going thump-thump, thump-thump along the road. And it's such a grand sound, I start jumping up and down, and Missus Purdy is waving away, and so am I.

'Oh,' she says, 'here's Mister John!' And Pea-in-the-pod comes past, looking just like old Mister Henderson, except not as stout. And behind him is the Drummond man, and Barney, and Poor Nora's husband whose name I've forgot, and a load of others, all staring ahead of them as if we're not here. And I let out a sigh of relief, as the last thing I want is the Drummond man shouting at me for being in his office that time.

'Well,' Missus Purdy says, when at last they've gone by, 'What a sight that was!' She turns to me. 'We're celebrating the glorious victory at the Boyne.' She wrinkles her forehead. 'Of course it all happened long before any of us was born. It was William of Orange started it.'

I'm wondering if he's the person who sells the oranges that Kate makes the marmalade with. But he must be as great a fellow as Sir Enda for everyone to be carrying on like this.

'I'm talking away, when you need to be getting back to the big house,' Missus Purdy says. 'And here's Kate come to collect you.'

I didn't know she was going to do that, but I see her hurrying up the lane towards us.

She gives a wave, and Missus Purdy says, 'Go along now, or you'll be late for your birthday tea.'

But I stay just where I am, listening to those drums and pipes still booming and tooting away. And I can feel them calling and calling to me to follow, so the next moment I'm taking to my heels, and running after that music for all I'm worth.

'Come back!' Missus Purdy cries. 'You don't want to be caught up in any trouble!'

But already I'm round the bend in the lane, and out of sight of the pair of them.

TWENTY-TWO

I RUN AND I RUN, UNTIL I COME TO A TURNING ON MY straw-foot side. I go down it, and keep on running, until I can't hear Missus Purdy and Kate shouting after me. When I reach another gate, with a patch of grass in the front of it, I'm all puffed out. So down I flop, and stretch out my legs.

I've not been in this part of the lane before. The hedge beside me is filled with a load of yellow and white flowers, with a fat bee buzzing away amongst them. It's grand to be lying here, with the sun all warm on my face, and no floors to wash, or spuds to peel, or pails to carry.

And as I close my eyes, I'm thinking that, when I've had another listen to the music, there'll be a big piece of cake waiting for me. Because although I've run off when I shouldn't, Kate won't stay cross for long, on account of it being my birthday.

*

When I wake, the sun is still beating down, and everything is very quiet and still. I take a good look about me, hoping to spot a pond or a stream, because I have a wild thirst after all my running. But all that's to be seen is the lane, with a bend at either end of it, and fields of dry-looking grass, with stone walls and fewsher bushes around them.

If I go back the way I came, I'll be at the house before I know it, with plenty to drink and eat. But then I'm thinking of those drums and pipes, and how they'll give me a chance to practise my steps, even though the tunes aren't near as good as the ones Dermot plays. And anyway, I just want another peek at those gorgeous banners. So I continue walking, listening out all the while for the music, because it surely must be somewhere hereabouts.

But everywhere stays very silent, and I'm thinking how strange it is that it's just myself out here, with no one working in any of the fields. All that's in them is a load of sheep and cows, and they don't give me a look as I go by.

After a good while, I come to a crossroads, and have another listen. If I was back in my village, this is where everyone would be gathered for the dancing, but the only sound is from some brown birds, cheeping in the hedge. Beside me is a tall post that has a sign with letters over it. I can't make head nor tail of them, so it's hard to know which way to go. So I choose the lane that has the most fewsher growing along it, and on I walk.

All the fierce heat has gone from the sun, so the afternoon is wearing on. And now I'm sorry to have run all this way because everywhere looks the same, and even if I turn myself about, it'll be hard to know which is the right road back. And what if I end up walking out here for years and years, and never clap eyes on Kate, or Mister Henderson, or Angus, or Missus Purdy, in the whole of my life?

My insides twist around, and I begin to run, as fast as ever I can. And I've not gone far when my foot catches in a big hole, and I fall flat in the road, so the breath is knocked out of me. I pick myself up. My knees are all sore, and there's a big tear in my skirt, and I'm just thinking of the scolding I'll be getting from Kate, when I hear a yowling kind of a noise.

On a wall beside me is a cat, black as coal, all except for its feet, which look as if they've been dipped in cream. It gives another yowl, and then it starts walking away, with its tail stuck in the air. I'm so glad to have some company that I start running after it, but it darts away. I've been so busy watching it, that it's only now I spot that the road ahead of me has a row of houses on either side. And I'm thinking that maybe there'll be someone there to give me a nice cool drink.

As I walk up the street, it doesn't take long to see that the place is very poor-looking altogether – not a patch on the town Missus Thompson took us to. For a start, the road is very narrow, with not a shop to be seen, and the walls of the houses are a dirty grey, with doors that haven't had a lick of paint on them for a good while. They're all shut fast, and there's no one about. The only sound is a kind of a screech-screech from a rusty-looking sign, with writing on it, moving backwards and forwards in the breeze that's sprung up. And I'm thinking that I don't like the feel of the place one bit.

But now the wind is carrying a great stink towards me, so powerful that I lift the edge of my skirt to my nose, and walk as fast as I can to be away from it. And when I come almost to the end of the houses, there's a field, with a low wall in the front of it, and a load of bushes. And I'm just stopping to draw in a breath of decent air when someone grabs hold of me. The next moment, I fall arse-over-tip into the ditch the other side. 'For God's sake!' a voice says. 'What do you think you're playing at?'

I wasn't playing, I was having a rest, but when I look up, who should be bending over me but a man with a beard, and hair that reaches to his shoulders? It's Dermot, and beside him is Carrot Hair, whose other name is Francis.

I'm so surprised to see the two of them that I open my mouth, and then shut it again.

'Is Kate not with you?' He grips my arm. 'Well, where the feck is she? Because I'm telling you that neither of you wants to be anywhere near this place. Not with what's about to happen.' He gives me a shake that makes my teeth go rattle-rattle. 'Bloody well talk to me, Brede! We need to warn Kate to stay out of sight. Do you understand me?'

I try to pull away, but his fingers are digging into my arm.

'You're wasting your breath,' Carrot Hair says. 'Sure, we all know this one's not the full shilling.'

I don't know what money has to do with anything, but I don't care for his tone one bit.

'Take a look up the road, Francis, and see if there's any sign of her. I need to stay here to…'

In the distance is a sound that at first I can't make out at all. Then my insides give a smile, because what I'm hearing is the boom-boom of the drums.

'Too late now,' Carrot Hair says. 'Oh, hold on a minute, who's this coming?'

Someone's running along the street towards us, and when I see who it is, I let out a sigh of relief.

'Kate!' Dermot calls. 'Over here!'

She comes up, panting away, and when she sees me, she says, 'Thank heavens you've found her, Dermot!'

'It was you I was worried about.' He pulls her over the wall. 'But for God's sake what are the pair of you doing out here?'

'What do you think? Brede just took off, and I've been running around these lanes for hours, half out of my mind with worry.' She turns to me. 'You stupid eejit of a girl! Give me one good reason why I should bother myself with you.'

The tears come to my eyes, because I can't think of one either.

'Well, there's nothing for it,' Dermot says. 'The two of you will have to stay till the march has gone through.'

She narrows her eyes at him. 'It's coming past here, then?'

'As it's done these good few years. But, God willing, this will be the last time the Barst Ards get away with it. Our people are ready for them.'

'For God's sake, Dermot…'

'Whatever happens, keep out of sight. Francis or myself will tell you when it's safe to go.' The next minute he's over the wall, and running into a house over the way.

Now Francis is waving his arm, and someone on a roof opposite us waves back.

'That's the signal. Just do as Dermot says, and remember to keep your heads down.' Francis runs along the inside of the wall, and disappears round the nearest house.

I can feel Kate trembling away. 'Oh, God,' she whispers, 'what have we got ourselves into?'

My belly gives a twist.

I can hear the tramp-tramp of feet, but it doesn't seem so grand a sound any more, because I've not seen her this scared since the time that dog sank his teeth into her.

And all the while, the music is growing louder, and when I take a peek over the wall, I see the banners are at the far end of the street, with the first row of men moving towards us.

Kate pulls me down beside her. 'For the love of God, Brede, not a sound out of you.'

A grey slater comes crawling along the ditch where we're crouched, and I'm just wishing I was back in the yard with young Rory, helping him put it into the box Missus Purdy gave me.

The drums and pipes are now so loud, I'm thinking they must almost be on us, and I clutch onto Kate for all I'm worth. Because what will we do if someone looks over the wall, and spots us? If it's Barney, it won't be so bad, because he's always nice and friendly. But suppose it's the Drummond man or Pea-in-the pod?

Something catches my eye, and I see these flashes of light above our heads. Then there's the sound of glass breaking. 'They're throwing bottles,' Kate whispers. 'What'll it be next?'

Above the drums and pipes, I hear someone screaming. Next minute, there's a whole load of bangs.

Kate blesses herself. 'Please God, let no one be hurt bad.'

The music stops, and a man calls, 'What's going on back there?'

'Someone's been shot!' another voice replies.

All goes quiet.

Kate has her eyes closed, so I take a peek over the wall. The first rows of men are very close to where we're crouched, but they all have their backs turned, looking up the street. There's more men there than I can count, and they're not in neat rows any more, but are milling about all over the place.

Then two big fellows come running up and a space is cleared around them. 'Four of you, come with us,' one of the men says. 'We need to teach these boys a lesson they won't forget in a hurry!' And he bangs on the nearest door, and keeps on banging for all he's worth. After a while, a woman steps out, with one, two wee boys clutching her skirt. In her arms is a babby that's bawling its head off, which is no surprise because if I wasn't so scared, I'd be howling away too.

'Who's in there with you?' another man shouts, and he pushes past her into the house.

He's not inside long, and when he comes out, he says, 'All clear.' And then the two fellows move on to the next house. And on the other side of the street, the other two men are also banging on the doors, and they've not gone far, when I see some figures being hauled out.

'Got them!' one of the men calls, and I can't rightly see what's happening, because a crowd of the ones marching has the fellows surrounded. And someone has a stick that he raises in the air, before bringing it down with a thwack. Again, and again and again, and with each thwack there's a scream. Then all goes quiet.

Kate pulls on my skirt. 'Get down, Brede. What do you think they'll do to us if we're spotted?'

I crouch by her again, squeezing my eyes shut.

Then a man calls, 'Let's show them what Prods are made of, Brothers!'

After a deal of shuffling and muttering, the drums and pipes start up, and then comes the tramp-tramp, and the crunch-crunch of glass, as they come by.

Kate and I stay where we are for a long while. Then Dermot's voice calls: 'Get up now, the pair of you.' He helps us over the wall, and we brush down our skirts. 'Right, let's get going.'

I wait for Kate to ask where it is we're going to, but she stays quiet and, as we walk back down the street together, I'm careful to stay nice and close to her. We're not going near as fast as I'd like, on account of having to step around all the glass that got broke. Ahead of us is a man, lying in a doorway. He's on his back, and as we get nearer, I see his eyes are closed and he has a piece of sacking over his belly. Another man kneels beside him, and Dermot walks over.

'Those Barst Ards,' he says.

'Is he hurt bad?' Kate asks.

'Nothing to be done for him now, poor fellow.'

'Come away, Brede.' She pulls me back, but not before I see him lift the sack away. Where the man's belly should be is a big hole with a load of pink worms sticking out of it.

My insides start to heave, and the next minute I'm sicking up all the food I ate, and it's going splatter-splatter down my skirt, and onto the ground.

'Don't say I didn't warn you,' Dermot says.

Kate seizes my hand, and I can feel her all of a tremble. And when I look up at her, she's all tight-lipped and her face is very pale. 'Let's get you back to the house, Brede.'

'Oh, and Kate?' Dermot says.

'Yes?'

'It goes without saying that you were never here.'

'But they'll be wondering where on earth we've got to.'

'Just have your story at the ready. Brede here ran off, and you found her way over the other side of the mountain.'

We start the long walk back, and all the way, I hold tight to her hand, waiting for the big telling-off she's bound to give me. But she says not one word, and I just wish I could tell her how sorry I am for the terrible trouble I've caused, but please, please don't send me away to the Poor House.

TWENTY-THREE

'ALL THIS RAIN,' ANNIE SAYS. 'IT REALLY GETS YOU down.'

Margaret gives a sigh. 'Can anyone tell me where that summer's gone?'

I'd like to know too, because it's a dreary old day, with the mountain looking as if someone's thrown a grey cloth over it, and the rain going beat-beat on the roof.

I'm meant to be in the scullery, peeling apples, so I'm hoping Kate'll not find me here in our room going through my things. She's not started on the lunch just yet, because she and the Mooney woman are in Missus Purdy's old room. The door's shut, so I can't have a listen as I wanted. All I can hear is Annie and Margaret talking away while they tidy one of the presses.

'That's us done,' Margaret says. 'So how long will you be gone?'

'I should be back within the week.'

'Well, I hope, Annie, you find your sister in better health and...'

Their voices move on past, so I have another look through my things. Under my second cap and apron there's a bird's egg, blue as the sky; a strip of bacon that I'm saving for later; and the gorgeous handkerchief Missus Henderson gave me and that I'm using to wrap a load of stones in. And there in the corner is just what I'm searching for – Missus Purdy's box that the looking-glass came in. I need the box for my next game of catch-a-beetle with young Rory, because the last one we found lay on its back, waving its legs in the air, and when I put it in my pocket for safekeeping, it ended being all squashed up. So I'm thinking the box will be a grand place to keep it.

I'm about to head back to the scullery, when Mister Henderson's voice comes from the hall. 'I'm sorry to disappoint you, John – and you also, Helen – but my mind's made up.'

'God knows I've done my best.' Pea-in-the-pod is very angry-sounding. 'And all I can say is, that if you continue this way, it won't be just you that suffers.'

Whatever Mister Henderson's going on with, I don't like to think of him in pain.

'It's you I'm most sorry for, Helen,' Pea-in-the-pod says. 'And what our father would be thinking, I can't begin to imagine.'

'Well,' Mister Henderson says, 'I can and I assure you, John, that it alters nothing. For believe you me—'

He doesn't get to finish because Missus Henderson says, 'Thank you for calling by, John. You'll be here for lunch as usual?'

'I'm sorry, Helen. Nothing to do with you, but the way things are, it's best to give it a miss.'

'What a coward you are!' Mister Henderson says.

'Better a coward than a traitor, William. And a bloody pig-headed one at that.'

'Get out of my house!' Mister Henderson shouts.

'Don't worry – I can't wait to leave.'

Steps go across the hall, and then the front door slams.

'Please, William, I'm begging you. Just listen to him,' Missus Henderson says. 'You know what all our friends are saying.'

'Cutting off our household supplies is hardly the action of friends.'

'Don't you see? If we give in to these Carth Licks, we'll end up losing our religion – our way of life – everything we hold dear. Does all that mean nothing to you?'

'Why can't *you* see that these Carth Licks are poor, starved creatures, who need our help? Now' – his steps move away – 'I've business in the city to attend to.'

'Don't do this, William!' she calls. 'Think of our future. Think of your son!'

The door bangs shut again.

In the silence, I hear the big clock going tick-tick, and then there's another sound. It's Missus Henderson, crying as if her heart will burst out of her. And I go all trembly inside, because it puts me in mind of the crying there was in our village when the sickness came.

I tiptoe into the hall, and stand beside her. The tears are running down her face, and her belly looks as if any moment the babby will burst out of it.

'Oh, it's Kate's daughter.' She looks at me before giving her cheeks a wipe. 'Whatever must you think of me, carrying on like this?'

I have a chew of my hair, because I don't know what to think.

'But can't you see how impossible it all is? Being put into a corner like this?'

She's in the middle of the hall, so I shake my head.

'No, of course not. I don't know what's come over me, talking to you this way.' She gets up and moves to the stairs. 'I need to rest, and haven't you work to be getting on with?'

I'm just back in the scullery, when Kate comes in the door. 'How are you getting on with those apples?'

I wait for her to give me a telling-off, but she has a faraway look on her face, like she's had ever since we were in that town and saw all the things we were told we didn't see. It was a good while back and she's never spoken of it since, so I think she's forgotten about it. And I'm just glad she's not sent me away.

Now she says, 'Quick as you can with those apples, Brede. I'm a bit behind myself today.'

When I've finished all the peeling, I move on to my next job, which is tidying the yard. The rain has stopped, so Angus comes out of his kennel and watches while I push the puddles of water away with the broom, and pick up pieces of twig that have blown off the tree. Next I wash the scullery floor, and by then, Kate has served up the

Hendersons' meal, and it's time for my own. Which I'm good and ready for after all that work.

I sit next to Sam, with Kate on my other side. Annie is away to her sister's, but opposite us is Margaret, Molly and the Mooney woman. When we've finished our stew, which is good and tasty, Kate dishes out the rice pudding.

'You're still managing with the supplies?' Margaret asks.

'It's mainly the sugar and flour that are running low.'

'No more pastry for us, then,' Sam says.

'Not until Mister Henderson gets in some stores from the city.'

'Would anyone mind if I had that last spoonful of rice?' the Mooney woman says.

Kate pushes the dish towards her.

Sam and I take turn-and-turn about with seconds, and today it should be his. He bangs his spoon on the table, and Annie gives him a look.

'It's not the only thing Mister Henderson has gone to the city for,' Margaret says. 'I heard him talking with Mister Johnson about some Home Rule meeting or other.'

'Whatever good will it do them?' Molly says.

'The dear knows.' Annie turns to the Mooney woman. 'Margaret says Missus Henderson was in a very poor way first thing. She was wondering where you'd got to.'

'Sure, all the woman needs is her rest. And as for my being late, you've only Kate to blame for that.'

Kate turns all red, and I'm thinking there's no call to be speaking to her that way.

The Mooney woman gives a laugh. 'The two of us were going over some menus together. Isn't that right, Kate?'

'We – I –' her voice has a wobble to it – 'want to make sure Missus Henderson is getting the right kind of food.'

Missus Mooney pushes back her chair. 'I could do with another lie-down. They worked me almost to death in my last place.'

'Pity they didn't finish the job,' Sam says, but he's speaking so low, it's only myself hears him.

'The child can give me a knock, Kate, if Missus Henderson needs anything.'

'Certainly, Missus Mooney.'

'The cheek of her! Ordering everyone around like that,' Margaret says, when she's gone out.

'You're the one who sees the most of her, Kate,' Annie adds. 'Do you think she's up to the work?'

Kate bites her lip. 'She can be a bit abrupt, but she knows what she's doing.'

'Well, let's just hope you're right.'

The rest of the afternoon, I'm busy clearing up in the kitchen. And I'm just cutting up more apples for tomorrow's pudding, when the Mooney woman comes back in. She stands, holding onto the door. There's a bit of rice stuck to her chin, and an odd kind of a smell coming off her.

'Good. I wanted to catch you on your own, Kate.'

'Can I get you anything, Missus Mooney?'

She gives a hiccough. 'No, thank you. But I trust you've not forgotten that little talk we had earlier? About your gentleman visitor?'

'I've not forgotten,' Kate's voice has gone all cold. 'But you'd do well to remember that we both have things we should turn a blind eye to.'

I can't make any sense of that, when the two of them can see perfectly well.

'I'll leave you to it then.'

The rest of the afternoon, there's not a word or a smile to be had from Kate, and I'm thinking it must be on account of the grey old day, with the rain still drumming away on the roof. When I take the dog his meal, the hens are clumped under the big tree, and the sky's gone all dark.

'There's a storm on the way,' Kate says, when I'm back in the kitchen, 'so you'd better head for the dairy. Go carefully now.'

As I turn out of the yard, it's fairly coming down, and in no time the wet is soaking through my shawl. There's a real blow starting, so the path under the trees is covered with pieces of twig, and the leaves go skittering about the place. Angus has a grand time chasing them, but all I want is to be back with Kate in the warm. When I climb higher, I see the cows bunched up in a corner of the field, and there's not a bird to be seen.

By the time I get to the top of the world, my skirt is sticking to my legs so hard, I can hardly take a step. And when I put out my arms to see if I can fly, I almost get blown clean away.

Angus watches as I collect the milk. The pail is a fair old weight, and as we go down the path, I slip on a piece of rock, and nearly land on my arse. Some of the milk spills out, but I carry right on. The rain and the wind are lashing even harder, so the dog stays right behind me, and when we reach the yard, makes straight for his kennel.

Kate is waiting by the door. 'Thank goodness you're safely back,' she says as she hands me my dry clothes. I'm just having a warm-up by the range, when Margaret comes in. 'I wish Annie hadn't gone to her sister's. Any sign of Mister Henderson yet?'

Kate shakes her head.

'He should have been back from the city long since, and Missus Henderson is getting herself all worked up.'

'Is Missus Mooney not with her?'

'Indeed she is. Sitting by the bed, telling her how harmful it is for the baby to be taking on so.'

'A big help *that* will be!'

'Well, let's hope he arrives soon, though it'll be a hard journey for him in this storm.'

'And I think, Brede,' Kate says, when Margaret's gone out again, 'that you could do with an early night. Go along now, and I'll tuck you up in a while.'

It must be all that walking about in the storm, but my eyes are so heavy, I can hardly take another step. So the moment I'm in my bed, I'm fast asleep.

*

The noise wakes me. It's going rush-rush, as if a load of water is tumbling about inside my head. I pull the blanket over my ears, but still I hear it, going on and on. I'm so tired, I want to yell, 'Stop that this minute!'

I open my eyes. It's another dark old morning, and soon Kate will be coming to tell me it's time for my breakfast. But the noise is carrying on worse than ever, and I'm thinking that if anyone can make it go away, it'll be her.

As I walk towards the kitchen, it grows louder, and now it's putting me in mind of the time my mammy and da and brothers and sisters caught the fever. It felt like a load of birds was flapping about inside me. And when they flew away into the sky, they took my voice with them.

So now I'm sick to my belly, because suppose something bad has happened to Kate?

I take a run at the door and kick it open. Then I stop in my tracks.

She's on a chair in front of the range, and on her knee, yelling fit to burst, is young Rory. He stops when he catches sight of me, but then he opens his mouth, and starts up again, worse than ever. His hair is stuck up all over the place, and there's tears and snot running down his cheeks. It makes me feel so bad just looking at him, that my own face creases up.

'You can stop that this moment, Brede,' Kate says. 'I'll not be having the two of you carrying on. And you're big enough to know better.'

Rory looks across at me. Then he gives a grin. 'Beetle,' he says.

Kate wipes his face with her apron. 'Draw up another chair, Brede. I'll give the child to you while I make us some tea.'

He settles onto my lap, and for a moment there I remember my little brother, and how warm and soft he

246

was to hold, when he wasn't going wriggle-wriggle. I wish it was him with us now, although young Rory is almost as good to have.

Kate smiles at us. 'That's a nice sight. Now, just keep sitting quietly there the pair of you while I fill the kettle.' She gives a big yawn. 'I need something to keep me awake.'

I stare through the window and see it's still dark outside.

Kate catches my look. 'Yes – it's the middle of the night, Brede. Did you not hear the earlier rumpus? Mister Henderson was no sooner in the door than Missus Henderson's pains started. Missus Mooney says she doesn't like the look of things, so he's away out for the doctor. She and Molly and Margaret are with Missus Henderson now.'

It's then I hear another sound from above our heads, and it's as sharp and high as the notes of Dermot's fiddle.

Rory's mouth turns down.

'No need for this fuss,' Kate says. 'Your mammy will be right as rain by morning.'

I'm just wondering what the wrong sort of rain would be, when he leans against me, and closes his eyes.

'We can't put him back upstairs,' Kate whispers. 'He'd never get a wink of sleep.'

The high notes sound again, louder than ever.

'Would you listen to the creature! Mister Henderson has been gone these two hours. Please God, he'll be back with the doctor soon.'

In the quiet, I listen to the cat lapping at its saucer of milk, and the kettle hissing away to itself on the range. I'm just dozing off when I hear a shout. 'Quick, Kate! A basin! And Margaret says we need more towels.'

'Well, I imagine they're in one of the upstairs presses, Molly. And I've had water on the boil half the night.' Kate lifts the kettle off the range, and begins filling a bowl.

Molly is walking up and down, talking away as she goes. 'If only Annie were here, she'd know what to do about Missus Mooney.'

'What about her?'

'She's been took sick. First she began singing away to herself, then she kept clutching at her head, and now she's lying stretched on the floor. And no matter how hard I shake her, she's not stirring.'

Kate gives a sniff. 'I can't think what possessed the Hendersons to allow her through the door!'

'She told Margaret and me that when the time comes, we're to use the big scissors, but we're afraid of cutting the wrong part. And there must be a gallon of blood already.'

'Ssh, would you!' Kate says, with a look across at me. 'I helped with two of my sisters, as well as my own mother, and not one of them made near this amount of fuss. And they didn't need some fancy midwife either!'

The high sound comes again.

'I don't know if I can bear her screams any longer!'

'It's not you that's having to do the bearing.' Kate puts her head on one side and listens. 'There's always a deal of noise and mess when babies come into the world. It's only to be expected.'

I give a nod, because I remember the screams my mammy gave when my brother was coming out of her. My da told the rest of us to wait outside, and I had a grand time with my sister, Sheila, giving me piggy-backs up and down the lane.

Molly picks up the basin, and she's shaking so hard that water spills over the floor. If it was me doing it, I'd be getting such a telling-off.

Kate sighs. 'Would you like some help up there?'

'Oh, *would* you, Kate?'

She turns to me. 'But this is not something for you, Brede.'

I pull a face, because I'd like to see Missus Henderson's babby arrive. Sam let me watch the sow pushing out her piglets. There was a load of them and they were all brown and slippery-looking.

'Come along now, Brede.' Kate lifts young Rory from my lap and carries him, still fast asleep, into our bed. 'I'll be in with you in a while,' she whispers, and gives my hair a stroke.

Rory and I lie together in the bed. He smells of milk and wee, and his breath is going puff-puff in and out. Then I hear Kate and Molly's feet going up the stairs.

I stay awake until the light from the outside shows a soft grey. The house is all nice and quiet again, but then there's the sound of horses, going clop-clop outside the window, and two men talking together. One of them is Mister Henderson's voice, and I'm thinking that the other will be the doctor.

And I'm recalling Missus Henderson's screams, and the water and towels that'll be needed to soak up all the blood, and I wish that Kate were here beside me, telling me that everything will be just grand.

Young Rory is muttering in his sleep, and then his legs start kicking against me. So what with that, and with all the thoughts flying around in my head, I'm afraid that the morning will never be here.

TWENTY-FOUR

I'M SITTING HERE, WITH MY BELLY GROWLING AWAY, just hoping there's not much longer to wait for my meal, because everything's arse-over-tip today.

Kate and myself and Molly and Margaret ate our bacon and eggs while it was still dark, and now the two of them are in their beds, even though the sun is shining. Kate said I could go to mine, but I don't want to just yet, because then I wouldn't be sitting here, listening to Mister Henderson.

He and Kate are side-by-side at the table, and I'm at the far end, wondering whether they'll notice if I creep a bit nearer.

He has a bottle at his elbow that's bigger than the one Dermot carries, but with the same kind of a smell to it. Kate and I are just having tea. She has on her grey frock, but no apron, because that's been put to soak on account of the load of blood on it. When I caught sight of it, my mouth went all wobbly. Then she said, 'Stop that, this minute, Brede!' so I knew there was no cause to worry.

'... the time my brother John was born,' Mister Henderson is saying. 'I was nearly six years of age. And what I recall is being shaken awake, bundled into the pony cart, and sent to stay with my cousins. It happened so fast that, as I went off down the track, I thought perhaps I was dreaming the whole thing.'

I'm wondering if Kate recalls the two of us running away from the Thompsons that time, but she just gives a yawn. 'Oh, I'm sorry, Mister Henderson. It's been a long old night.'

'And Doctor Russell may be a while upstairs. Would you rather—?'

'No, I'm fine.' Her face goes very soft when she looks at him, and I'm thinking that these days she's not near as pleased to see Dermot.

'So what happened then, Mister Henderson?'

He swallows his drink. 'There were several children, all older than myself, but they treated me kindly.' He gives a smile that makes his moustache jump. 'We played tag for hours on end. Then their mother fed me chops and griddlecakes, before returning me home.'

I could be doing with some of those chops now. I look over at Kate, because she can always tell when I'm in need of my food, but she's too busy looking at Mister Henderson to notice me.

'I remember the quiet feel of the house. God knows

what I thought to find, but as I went into my parents' room, my father gave me such a severe look, I feared I'd done something terrible.'

'Oh dear.'

He pours more drink into his glass. 'My mother was lying in the bed, her face very pale. "See what the stalk has brought," she said. "A wee brother, John, for you to play with." And she pointed down at this red-faced scrap of a thing in the cot beside her.'

'That must have given you a surprise!'

'I think I was too busy working out what a stalk had to do with it.'

Kate gives a smile. 'Even Brede would be wondering that.'

I nod my head, because this talk of plants makes no sense at all.

He gulps his drink. 'I wanted to ask what a stalk looked like, but I was afraid of angering my father even more.'

'So what did you say?'

'The first thing that came into my head: "Will he be big enough by next summer to ride the pony?" "You'll have to give him a bit longer than that!" my father said. And then he and my mother laughed. And do you know, Kate, I walked out of that room without giving the baby a second glance. Because of what use was a brother if he wasn't going to be running about the place with me?' He pauses. 'I hope I'm not tiring you?'

'Not at all.' She sips her tea. 'I always imagined that someone like you – you know –' she waves her hand around the room – 'having all this. That you wouldn't feel the same as the rest of us. But for all that my family lived very plain, my da was a sight kinder than yours.'

I never thought of her having a mammy and a da. I think they must have got took by the sickness too.

'You're right, Kate. And I could never work out why my father was always so bad-tempered – why whatever I did was never good enough. Though later on, when it was plain that John was the son he loved best… Do you know—?' He breaks off. 'I've never told anyone this before – it must be the whiskey talking.' He picks up the bottle and peers into it. 'It still angers me to remember the kind of things my father said. "As well give the vote to a pig as to a Carth Lick!" and "If I'd my way, I'd shoot the lot of them!" He wasn't joking, either.'

I'm thinking that Kate and I are Carth Licks, and how much I'd hate for either of us to be shot. And I'm about to slip out of my seat, when the door opens.

'Dada!' Young Rory, in a nightshirt, and nothing on his feet, makes a rush at Mister Henderson, who lifts him onto his lap.

'Well, what do you make of your new sister, then?' He gives the top of his head a kiss. 'But whatever it is, you'll always be a splendid fellow. D'you hear me?'

'You smell funny, Dada!' And Rory slides off his knee, and is out the door again.

Mister Henderson gets to his feet. 'It's time I…' He's swaying from side to side.

Kate takes hold of his arm. 'Will you be all right?'

'Just fine, as long as I can lean on you.'

'Steady now!'

'Ah, William,' a voice says. 'I came to tell you that Helen is sleeping, and all's well with the baby. None of those unfortunate difficulties we had the last time.'

The man has dark hair with pale bits at the edges, and his beard is grey and fuzzy-looking. There's a pair of spectacles with gold-coloured frames on his nose, and he carries a big bag.

'Doctor Neil Russell! The very man I was on my way to see!'

'I see you're already celebrating. And with good cause.'

'Yes, thank God!'

'And thank God for this young woman here.' The doctor gives Kate a smile. 'Without her, it might be a very different story.'

It makes my insides all warm to think how she's helped Missus Henderson push the babby out, and how the two of them are sleeping, with all that blood washed away.

Mister Henderson squeezes Kate's arm, just as I've seen Dermot do. 'How can we ever repay you, Kate?'

She takes a step away. 'I was just glad to be of help, Mister Henderson.'

I hear feet coming along the passage, and the Russell doctor whispers, 'That'll be the midwife now. Not before time, I might add.' He gives Mister Henderson a look. 'I won't repeat what I'd like to do with her!'

Margaret comes in, and behind her is the Mooney woman. 'You've no cause to be turning me out like this, Mister Henderson!' Her eyes are as hard and black as two pieces of coal. 'It's hardly my fault I was taken ill.'

His face has a very angry look to it. 'I can assure you, Missus Mooney, that there is every cause. Sam will take you as far as the town – just be thankful we're not making you walk.'

She gives a sniff. 'Well, I'm telling you now that you'd do well to think about who you employ in this household.'

'What do you mean?'

She points a finger at Kate, and I move over so I'm next to her. 'Standing there as if butter wouldn't melt in her mouth.'

'You're making no sense, woman,' the doctor says. 'This is the person whose prompt action saved the life of Missus Henderson and her child. And I might add, while you were lying on the floor in a drunken stupor!'

'That's as may be.' She looks across at Kate. 'But, I can tell you a thing or two about your precious cook, Mister Henderson. Carrying on with that wild-looking fellow. A Feen Yun, I shouldn't wonder. And her not married. Can you credit it?'

Kate is all of a tremble beside me, and it makes me so scared that I reach for her hand. 'It's all right, Brede,' she says.

Mister Henderson draws in his breath. 'Let me tell you very plainly, Missus Mooney, that any carrying on in this household has not been done by Kate!'

'Well, have it your way. But don't say I didn't warn you!'

'Margaret, Missus Mooney is leaving,' Mister Henderson says. 'Would you show her the door?'

I recall the day she arrived, and found Dermot and

Kate in the kitchen together. And I'm just glad to be seeing the back of her.

She goes into the yard, and I hear Angus give a growl as she goes past.

'Well,' Mister Henderson says, 'I'd better let you get on, Kate. Just a cold meal will do everyone fine today. And' – he turns to the doctor – 'how about something to wet the baby's head?'

It doesn't seem a very nice thing to be doing to a babby, but the doctor says, 'I wouldn't say no. Although it looks to me as if you've made a pretty good start.' And they go off down the passage together.

'Did you ever hear such a carry-on?' Margaret says. 'The things Missus Mooney was saying about you, Kate!'

'Well, never mind all that. At least she's gone.' Kate moves to the range. 'Will you take some tea?'

'Not for me. I'm away to my bed again.' She heads for the doorway. 'Annie will be back before supper. Just wait till she hears what's been happening!'

When Margaret's gone out, Kate turns to me. 'Mister Henderson's said we can have the rest of the day off, and I could do with some air. So how about we have some bread and cheese, and then take a walk to the dairy?'

As Kate and I go up the path I'm smiling away, thinking of the Mooney woman gone from the house, and Missus Henderson's babby safely out of her.

Angus gives a bark, and I see Barney coming towards us. 'Good day to you, Kate. Any news?'

'There is indeed. Missus Henderson has a daughter, and they're both doing grand.'

'Extra porter for us men, then. Do you know what they're calling the child?'

'Is a bell,' Kate says.

It seems a funny kind of a name to me, but Barney says, 'That's nice.' And he touches his cap and is off down the track.

Kate and myself continue our climb, and when we've filled the pail with milk, and collected the cheese, Kate says, 'Let's have a bit of a rest, Brede. Goodness knows, we've earned it.'

So we sit on a piece of rock, and look out over the fields. Everything is turning very brown, and the trees are very bare-looking.

'I've not been up here for a while,' Kate says. 'At least at this time of the year you get a good view of the town.'

She points to the roofs, and the spike on one end of the Prod church, and the street like a piece of ribbon running past it, and beyond that the river, with the mill beside it. I squeeze my eyes shut, trying not to think of the Drummond man walking about in the town.

'I'm not surprised you're so tired,' Kate says. 'After the night we've had. Let's give ourselves a bit of a treat.' She gets up, and comes back with one of the ladles that she dips into the pail. 'Go on!' she says, holding it out. We take it in turns to drink, and it's grand to feel the milk sliding, all warm and creamy into my belly.

'Remember all those times when we were walking the countryside, with nowhere to call home? Just think of what we've escaped from, Brede. So aren't we the lucky ones?'

I don't rightly know what we've escaped from, but sometimes I wish we hadn't, because then my mammy and da, and my brothers and sisters would still be here.

Kate once said that if someone's not here, it doesn't always mean they're dead, but when they're dead, then they're in heaven, but that isn't the same as being up in the sky. Which leaves me thinking what a puzzle it all is.

I take another mouthful of milk, and Angus settles beside us, with his head on his paws. He closes his eyes, and I'm so tired, I wish I could do the same.

'Poor Missus Henderson,' Kate says. 'Lying in her bed, all white-faced and frail. She didn't think she'd survive the night, or the baby either. You should have seen the look she gave when she heard its first cry.'

Crying is all it seems to be doing, so I'm hoping it'll stop soon.

'Now we're alone up here, I want to talk to you about Dermot.' Kate puts her hand on my arm. 'I know how much you like him, Brede, and there's no denying the kindness he's shown us. But we need to tread carefully with him. Do you get my meaning?'

I give a nod, because I always make sure not to bump into him when I'm practising my steps.

'I knew you'd understand.' Kate wipes the milk from my mouth with the edge of her skirt.

Angus gives a growl.

'Whatever's up with him?'

I look around, but all I see is the sun shining down on the fields, and the white backsides of the sheep feeding on the slopes.

Now Angus goes flat on his belly, showing his teeth.

Kate jumps up. 'Who's there? Come out at once!'

I wait for someone to answer, but the only sound is the dog, who's still growling away.

I get up, and take hold of Kate's hand.

'We've been here long enough. I'll just return this ladle, and then we'll get back to the house.'

'That's a pity!' a voice says, and the next moment Dermot appears round the side of the shed.

I give a jump, and Kate lets out a shriek.

'No need to act so scared. It's only me.'

'What do you mean, no need?' Kate says. 'You've frightened us near out of our wits!'

'And for that I apologise.' He gives a grin. 'But to make up for it, I've brought someone to see you.' And round the corner comes Francis, who waves his hand at us.

'What on earth are the pair of you doing up here, Dermot?' Kate's voice has gone all cold.

'Come to share the good news. It *is* good news this time, I take it?'

'Missus Henderson and the baby are doing fine, if that's what you mean.' Kate looks about her. 'Suppose someone spots you?'

He gives a laugh. 'Barney went off for his morning tea a while ago, and as you can see, there's just the four of us – unless you count that pair of magpies.'

I look over and, right enough, there's one, two birds with lovely black and white feathers hopping about under the tree.

Kate picks up the pail. 'We need to be getting back.'

'Of course you do.' He gives another grin. 'I'll be round Sunday. You can show me more of your steps, Brede.'

As Kate and I start down the path, I give him a wave. She slaps my arm. 'Stop that!'

I can't think what's put her in such a mood.

'See you, darlin'!' Dermot calls after us, but she doesn't answer.

TWENTY-FIVE

I T'S THE GOLD THAT CATCHES MY EYE – A GREAT, round circle of it. At first I'm thinking it's the ball young Rory plays with that's got itself caught in the tops of the trees. Then I feel a right eejit, because it's only the sun shining down from above the lane.

It's a cold old morning, with the frost like a sprinkle of sugar over the ground. It goes crunch-crunch under my feet and I'm thinking of the time when I'd have given it a lick. It's not something Missus Henderson or Missus Thompson would do and now I've my very own looking-glass, and a handkerchief with flowers across it, I'm aiming to be every bit as good as the pair of them. And anyway, the frost never tastes anywhere as nice as it looks.

I throw down the grain, and the rooster flies from the fence, and the hens come running over and start pecking it up.

Kate is at the kitchen door. 'Is he not here yet?'

'Neither hide nor hair of him,' Margaret says.

'Thank God the Christmas puddings and cakes were made weeks back.'

'But it won't be the same if we can't have all the trimmings.'

What lace and ribbons have to do with it is beyond me. The only thing I do know is that we just had the one strip of bacon and some spuds for our lunch again, and there's been no scones or cakes for a good while.

Angus gives a bark.

'Is that wheels I hear?' Kate says.

And sure enough, a big cart, with a load of stuff piled on the top, is rattling down the track.

Sam opens the gate, and a man with a great big beard and hair the colour of dish-water jumps from the cart. He's very short, and his legs have a kind of a curve to them.

Annie comes out of the house, with Kate and Margaret beside her. 'Joe Dooley?' Kate says.

He touches his cap.

'Well, you certainly took your time!' Margaret says.

'That's a terrible hard road over the mountain, Missus. I'd have been here earlier, only the mare lost a shoe.'

That's no surprise, because it'd be easy to lose anything on that mountain.

'Get the mare some water, Sam,' Annie says, 'and then help Kate in with this lot.'

I'm glad the animal is being given a drink because it looks in a very poor way, with bits of spit around its mouth, and its sides heaving in and out.

Sam and the Dooley man start unloading the wagon.

'Stand back, Brede,' Kate says.

So I wait with Margaret under the tree. Soon there's great piles of sacks all along the ground. 'That'll show them!' she says, but when I look around, it's only ourselves and the chickens watching.

Inside, Kate's busy telling Sam where all the bags should go, and it makes me want to skip, knowing the stores are being filled up with all these good things.

'I'll just run and tell Missus Henderson the food's arrived,' Annie says. 'And then we need to get ready.'

Kate turns to me. 'Come along, Brede.'

I'm not sure what we're getting ready for, but I'm all excited to be putting on the clothes that I wore at Easter. First there's my skirt that's a lovely grey colour now all the bits of food are washed out of it. Then there's my blouse that's white with a kind of a frill at the top. I smooth my hair down with my fingers, and then I lift out my looking-glass. As I hold it up to my face, I recall Margaret telling Missus Purdy one time what a very plain girl I was, and Missus Purdy saying: 'Isn't it lucky children pay no heed to that kind of thing?' But that doesn't stop me wishing that my hair had a bit of a curl to it, and that my cheeks weren't so fat. But maybe one day soon I'll turn out – if not as lovely as Missus Thompson, for who can ever match her? – then at least as pleasant-looking as Missus Henderson.

I pick up the ribbon I found in her sewing room. It's a lovely purple colour, and I'm just tying it into my hair, when Kate says, 'That's not yours, Brede. Wherever did you get it?' She tries to take it off me, but I push her away.

'I give up,' she says, but she has a smile on her, so I know she's letting me keep it.

She looks very well in her best green frock and when we join Annie, Margaret and Molly they're in their Easter clothes too, smiling away at one another.

'Come along then,' Annie says, and we follow her across the hall and into the room that's beside the front door. It's the place where Mister Henderson and Pea-in-the-pod do all their yelling at one another, and it's the only room I've not been in before. It's bigger than Missus Henderson's parlour, with red curtains at the windows. There's a good fire in the grate, and on the wall above is a picture of old Mister Henderson, with a black ribbon across his chest. His eyes look straight at me, and I suck in my breath, waiting for him to shout: 'Freedom, my arse!'

When I'm certain he's staying quiet, I take a good look at the best thing in the room. It's a great big tree, with a load of coloured balls, and candles burning away on it, and right at the top is a very small lady with wings and a gold frock on her, who puts me in mind of Missus Thompson.

Annie and Kate and Molly and myself stand in a line, and I'm just thinking that maybe this is a chance to show my steps, when Kate whispers, 'Not now, Brede.'

But she doesn't sound one bit cross, because the room's so lovely and warm, and the tree's so gorgeous. Only Sam, who's standing beside it with a bucket, has a very long face on him.

'What in the world are you doing, Sam?' Molly whispers across.

'I'm in charge of the water,' he whispers back.

'It's in case the tree catches fire,' Annie says. 'One of the Hendersons' friends had their house burned to the ground a few Christmases ago. So you can't be too careful.'

I have a chew of my hair because if that happened here, where would Kate and I go?

'Don't look so worried, Brede,' she whispers. 'We're perfectly safe.'

So I smile up at her.

Then Mister and Missus Henderson come in. She has on a brown and white frock, and a hat with a brown feather, and her face has a good colour to it. Mister Henderson looks very well too, with his boots all polished, and a jacket with a red scarf tucked into the neck.

'A very happy Christmas to you all,' he says. 'Missus Henderson and I have just come from visiting the Ten Aunts and other workers, and now it's your turn.' He starts talking away about someone called Good Will, and what a great job we've done through the year.

I'm thinking of the load of spuds and carrots I've peeled, and the floors I've swept, and all those trips to the dairy, and I'm glad he's remembering them too.

'Right,' he says, 'time for your presents. Annie, you first.'

She steps forward, and Mister Henderson gives her some paper, which she puts in her pocket, and Missus Henderson hands her a square that's the same shape as the soap I had for my birthday. Then it's the turn of Margaret, Molly and Sam, who get given the same. And they've all got very pleased looks.

'And now for Kate,' Mister Henderson says. 'And Brede, of course.'

Kate's given a square of paper too that she tucks into her pocket. Then Missus Henderson reaches behind her and lifts out a parcel. It's about the size of the board I use for my steps, so I'm hoping this is a new one.

'We wanted you to have this, Kate,' Missus Henderson says, 'on account of all you did to see our beautiful daughter safely into the world.'

'Oh,' Kate says.

'Well, aren't you going to open it?'

She tears off the paper, and then she turns all pink. From behind us, I hear a gasp, but Kate and I just stand and stare, because what's inside is something I've not set eyes on since I lived with my mammy and da. It's the Sacred Heart, with the same long white frock on him that I remember. There's a lamp shining out from a hole in his chest and his feet are all bare. It's no wonder his eyes are sad-looking.

'Oh, I couldn't have asked for anything nicer!' Kate's voice has a catch to it, and Mister Henderson gives a cough. 'We're glad you like it.'

'We'll put it up in your room, Kate,' Missus Henderson says, 'but in giving you this, Mister Henderson and I wanted to make it very clear to this household that it is one that is open to all.'

Mister Henderson gives her hand a squeeze. 'Thank you, Helen.'

Margaret steps forward. 'Haven't we always been welcoming to her?'

'Of course you have, Margaret,' Mister Henderson says. 'And it's much appreciated.'

'But now,' Missus Henderson says, 'here's something special for Brede too,' and she hands me a parcel that's small and very soft under my fingers, and when I open it, there inside is one, two, three ribbons. One is red, one is green and one is yellow, and they're simply gorgeous.

'Isn't that kind, Brede?' Kate says, and I give a grin.

'I was thinking that now she has some of her own,' Missus Henderson says, 'she can maybe stop using mine.'

I put a hand up to my hair, and everyone gives a laugh.

'You're all to have the rest of the day off,' Mister Henderson says, 'and you can crack on with preparations for the Christmas lunch in the morning. And now that Kate has a good supply of flour, I'm sure none of us will go hungry.' He smiles at her, and she goes all pink again.

*

'Who's the Hendersons' little pet, then?' Margaret says, when we're back in the kitchen.

The only creature in the house is the cat, and it's fast asleep in its box.

'I didn't ask them to do that,' Kate says.

'No, but I kept telling you that midwife was up to no good, Kate. Maybe if you'd listened, the Hendersons would have replaced her and there'd have been no need for your help.'

Kate's looking all hot and bothered, as she always does whenever there's any mention of the Mooney woman.

'Now, there's to be no arguing today,' Annie says, 'because haven't the Hendersons been just as generous as always?'

'True enough,' Molly says. 'I'll be able to get that material from Whelans that I've had an eye on.'

'And I'm after a new pair of shoes,' Margaret says. 'How about you, Annie?'

'Oh, I'm saving for my old age.' She gives a laugh. 'Now, a cup of tea would go down well. And I'm sure you'll have scones for us later, Kate.'

And then everyone starts talking away, and we sit round the table, listening to the rain against the window. And I feel all warm inside.

A while later, when Molly, Annie and Margaret have taken themselves off to their rooms, Kate and I sit on by the range.

'What a great day, Brede.' She pats her pocket. 'You know the Hendersons gave us some money too? The most I've ever had. But best of all, now we've that picture of the Sacred Heart, it's all right for us to be Carth Licks again.' She gives a yawn. 'Ah well, we've an early start in the morning, so let's—'

Someone goes rap-rap on the yard door.

'Who on earth would be visiting at this time of night?' Kate picks up the poker, and moves across very slowly. 'Who's there?' she calls, but all that's to be heard is the rain on the roof.

She unbolts the door.

'Just come to wish you girls the compliments of the season.' And in steps Dermot and Carrot Hair, with the water dripping off their jackets.

I'm sorry Dermot doesn't have his fiddle with him, but maybe he'll bring it next time.

'Dermot Friel – the fright you gave me!'

He goes to give her a kiss, but she pushes him away. 'You've been drinking!'

'Just a drop to keep out the damp. Isn't that right, Francis?'

'Right enough, Dermot,' and they both move to the range.

'You shouldn't be here,' Kate says. 'Suppose someone comes in?'

'Sure, the Hendersons and the rest of them are away to their beds.' Dermot settles himself in Missus Purdy's old chair. There's a hole in one of his boots, and his jacket has a big tear in it. 'Francis and I were thinking you might spare a couple of hungry fellows some food.'

Kate bites her lip. 'Very well. But you're to leave the minute you've finished eating.'

She pours out tea, and puts the heel of a loaf and some slices of ham on a plate.

'How are you doing then, Kate?' Carrot Hair says. 'All well here?'

'Just fine.'

He bites into his bread. 'Wish I could say the same.'

'What do you mean?'

'The Thompsons. At each other's throats all day long, and treating everyone else like shite.'

'She's not been seen in the town these weeks past,' Dermot says, 'and all those purchases from the city have stopped.'

'I'll be driving the pair of them over here for the Hendersons' Christmas party,' Francis says.

Dermot gulps his tea. 'You'd best keep out of their way, Kate. They're not the sort to forgive you for running off like that.'

I have a chew of my hair, because I don't want to set eyes on them again either.

Dermot stretches his arms above his head. 'Well, we're for the off.' He looks around the room. 'I heard the supplies came through, so I suppose the cupboards are all filled up again?'

'If you're thinking, Dermot Friel, that there's any food to be taken away with you,' Kate says, 'you can think again!'

'Well, there's always other places. Which reminds me – did you get much cash off Henderson?'

Kate puts a hand to her pocket. 'Only a lovely picture.'

He gives a laugh. 'Well, enjoy yourself – while you can.'

And then he and Carrot Hair step into the night.

TWENTY-SIX

'I WAS JUST PASSING THE DOOR.'

It's been such a while since I've seen Sausage Arm that I've clean forgot about her. But she's as thin-looking as ever, and her hair's the same dirty colour.

'You know you're always welcome, Bridget.' Annie folds a blouse of Missus Henderson's that's been airing over the range. I'm busy sweeping the floor, and Kate's at the table, rolling out her pastry.

'So, how are you this festive season?' Annie's been in a very good humour ever since she had her present off Mister Henderson. 'I'm sure you'd welcome some tea on such a cold morning.'

It is that all right. When I was up at the dairy earlier, snow was coming out of the sky in great pieces, and now it's as if someone's taken a load of sheets from the wash and spread them over the ground.

'You're just in time for one of my scones, Bridget,' Kate says, lifting them onto a plate. They smell grand as always, and what I'd like best in the world is to get my teeth into the big one in the middle.

Sausage Arm sits at the table, and I move closer to have a better look at the place where her hand is missing.

'So, you've not got Deidre with you the day?' Annie asks.

'Did you not hear?' She doesn't wait for an answer. Instead, the tears come running down her face.

Just looking at her makes me feel so bad that my own eyes start to water.

'Stop that, Brede!' Kate says.

Sausage Arm wipes her face with her shawl. 'It happened two days ago. It was very sudden.'

'Oh, the poor child!'

'And I can't tell you how terrible it was, Annie, to see her so failed. We had the doctor out, but he could do nothing for her. And there was never any medicine to be had.'

Kate blesses herself. 'At least she's at peace, God rest her.'

That's what people say when someone's gone to live with the saints, but with her cough-coughing about the place, I'm thinking the poor things won't get a moment's quiet.

'So, what will you do now?' Annie asks.

'I'm still at my brother's, though I'm not sure how long he'll have me. There's little enough to go round as it is.'

'Maybe Mister Henderson could find you something?'

'Sure, what am I good for now?' She holds up the arm that has the hand missing from it. 'You tell me that.'

I'm not surprised no one answers her, because it's hard enough peeling spuds and washing floors when you've both your hands.

'This'll make you feel better,' Kate says, setting the tea and scone in front of her.

Sausage Arm puts the scone in her pocket. 'I just came in with the news, so I'll not hold you up any longer.'

'Don't be rushing off. Stay a while longer,' Annie says.

But she's already at the door.

'Well, come and see us again soon.'

She goes out without another word, and Annie lets out a sigh. 'What that woman's been through.'

'It doesn't bear thinking about,' Kate says. 'Just think, if it wasn't for her calling in here that time, Brede and I would have ended up in that mill.'

Annie gives a smile. 'Well, thank the Lord you didn't. I know Margaret has a sharp tongue on her sometimes, but we're still one big family, aren't we? And—'

A man is shouting something, and then steps come running along the passage. The three of us look up as the door bangs open, and in comes Pea-in-the-pod, with Margaret after him. I've not set eyes on him since that afternoon when Missus Purdy and I stood in the lane, and he and the other men came marching past, waving their flags and playing that gorgeous music.

'Do you know where Mister Henderson is, Annie?' Although, he's not got his hat and gloves on, he's still very sweaty-looking.

'He was in the stables a while ago, Mister John. But I think now he'll be up on the farm somewhere.'

'I must speak with him.'

'Shall I send Sam to find him?'

'Please do. And tell him to say it's a matter of great urgency.'

'John?' Missus Henderson is in the doorway. The toes of her shoes are brown, and she has on a green frock, with a black ribbon round her neck. 'Whatever's the matter?'

'Nothing to concern yourself with, Helen.'

She gives him a look, like the kind Kate turns on me when I'm doing something I shouldn't.

'Oh, very well. If you insist. But let's talk in private.'

As they go off down the passage, his voice carries back to us. 'The same as at Jim Baxter's place... four of my best bullocks... barn burnt to the ground... but for the dog...'

'A bad business,' Annie says. 'And at Christmas time too.'

'Is it Feen Yuns again?' Margaret asks.

Kate's gone back to her pastry, slap-slapping it onto the board as hard as she can go.

'I shouldn't wonder, Margaret,' Annie says. 'Though worrying about them rebels is not going to get us anywhere. Best to be like Kate, and just get on with our work.'

But it's hard to do that because now Sam comes rushing in from the yard. 'Could someone tell me what in the world's going on? Barney says all the cows are to be rounded up into the lower field; Mister Henderson and his brother are outside the house, arguing their heads off.

And now there's some men on horses coming along the far track at a fair old lick.'

'Wait till I tell you, Sam...' Margaret says.

I slip out of the door and across the yard, so I can get a look at the horses. The snow is flying out from under their hooves, and as they get near, I can see the breath, like white smoke, coming out of their noses.

The first rider is the James man, who gives a nod as he goes by. Next is the doctor, who was here when Is A Bell was born. But when I see who's coming behind them, I put a hand to my mouth. It's Mister Thompson, and beside him is the Drummond man. He still has his jacket with the green and orange squares, and the orange scarf around his neck. As they go past, he turns. I duck, but I'm not quick enough, and he looks straight at me. I feel myself go all cold inside, because I know he's remembering that time in his office, when he and Missus Thompson were trying to make babbies. Then his horse carries him on past, and I go running back to the kitchen, as fast as my legs will take me.

Mister Henderson must have come in by the front, because there he is by the range, talking away to Annie and Kate. I'd like to be the one standing next to him, but the other two are in my way.

'... And I've asked Barney to rig up an overnight shelter by the dairy,' he's saying. 'Just to be on the safe side. I know it'll be pretty cold up there, but I'm sure Brede will manage fine.'

My chin starts to wobble, because I don't want to be left up there all on my own, and supposing I'm not allowed to take my blanket?

Kate looks across at me. 'The shelter's not for you, Brede, it's for Angus. So he can guard the milk.'

I don't know why it's not safe enough with just the door locked, but I'm so happy to be sleeping in my own bed that I give a skip.

'Well, at least someone's pleased,' Mister Henderson says.

'Will the other gentlemen be wanting refreshments?' Annie asks.

'No, they're not stopping, and Missus Henderson and myself will be setting off for her mother's shortly. We'll only be away the night.' At the door, he turns towards us. 'I wish this business with the cattle hadn't happened.' He moves his finger and thumb together until they're almost touching. 'But I can tell you now that Glad Stone is very close to an agreement.' He smiles at Kate. 'And the sooner Carth Licks get their rights, the sooner all of us will sleep easy in our beds.'

'All well and good for him,' Margaret says, when he's gone out. 'And for you, Kate. But what if it's Prods' throats next?'

'Sure, we've said that before and nothing happened,' Annie says. 'So now what I'm thinking is that we've this lunch to prepare.' Annie looks across at me. 'Why don't you take the dog a dish of tea? It'll help keep out the chill.'

The tea is the colour of turf, and when she's added milk to cool it, I carry it into the yard, walking very slowly so as not to spill any. Angus comes rushing out of his house, his tail wagging away. I put the bowl in front of him, and he starts lapping it up. But I don't stay to see him finish, on account of the cold.

And because I'm busy in the scullery, I don't see the wild horses galloping away but later, when I'm giving the hens their feed, I hear a clatter of wheels and the Hendersons' carriage, with the black horse pulling it, comes past. Young Rory presses his face to the window, and sticks out his tongue at me. So I poke mine out at him, and then go running back to the kitchen.

Kate, Margaret and Sam are already at the table, and Annie is ladling out the stew.

'You're off to your mother's for the night, Margaret?' Kate asks, handing me my plate.

'If it's still all right with you, Annie, I'll get the table all set up before I go.'

'Of course you'll be wanting to see in the New Year with your family,' Annie says. 'As Sam does. So, as long as you're both back first thing, Kate and I will manage here just fine.'

It's my turn for seconds of pudding– fruit pie, with a load of custard on the top.

Sam gives me a nudge. 'Any chance of some of that?' His voice has gone all deep, and I can see a load of hairs on his chin that I hadn't noticed before.

'That's a nice idea, Brede,' Kate says. 'How about sharing for a change?'

So I cram in one, two more spoonfuls, and then I push the plate over. He grabs hold of it, and has the rest finished before I can take it back.

'The child's coming along really well,' Annie says. 'And it's been a while since she's broken anything.'

'Yes, she's become a real help,' Kate says.

'For the minute anyway.' Margaret pushes back her chair. 'I'll see you all in the morning. Shall we get going, Sam?'

He gives me a wink. 'Thanks for the pie, Brede.' And I feel my cheeks go all hot.

'I know it's still early,' Annie says, 'but I'm for my bed. It'll be a long day tomorrow. You'll lock up, Kate?'

'Of course, Annie.' She looks at me. 'There's still a deal of clearing to do, but I want you to take Angus up to the dairy while it's still light.'

I fetch my shawl, and the pail, and Kate sees me off at the door. 'I wish they'd send Sam,' she says, 'but you'll be all right as long as you tie Angus up and come straight back.'

Outside, it's a cold old afternoon, but some of the snow has melted away, and as I go along the track under the trees, there's a load of puddles that I'd be jumping over if I didn't have the pail to carry.

Everything is very quiet and still, and I'm glad there's still enough light to see my way. Angus runs ahead, and when I get to the top of the world, there's the shelter that Barney has built for him. It's made of stout pieces of wood, with a space at the front to get in and out of, and I'm thinking he'll be snug enough inside.

While I collect the milk and cheese, he runs around in circles. I put the pail down by his new house, and while he's having a nice drink from the bucket, I fasten the rope round his neck, and tie the other end to the hook. *Kate will be baking first thing*, I tell him in my head, *so I'll bring you a slice of fresh soda-bread for your breakfast.*

He lies down, with his nose between his paws. He could go into his kennel, but instead he stays outside, watching as I go back down the path.

The mountain's a dark shape behind me and the wind has started moaning away to itself. I'm trying not to think of the cows lying with their throats cut open, and the blood running out of them. The pail feels heavy, and my shoe is catching on a sore place on my heel, so I'm glad to see the lights of the house, and to be turning into the yard.

Inside the kitchen is all lovely and warm. I'm looking about for Kate when a voice says, 'How are you doing, Brede?' I give a jump so that some of the milk spills out of the pail.

Dermot is in the chair by the range and Kate's busy putting plates away in the press. When she sees me, she says: 'Oh good, you're back.'

'Would you not be sorry for that dog?' He stuffs some bread into his mouth. 'Left in the cold to guard a load of milk and cheese?'

'There are some nasty goings-on around here, Dermot Friel, in case you hadn't noticed.'

He reaches for another piece of bread. It's from the fresh loaf that Kate was saving for later. Her lips are set in a line, so I know she's none too pleased.

'I hear there's been a great carry-on over this cattle business,' he says. 'Henderson's brother running around like a frightened rabbit, and another meeting planned in the town.'

'Well, can you wonder at it? People are afraid.'

'If the Feen Yuns intended to cut a person's throat, do you not think they'd have done so? I mean, why kill harmless animals?'

She gives him a look. 'As a warning?'

'You've a good head on your shoulders, Kate O'Hagan.'

'And you'd do well to remember it.' She gets up. 'Off to bed with you, Brede. I'll be in to say your prayers.'

I was hoping for a chance to show Dermot my steps, but I know from her voice there'll be no dancing for me this evening, so there's nothing for it but to walk over to the door. I push it nearly closed after me, and then I stand and have a peep through the crack.

'I think it would be best if you stayed away from the house, Dermot. Until all this business blows over.'

He takes a drink from his bottle. 'Well, well. I can tell the Hendersons have you in their pocket.'

'They're good people. And I don't want Brede picking up on anything. Sometimes I catch her listening at the door.'

'Where's the harm in that? Sure, she can't string two words together.'

There's a piece of string in my drawer, but I don't know how anybody would fasten words to it.

'Maybe not. But she used to get such terrible nightmares, and I don't want them starting again.'

I hear the clink of his bottle. 'But don't think we're going to take much more of this, Kate, without a fight.'

I'm remembering my cousin, Liam, who knocked out the rent man's teeth that time, and had to go away across the water; and of Mister Henderson and his talk of fighting. And I go all cold inside to think that maybe he and Dermot will get themselves hurt.

'You heard of wee Deidre's death? Though much those Fekk Ing Prod Barst Ards care about it.' He gets to his feet. 'But enough of this. Have you missed me?'

'I need to say goodnight to Brede.'

'She can wait for once, can't she?'

He starts undoing the buttons on her blouse, and she unfastens the buttons on his shirt, and why they can't just take their own clothes off is beyond me. They move the chairs away from the range, and he pulls her down so they're lying on the floor, with him on the top.

'Suppose someone comes in?' Kate says.

'With Annie in her bed, and the rest of them away?'

He takes down his breeches, and I see his arse, all white and smooth, moving up and down on top of her. I'm glad they're doing it properly, like my mammy and da used. They're panting, and laughing and kissing away, and I'm wondering what it would be like to try it for myself one day – maybe with Sam, if he'd be up for it.

I tiptoe to the privy, and when I'm undressed, I get into my bed. The moon is shining away, and I think of the dog in his house under the mountain, and hope he's not too lonely. I say goodnight to him in my head, and then I look up at the Sacred Heart in his lovely white frock, and try to sort out my prayers.

Kate says that, as long as I'm a good girl, He'll always keep an eye out for me.

So I ask Him to give me my voice back, because those bad words Dermot used have such a grand ring to them,

I'd like to shout them as loud as I can. But when I give it a try, only a load of spit comes out, so maybe the Sacred Heart's not listening hard enough.

I squeeze my eyes shut, and into my head comes a picture of those men in their gorgeous sashes and banners, marching along the lane to the pipes and drums. And I'm thinking it's no wonder Dermot's no patience with them, because they only do the one kind of a step, and they don't keep their arms by their sides, or point their toes.

So I shape the words that he used, and listen to them echoing away in my head. *Prods*, I shout. *Fekk Ing Prod Barst Ards*.

TWENTY-SEVEN

'UP WITH YOU, BREDE!'

When I open my eyes, I see it's another cold old day, with the trees looking as if someone's sprinkled flour over the top of them.

'Eighteen ninety-six!' Kate says. 'Who'd have thought it?'

I never knew there were that many numbers in the world either.

'Quickly. I've something to show you.'

I can tell from the way she's smiling that it's a good kind of a thing. There's been such a load of them lately and, while I'm pulling on my clothes, I count them up: a bar of soap the colour of sunshine, a gorgeous looking-glass with a silver edge to it, a straw mouse, the ribbons from Missus Henderson, along with the handkerchief with flowers across it. And as if that's not grand enough, there's all the pies and cakes and puddings that Kate makes for us.

She says the best present for her is the Sacred Heart. His feet put me in mind of the time I had to walk the countryside with no shoes on me. I liked the feel of the grass on a warm day, and the fun I had – until Kate turned all cross – jumping into cowpats, and feeling them go squelch-squelch between my toes.

But in the winter, my feet were so cold and sore, I could hardly walk. So I tell the Sacred Heart I hope he'll get some shoes soon, and follow Kate into the kitchen.

'Careful not to knock into anything.'

And it's no wonder, because everywhere I look there are bowls. Big bowls and middling bowls and little bowls filled with vegetables, and sugar, and loaves of fresh bread, and eggs. The top of the dresser has fruit pies on it, and the jugs for the custard and gravy are lined up at the back of the range, and everything's giving off a grand smell.

'There's something else I want to show you. But quiet as a mouse now so we don't wake Annie.'

The hall with the lovely squares is the same as always. There's the clock that reaches nearly up to the ceiling and is still tock-tocking away to itself. On the far wall is the painting of the ship, and beside it the cupboard with yellow handles, and on the top of it the vase with flowers and the birds with great long tails on them.

Kate tugs me forward and we go down the passage and into the room with the big table. I stand by the door while she lights a lamp, and although I've seen it all before, I still suck in my breath. Because the light's shining on the white

cloth, and the load of glasses, and the knives and forks –
like the ones we eat off, only shinier. And there's the same
green and gold plates on the table with a pattern of fruit
and leaves around the edges.

'I wanted you to see why we're all working so hard for
this New Year meal, Brede. Because we have to make food
that's fit to put on these plates.'

I think it would taste just as good on the ones that we
use.

She points to the silver tree, with the two horses with
wings sitting underneath, and the round dish on the top.
Today there's nothing in it, but it puts me in mind of the
time I was in here before, when I had a bite of that plum,
and Molly helped me with the silver pots. And Missus
Henderson gave me a lace cap and apron to wear.

I'm glad to see that the marks from the slugs have gone
from the carpet, because they were horrid old things.

Kate put her arm round me. 'Remember what it was
like before our family went to live with the saints? Hardly
a crumb to eat, and the rain pouring through the roof.'

I don't want to think about any of that.

'You're right, Brede. We've no call to be dwelling on
the past. And do you know what the best of being here is?
When all the people go away again, there's always plenty of
leftovers. Do you remember after Christmas, when we had
those platefuls of meat and gravy, and some of that cake
with the cherries?'

I remember the cherries all right.

'So we must never forget all we owe Mister and Missus
Henderson.' Kate reaches out her hand and strokes one

corner of the cloth. I do the same, and it feels all smooth and soft, like when I dip my fingers in the milk. She gives a sigh. 'But it's still a deal of potatoes to peel, and a deal of meat and pies and puddings to cook. But maybe there'll be time for your steps when things quieten down.'

She snuffs out the lamp, and we creep back to the hall. The black and white squares gleam in the early light and, but for the tick-tick of the clock, everywhere is silent. She puts her finger to her lips and walks to the middle of the floor. Then, with her hands down by her sides, she starts to dance.

First foot: Tip down, tip tip down,
tip tip down, tip tip down,
tip tip cut, tip tip hop back;
Other foot: hop back;
First foot: cut up, and out hip hop down.

And as I watch, I'm put in mind of a time long ago when a man with a fiddle came to the village. And it must have been on a summer's evening, because the air was lovely and warm, with a bit of a moon hanging above us. And my young brother and myself sat on a pile of hay, watching a load of people, mammies and das and uncles and aunts and cousins, dancing away to the music. And we didn't have to go to our beds, but stayed watching until it was nearly morning, and when I did go to sleep, I could still hear that fiddle playing away.

Other foot: tip down;
First foot: tip hop, heel down, tip tip cut, up tip hop back;
Other foot: hop back 2,3,4.

It's the St Patrick's Day reel that's too hard for me. But her feet are moving quick as a flash, and she has her chin

287

held high like she tells me. Her hair flies over her face and she's smiling fit to burst.

'Come on then!' she whispers.

So I join in with the Beginner's Reel.

First foot: heel up, down.

Slide, step, step

Straw foot: heel up, down.

Slide, step, step.

And the two of us go dancing up and down the big squares, so that I feel as free as one of the queens of Ireland. Backwards and forwards we go, turning around and around, our feet going click-click click-click on the floor.

Just as suddenly, Kate stops. She looks over at me, and then she balances on one leg, and I copy her. And the two of us go hopping along the passage and into the kitchen.

We sit at the table, panting away.

'Wouldn't it be grand,' she says, when we've got our breath back, 'if it was just the two of us in a fine big house like this, with plenty of space to dance in, and only ourselves to cook and wash for?'

I'm thinking that I'd be happy enough to be in a house like Missus Purdy's, but then Kate starts to giggle, and she's still laughing away when Annie comes in, tying her apron over her frock.

'Well, you're in very good humour. A happy New Year to you both.'

Kate dabs at her eyes with her apron. 'And to you, Annie.'

'The Hendersons aren't back yet, are they? I could have sworn I heard them in the hall just now.'

Kate goes all pink. 'I'd say they'll be here soon, because they'll need to get themselves ready, and Missus Henderson will want to check the menu.'

Annie waves her hand at the basins of food. 'You seem to have things well under way in here. And Margaret set the table before she left. It's quite a sight – you should take a look.'

'Thank you. I'd like that.'

I give another grin, and Kate says, 'Don't just sit there, Brede. Pass Annie the sugar. And then up to the dairy with you!'

*

It's grand to have Angus waiting by his new home, his tail wagging away. He's not one bit put out by the cold, so I give him his slice of bread and the two of us head back to the yard.

Missus Henderson is in the kitchen. She has on a green coat with grey buttons down the front. 'I wanted to check that everything's going along as it should, Kate.'

'It certainly is, Missus Henderson. Do you want us to go over the menu again?'

'No, I'm sure it's all fine. But what I wanted to say also was that, with Margaret needed to serve at the table, I'd like Brede to help Annie with the coats.'

'Well, if you really think...?'

'She did such a good job the last time.'

I chew my lip, because I don't want Mister and Missus Thompson and the Drummond man catching sight of me again.

But Missus Henderson says, 'That's settled then. I'll ask Annie to look out a clean apron and cap. Now, I'll leave you to get on.'

Kate gives me a smile. 'I'm really proud of you, Brede, doing so well. But for now, you're best in the scullery. You'll only get in everyone's way here.'

Sam passes me in the passage. 'Hello there, Brede.' He's carrying a basket of logs that he lifts into the air, so I can duck underneath. As I straighten myself, he gives another wink, and my insides turn all warm wondering if there's anyone he huffs with.

The two barrels are still in the scullery, but this time I'll not be putting the coats in them. Instead, I'll hang them on the hooks, like Annie has shown me.

She and Margaret keep rushing past with trays filled with dishes of butter and baskets of bread, and jugs of water, so I sit on one of the barrels, and swing my legs up and down while I wait.

Margaret comes to tell me all the people will soon be arriving, and she gives me an apron and one of the caps with a frill around it. 'It goes the other way round,' she says. 'And you tie the apron like this.' But although I'm glad to be wearing them, it doesn't stop my belly twisting inside me.

'It's such a cold day the Hendersons have decided to greet everyone by the dining-room fire. And here's the first of the guests now.'

It's the Bosom woman, and I drop her a curtsey.

'I see your manners have improved since I was here last, Missie.' She hands me her coat. It's black with brown fur round the collar, as if someone's stuck a rabbit onto it. Behind her is Pea-in-the-pod, and Poor Nora, still with those pink patches.

I'm so busy placing all the coats on the chair beside me, and picking up the ones that keep sliding off, that it's only when I look over that I see something I'd know anywhere. It's Missus Thompson's boots with the currants running up the sides. She has on her hat with the feather, and a dark-coloured coat I've not seen before, and she's still as gorgeous-looking as ever.

'And how are you today, Brede?'

She's smiling away, and I'm so surprised that I forget to curtsey.

And then, as I take her coat from her, I get another shock. Because I see from her belly that she has a babby inside her.

'Go and find yourself a seat, Adelina,' the Bosom woman says. 'Give her your arm there, Alexander.'

He leads her out of the hall with a face less cross-looking than I've ever seen it.

But there's no time to think about them, because a load of others are arriving, so thick and fast that when I'm handed a green and orange coat, there's time for only a quick look at the Drummond man, and as he walks on through, I feel my insides untwist themselves.

'Well, that's the last of them, thank goodness,' Annie says. 'I need to see to things in the dining room, so back with you to the kitchen.'

It takes me one, two, three trips to hang the coats, and all the while the kitchen door keeps opening and closing, as Margaret and Annie go backwards and forwards with all the grand-smelling food. I know to keep out of the way, so I stand beside the clock in the hall, listening to the talk and laughter from the ones who are eating.

Every now and then, one of the men comes along the passage and into the small room they use for their privy. When I had a peek inside at the last big meal, there were all these china pots lined up on the floor. They had a load of yellow wee inside them, and I'm just glad Sam's the one who has to empty them, because they don't smell nice and, anyway, I'd only get a scolding for spilling the stuff over the floor.

That room is not where the ladies go to wee, because when Missus Thompson comes out of that dining room, Annie leads her up the stairs.

'That's us almost done,' Margaret says to Annie, as they come past again.

So I'm just thinking that now's maybe a good time to go back to the kitchen, when along the passage comes Mister Henderson and the Drummond man.

'Our polly ticks may differ, William,' the Drummond man's saying, 'but I could get you a decent rental for that field.'

'That's good of you, Bob. Why not take a look from the dairy? You'll get a better idea of it from up there.'

As they go into the weeing room, I'm thinking I'll need to take good care not to be at the dairy anytime he's there.

Margaret comes past again. 'Not long now until they leave,' she says to me. 'Be sure to be ready with those coats.'

And now Missus Henderson is walking towards me, with Missus Thompson leaning on her arm. 'I can't tell you how delighted I am for you, Adelina,' she's saying. 'After all this time.'

'I'm certain it's going to be a girl, Helen. We're going to call her Augusta.'

'That's not one you hear often.'

And I'm thinking it's a funny thing to name your babby after a month.

'I just need a quick word in the kitchen,' Missus Henderson says. 'I'm sure the others will be out in a moment.'

Right enough, I can hear the scrape-scrape of chairs, and then Mister Thompson walks along the passage and into the weeing room.

Missus Thompson is looking up at the picture of the sailing ship, smiling away to herself, so I collect up all the coats. And as I pile them onto the chair, who should come into the hall but the Drummond man.

I look about me, to see if there's anywhere to hide, but he only has eyes for Missus Thompson.

'There you are, dear!' He's swaying as he talks, and his nose has gone all red. He rights himself on a chair. 'I've been trying to have a word all—'

'I've nothing whatever to say to you.'

'Don't be like that.' He steps closer to her. 'I must say I was as surprised as everyone else.'

'What do you mean?'

'To see you in the family way, dear.'

'Ssh! Would you. Someone may come.'

He looks over his shoulder. 'No one here but us.' He places a hand on her belly. 'We both know all about this, don't we?'

'Stop that at once!'

'Have it your own way.' He gives a laugh. 'But I'll be looking to see if he has the Drummond nose.'

Missus Henderson is coming back from the kitchen, and Missus Thompson turns towards her. She gives her hair a pat. 'Bob was just saying how well I looked.'

'It's such good news, isn't it Bob?' Missus Henderson says. 'And here's your husband, Adelina, to see you safely home.'

Mister Thompson steps forward, and I'm wondering how long he's been standing in the passage. 'We certainly wouldn't want my wife to come to any harm.' He's not smiling, and neither is she, and I get a kind of a cold feeling inside.

But then I'm busy handing out all the coats, while Mister and Missus Henderson stand inside the door, waving everyone off.

The Bosom woman is the last to leave. 'It seems you've come to your senses at last, William,' she says, as she pulls on her gloves. They're black with more of that fur stuck round the top of them.

'I promised Helen there'd be no polly ticks today,' he says, 'but I'm afraid, Honoria, my views are unchanged. In fact, Home Rule is nearer than it's ever been.'

'I've never known such a pig-headed man. Make him see reason, Helen. Before it's too late.'

'Can I offer you my arm down the steps?' he says.

'No – my daughter can do that. Come along, Nora.'

Poor Nora gives a nod, and the two of them go out the door.

'I think that all went off rather well,' Mister Henderson says. Then he turns to me. 'You've done really well again, Brede,' and my insides give a big smile.

'Let's say goodnight to the children,' Missus Henderson says and the two of them go up the stairs together.

And as I go hop-hopping along to the kitchen for my dinner, I'm thinking what a pity it is that Mister and Missus Thompson can't be as happy-looking. Though it's no wonder they're both in such a mood, because who would want a babby with a nose as red as the Drummond man's?

TWENTY-EIGHT

I T'S MID-MORNING, AND MISTER HENDERSON IS IN the kitchen, taking his tea. He usually has it with Missus Henderson, but she's away out visiting her sister, Missus Thompson. Margaret says that she's feeling rather low and I'm thinking she could do with another frock to stop her fretting about Mister Drummond's nose. But from the way Mister Thompson was glaring at her, I doubt he'll buy her anything new.

The range is giving off a great heat, and Mister Henderson has his jacket off and his sleeves rolled up. I'm sitting right beside him, so I can get the nice outdoor smells off him.

'So you see, Kate, how tricky the whole situation is.'

She looks up from her pastry, and gives a nod.

'Everyone's concerned about their animals – and rightly so – but my fear is that they'll take it out on innocent Carth Licks. And that won't get us anywhere.'

His moustache is moving up and down as he talks, and when he sips his tea, some of the wet stays on the ends. I put out my hand to pat it away, and Kate says, 'Move further away, Brede.'

'No – she's fine where she is.'

I give him my best smile.

'Well, if you're sure she's not—'

Margaret puts her head round the door. 'Kate, have you by any chance seen—?' Then she stops, and looks from him to her, and back again. 'Oh, I'm sorry, Mister Henderson. I didn't realise you were here.'

There's no need for her to act so surprised, because he's often in the kitchen.

'Good morning to you, Margaret. I was just having a quick word with Kate.'

'I'll leave you to it then,' and she's away out before Kate can ask what it is she was wanting.

He gives a sigh. 'As I was saying: Heaven knows what my neighbours hope to gain by calling this meeting.'

'It's just about what happened to the cattle, then?' Her voice is very tight-sounding.

'I know what everyone's thinking, Kate. Wherever will it end? Barns torched, and innocent animals with their throats cut.' He takes another gulp of his tea. 'But any day now, and I'll be reporting that the deal between Glad Stone and Pa Nell is done.'

I can't for the life of me work out whose da that is.

'And then my brother and the rest of them can stop their marching.'

There's a pot of soup on the range, and she moves

over to give it a stir. 'And the shops will start serving us again?'

'God willing.' He pushes his chair back. 'It's a comfort to be able to speak about all this, Kate. Sometimes I feel such a lone voice.'

I don't know what he's on about, because everywhere you go there's people talking.

'Well, I'd best be off.'

'I hope the meeting goes well for you, Mister Henderson.'

'Thank you, Kate.'

I'm wondering if it will be like the one that was held in the barn, with all the men jumping up and down – all but Mister Henderson and his friend, the James man.

When Mister Henderson's gone out, Kate says, 'Are you going to sit lazing here all morning, Brede? Time to fetch the milk.'

I don't care for her tone one bit, so I drum my feet on the floor.

'I know – I wish it wasn't such a long old haul up to that dairy, but spring's almost here, and at least all that ice has gone.'

Many's the time I've gone arse-over-tip on that track, so I'm glad that now there's just last night's rain on it. The sheep are bleating away in the big field, and one of the new lambs is taking a suck from its mammy's tittie. I watch another lamb jump up, with its legs in the air, and I'm thinking that maybe it's called spring because of all the leaping around they do. I tried it myself once, but I just ended up with a sore place where I'd kicked myself.

When Angus sees me, he comes rushing out of his kennel to say good morning, and as we go back to the house, I'm thinking how grand it is to have him as my special friend.

Back in the yard, I feed the hens, and then go over to the corner where Rory and myself build our towers. We haven't made any for a good while, but the stones are still there, so I start piling them up to make sure none is missing.

'Brede!' A voice whispers, and I give a jump.

Dermot is leaning against the stable door with his arms folded over his chest. And beside him is Francis, with the same carroty hair sticking out from under his cap.

'Did we scare you?' Dermot says.

He's not got his brown bottle or his fiddle with him, but at his feet are four big sacks. They're very dirty-looking, and are tied at the top with pieces of string. They put me in mind of the time Mister Thompson had a load of kittens that he was taking off to be drowned. I didn't like him doing that one bit.

I reach down to the sack nearest me, but before I can touch it, Dermot gives my face a slap. 'Stop that!'

My cheek is burning hot, and the tears are in my eyes, because I was only checking to see if there were any kittens inside.

'I didn't mean to do that, Brede.' He nods towards the sacks. 'But did no one ever tell you not to meddle in what doesn't concern you?'

I have a chew of my hair.

'Kate's inside on her own, so Francis and myself are going to have a little talk with her. You're to stay out here until we call you.' They start dragging the sacks after them, each one going clunk-clunk across the yard. And I'm thinking Kate will be none too pleased to have them cluttering up her kitchen.

I sit on the top of the gate, swinging my feet and watching the hens scratching about. They're always busy doing something – just like Kate or Mister Henderson, when they're not sitting talking.

Angus has gone into his kennel, and I'm just wondering whether to build a new tower, when the rain starts going splash-splash onto my head. I go over to the window and take a look inside. Dermot, Carrot Hair and Kate are talking away in front of the range. They have their backs to me, so I push open the door and, quiet as a mouse, I creep to the table, lift up the cloth and slip underneath.

Dermot is saying something that I can't hear, and then Kate says, 'Everyone else would have left us to starve. I'll do nothing against them.'

'For God's sake, Kate! When the day comes, and you stop being of use to them, the Hendersons and their kind won't lift one of their little fingers for you. Anyway, it's time you started thinking of your Feen Yun loyalties!'

Their voices have grown very loud, so I peek round the edge of the table.

'There's no risk to you, or I wouldn't ask.' He moves over to the turf store.

'You've asked me whether I agree, Dermot Friel, and I'm telling you loud and clear that I do not! Anyway, suppose someone walks in on us now?'

'Why else do you think Francis and I picked a day when all the fat Barst Ards are at their meeting? And as for Annie and Margaret, they're busy upstairs and won't be down for their tea for a good while.'

'You've been spying on us!'

'Listen to me now. It's only for a short time. So where's the harm?'

'I'll tell you where the harm is.' Kate's voice has an edge to it, as if she's sickening with a cold. 'The harm is when the three of us get lined up against a wall!'

I can tell from her voice that being lined up like that wouldn't be for the dancing, but would be for a very bad thing indeed.

'No need for you even to know what's in the fecking sacks, Kate.' Dermot's voice has gone all hard. 'And if anything goes wrong, sure you just thought it was some old farm tools.'

She folds her arms across her chest. 'I've said no, and I mean it!' But her voice has a wobble to it that makes me want to jump up, and take hold of her hand.

'It's too damp to leave the stuff out of doors.' Dermot stoops down, and looks into the store, like he did that day when I was showing him all the cupboards. 'This one here will do nicely. There's that good amount of space at the back.'

'And the answer's still no!'

Suddenly, Dermot reaches out, and puts both his hands round her throat. Then he brings his face very close to hers. 'You'll fecking well do what you're fecking well told!'

I open my mouth to shout something, but not a sound comes out, and my knees are stuck fast to the floor.

'Leave go of me!' Kate's face has gone very red, and her voice comes out all croaky.

He drops his hands, but stays standing right in front of her. 'Take the turf out of the cupboard, Francis.'

He begins lifting out the pieces and bits go flying around him in the air. I wait for Kate to give him a good telling-off, but she just stands, giving her throat a rub.

'Good,' Dermot says. 'Now bring the first sack over.'

They're by the table, and as Francis starts dragging the first one towards him, he looks over his shoulder. I go to duck under the table, but I'm not quick enough.

'Jesus, Mary and Joseph, Brede! You frightened the life out of me!'

Dermot swings round. 'Fecking hell!' He comes across, and I wait for another slap. But, 'Get up!' is all he says.

I go and stand beside Kate, and it makes my belly twist around to see the scared look she has on her. As bad as when that dog took a bite out of her leg, or when Missus Thompson told us she didn't want to see our faces ever again.

'So, how long's she been here, listening to every word?' Dermot says.

'She's just come in this minute. I promise,' Kate says.

'Well, maybe it's no bad thing. Because we all care about Brede. And it would be a pity if anything were to happen to her.' He gives a smile. 'Remember her safety's in your hands.'

She turns to me and her voice comes out all in a rush. 'How many times do I have to say it, Brede? Go and make a start on those vegetables. *Now*!'

There's no arguing with her when she's in this mood, and I wish I had the words to tell her that with Dermot as well as Mister Henderson looking out for us, there's no need for her to be so worried.

As I go out, Francis is putting the last of the sacks in the store, and I hear Dermot say: 'We're for the off. But I'll be back on Sunday as usual to keep an eye on things.'

Kate doesn't answer, and for the rest of the day, there's not a smile or a word to be had from her.

'Are you sure you're not sickening for something, Kate?' Annie asks, when we're having our meal. 'You're terribly quiet.'

'I've a bit of a sore head, Annie. I'll be fine in the morning.'

But I can't stop myself looking over at the store and picturing those sacks tucked away in the back. Annie, and Margaret and Sam are busy eating, so they don't notice, but Kate catches me staring, and shakes her head at me.

Much later, when it's time for my bed, I go on through to our room. I like being in here, because it's Kate's and my special place, and no one else comes in, not even Missus Henderson. I like the bed that's big enough for the two of us, and the chair for our clothes, and the chest with the drawer that's my very own.

I look up at the Sacred Heart, and ask Him to please put Kate in a good mood again, so I don't end up in the Poor House. And the thought has me so worried, that I'm still awake when she comes in.

She puts the lamp on the chest. 'Sit up a moment, would you, Brede? I need to tell you something important.'

I lean against her and she gives my hair a stroke. 'What you saw and heard in the kitchen earlier – you're to forget all about it. It was just Dermot and me having a bit of an argument. But we're friends again now.'

There's red marks on her neck, and when she sees me looking, she puts her hands to her throat. 'He'll bring his fiddle with him on Sunday, and we can go over our steps. You'll like that, won't you?'

I chew my lip.

'So if anyone ever asks if you know about those sacks, you're to shake your head. Because it's just a load of farm tools in them – of no use to anyone. You'll do that for me, won't you?' She kisses me like my mammy used, her hair brushing my face. 'We'll get through this somehow, Brede. Sleep tight, then.'

But I stay awake for a long while, trying to puzzle out what it is we're having to get through. And why, when Dermot only wants to keep us safe, Kate lies trembling away beside me.

TWENTY-NINE

O NE, TWO WEEKS HAVE GONE BY, AND MY HEAD'S in more of a muddle than ever. As I clear away the breakfast, I try to work out what it is that's most puzzling.

First, Kate makes me get up extra early each morning, because she says we've a mountain of work to get through, and she can't afford to make any mistakes. But that makes no sense, because when has she ever burnt a stew or put lumps in the custard like the Nellie woman did? And besides, with no more of those big parties, and no visits from Pea-in-the-pod or the Bosom woman and Poor Nora, there's just Mister and Missus Henderson to cook for, along with the kitchen food for the rest of us.

Second, anytime I want to try out my steps, Kate tells me to stop, because we mustn't on any account make too much noise. But she's never bothered about that before, and now I'm afraid that when she does let me have a go, my feet will have forgotten where to put themselves.

And third, Dermot hasn't been back to see us, even though he promised he would. A part of me is sorry, because I like nothing better than when Kate and I are dancing away to his fiddle. But another part of me is thinking of the temper he had on him the last time he was here, and that maybe it's best that he stays away, until he's in a better mood.

I'd like Kate to explain it all, or at least to talk to me like she used, but this morning her mouth stays set in a line, and there's still not a cheery word to be had out of her. So the best thing to do is to just get on with my work, until she wants to be friends again.

I give the porridge a stir. It's the colour of the dog's fur, with a load of bubbles on the top.

She's cracking eggs into a bowl when, all of a sudden, one of them slips out of her hand, and spreads itself across the table. 'Feck it!' She scoops it up. 'You didn't hear that, Brede.'

I give her a stare, because how can you un-hear something once it's said? Or not see something once you have?

'The others will be in for their breakfasts soon, so go and give the hens their feed.'

I wrap my shawl around me and step into the yard. Everywhere I look has a coating of frost over it, and when I go to the corner, I see that Kate's forgotten to bring in last evening's washing. Young Rory's shirts and stockings are still pegged to the line, along with a row of Missus

Henderson's bloomers. Missus Thompson had lovely pink ones with a frill round the edges, but these are just plain old white. And there's the blue jacket with the holes that Annie says Missus Henderson wears in bed, though I'm thinking she'd keep a sight warmer if she stitched them up.

I've always liked the feel of the wool, but this morning the jacket's as stiff as the board I practise my steps on, and I can hardly feel my hands for the cold. So I place the bowl on the ground, and jump up and down a bit, like Dermot does when he wants to get his blood flowing.

The rooster's sitting on the roof, because his wings have grown such a deal, there's no catching him. But he'll not stay perched there once I bring Angus back here for the day, and my insides feel all warm with knowing I'll be seeing him so soon.

I lift the door to the hens' house, and they come tumbling down their plank all in a fluster, and go peck-pecking after their food.

Then I hear the clip-clop of a horse coming along the track. I go over to the gate, and crouch down, ready to run inside, in case it's one of the people I don't care for. Then I let out my breath, because it's only the James man, swinging himself out of his saddle, and tying his horse to the post. The animal is brown and when it gives a snort, steam comes out of its nose, like the kettle when it's on the boil.

'Hello there, Brede!' he says. He has on a dark coat and hat, and his beard still looks as if it's been painted on him. I'm just wondering how it would feel under my fingers, when he says, 'Is Mister Henderson out of his bed yet?' He pushes open the gate, and comes past me. 'Never mind, I'll go in the back way, so as not to disturb Missus Henderson.'

When I follow him into the kitchen, there's a grand smell of bacon frying, and Annie and Margaret are at the table. When they see him, they scrape back their chairs.

'I'm sorry to trouble you all this early.' He takes out a big piece of paper with a load of writing across it. 'I need to show this to Mister Henderson.'

It beats me why there's a need for people to go writing things down, when they can talk to one another perfectly well.

He turns to Annie. 'Could you go up and tell Mister Henderson there's important news just come in?'

She gets to her feet. 'Of course, Mister Johnson. Would you like to wait in the front room? Kate here will make you some tea.'

'That would be grand,' he says, and follows Annie out.

'Well, whatever the news,' Margaret says, 'you can bet your life it'll not be pleasing everyone.' She pulls the passage door open to have a listen, and Kate and I join her. We hear feet running down the stairs, and Mister Henderson's voice calling, 'James?' And then the James man shouts, 'He's done it, William! Glad Stone's finally got it through!'

'My God!' Mister Henderson says, 'I never thought I'd see the day!' And there's the slam of a door cutting off the sound.

I look at Margaret and Kate to see whether they've a frown or a smile on them, but Kate goes back to the range, and Margaret seats herself at the table again. It's strange they're not speaking, but maybe they're just thinking about their breakfasts.

When Annie comes back in, along with Sam, I know the news isn't the good sort, because everyone's very quiet, and no one looks at Kate. And we're still eating away in silence when the door opens, and in walks the James man along with Mister Henderson. His shirt is half out of his trousers, and his cheeks have a coating of hair across them because he's not yet shaved himself. But I'd still like to be standing right up close to him, breathing in his smell.

'Why all these long faces? Have you not heard?'

'Heard what, Mister Henderson?' Annie says.

'That Glad Stone and Pa Nell have struck a deal.'

'So Home Rule will be in before we know it,' the James man says.

Mister Henderson and Kate are smiling away at one another, so I give a grin too.

'That's more like it!' Mister Henderson says. 'Now, we must have a toast.'

I wait for Kate to start slicing the bread, but Mister Henderson says, 'If I remember rightly, there should be some of last year's cordial left.'

'Just the one bottle,' Kate says, 'but Missus Henderson was saving it for—'

'Perhaps you'd fetch it then, Margaret? And, Kate, you can put out the glasses.'

We had some of that drink at Christmas time, and it was one of the nicest things I've tasted in the whole of my life – as if I was swallowing a whole load of the fruit without the bother of chewing it. So I can't wait for more.

When Margaret returns, Mister Henderson takes the bottle from her and pours out the drink, and Annie tops up each glass with water. Then we all stand around – Mister Henderson, the James man, Kate and myself and Annie and Margaret, and Sam. Everyone is very quiet, and when I take a gulp of my drink, Kate nudges me to stop.

Mister Henderson lifts his glass in the air. 'To Home Rule!' And everyone starts drinking, so I know it's fine to finish my own.

'But what does it mean exactly?' Margaret asks.

'It means,' Mister Henderson says, 'that from now on everyone in Ireland, be they Prod or Carth Lick, will have a home and a decent wage. And, what's more—'

'I wondered where you'd got to.' Missus Henderson is in the doorway, dressed in a blue skirt, and a blouse with folds down the front that Margaret says is the very devil to iron.

Missus Henderson looks at each of us in turn, and my feet start to shuffle around.

The James man holds out the square of paper. 'I'm afraid this is all my doing, Helen, and I'm sorry for waking you so early. But this report's just come in from London.'

'We're drinking to celebrate Home Rule,' Mister Henderson says.

'Indeed,' Missus Henderson says. 'And with the last of my raspberry cordial, I see.'

'Please, Helen,' Mister Henderson says. 'Let's all just…' but she turns away from him.

'You ask what it means, Margaret,' she says, 'as well you might. Because what it means is that we're to come under papist rule. What it means is that as like as not we'll have our homes taken from us. Like as not, we'll be the ones out in the fields, with the Ten Aunts living it up in this house.'

'Now you're just being ridiculous!' Mister Henderson says.

'Am I?'

I can see she's not one bit pleased with him, which is no wonder, because I wouldn't want to be back sleeping in a ditch either.

Annie steps forward. 'I think you should know, Missus Henderson, that not all of us here agree with this Home Rule business. Isn't that right, Margaret?'

Margaret gives a nod.

'Well,' Missus Henderson says, 'thank goodness *some* in this household still have their wits about them! Come on through with me, both of you, so we can go over what needs doing today.' She gives Mister Henderson a look. 'When you've quite done celebrating, I'll be in the front parlour.'

And then she's gone, with Annie and Margaret following after.

'Is there anything…?' the James man begins.

'Thank you, James, but no. She'll come round in the end, like all the others. But I'm grateful to you for riding over. We'll meet again tomorrow.' He turns to Sam. 'Give Mister Johnson a hand with his horse, will you?'

They go out, and Kate and I are alone with Mister Henderson.

'There'll be plenty more opportunities to celebrate. But I promise you this, Kate. That there'll come a time –

sooner perhaps than anyone here realises – when Carth Licks will be treated the same as everyone else.'

'You really believe it?'

'I do.' He moves over to her. 'All this marching business will be put a stop to. Carth Licks will own their own land; their families will have food on the table. God knows, this country is rich enough to provide for everyone.'

'So does this mean there'll be no need now for any guns?'

Some of her hair has escaped from under her cap, and he reaches forward and brushes it off her face. 'None at all.'

I pull some of the hair from out of my cap, and look across at him. But he takes no notice.

Kate steps back, and I can see she's gone all pink, as I would do, if he'd just look the same way at me. 'Thank you, Mister Henderson. For everything.'

He bites his lip. 'Well, enough of all this – I'd best be getting on.'

So now it's just the two of us in the kitchen.

Kate looks up at me. 'Everything's going to be all right, Brede. Isn't that great?'

And all of a sudden, she starts dancing around the room, and I hop along behind her, and she doesn't get cross when my elbow catches a bowl, or I knock into the table, because she's too busy humming away to herself.

But as we start washing the glasses, I'm thinking that this new rule is even more of a puzzle. Because Mister Henderson and Kate are happy enough about it, but Missus Henderson, and Annie and Margaret don't like it one bit.

Suddenly, my insides are all unsettled, because I don't know whether to be dancing or having a long face on me. And what I'm wondering is this: Will there ever be a day when everyone is happy about the same thing?

THIRTY

It's a misty old morning, with the grey damp pressing itself against the window.

'I know it's still early, Brede, but I need that milk.'

I'm peeling carrots by the range, and I'm so nice and snug, I can hardly stir.

Kate lifts up the empty pail. 'I'm hoping Dermot will be along later.'

I look over at the turf store.

'No doubt he'll have heard the news, so he can remove those wretched sacks.' She sighs. 'And I can't wait to see the last of them.'

It seems to me there's been a deal of fuss about a load of old farm tools, but I'm just glad that Kate's in a good humour again.

'I've saved some of yesterday's meat for Angus,' she says, 'and here's the heel of a loaf for him to be getting on with. Oh, and you know he can sleep back in the yard tonight?'

I'm so happy to hear it, that I jump from my seat, and the carrots go rolling across the floor.

'No worries,' she says, 'I'll pick them up. You get on your way. And when you're back, I'll have your breakfast on the table. An extra helping for all of us today.'

As I close the door, she's humming away to herself, so I go skipping across the yard, and onto the track. Even without the sunshine, it's grand to be out in the open, with just a bit of a wind on my face. One, two rabbits go running across the field, and there's a load of sheep lying by the track, all nice and warm in their coats.

Most days, as I go climbing up the path, Barney will be coming along towards me. He's so stout, there's not room on the path for the two of us, but he always steps to one side. 'How are you doing?' he says, and touches his cap that's a dirty brown colour.

Today I'm too early for him, but I can't wait for the moment when Angus catches sight of me, and starts barking and waving his tail in the air. I like sitting beside him while he eats his breakfast, swallowing down the bread as fast as I give it him. And after I've filled the bucket and collected the butter and cheese, I untie his rope and he starts running down the hill, scattering the rabbits as he goes.

This morning, there's a load of mist at the top of the world, swirling around the place, and blowing towards me. It's so thick, it's making me cough, so when I reach the stile I stop, and put my bucket down. Suddenly, the mist raises itself into the air, and I see the dog stretched out under the tree, having a bit of a lie-in.

I drop the bucket over the stile to let him know I'm here. It goes clash-clash onto the ground, but he stays nice and quiet, so I set off up the last stretch of path.

I can hear the cattle mooing in the big field, and ahead of me, comes a snapping sort of a sound, as if someone's treading on a load of twigs. I can't see anyone else about, but when I'm almost at the tree, I put the bucket down again and stare about me.

It's turned very warm, and there's a powerful smell in the air. Although the mist has grown thicker, every so often the wind catches it and blows it away. I blink my eyes, one, two times, and then I squeeze them shut, because this can't be right. When I open them again, and look for the dairy ahead of me, for the life of me, I can't see it. The milking shed is there all right, but the dairy's gone.

I walk over, and give the dog a nudge with my foot to wake him. Then, as I bend closer, my insides turn all cold. Because, Jesus, Mary and Joseph! There's a big patch of red under his chin, and his eyes are staring up, like old Mister Henderson's, when he was stretched out in the hall that time. And in my head, I'm calling: *Wake up, Angus!* But it's no good, because even when I give him a poke, he doesn't stir. And it puts me in mind of how my mammy and da never woke either, and I feel so scared, I can hardly move.

Then, something brushes against my face and when I put my hand up to wipe it away, my fingers get covered in grey flakes. Snow, I think to myself, but then I realise that of course it's not snow or the mist. Whatever put it into my

316

head to make that mistake? It's smoke, the sour smell of it catching my throat and making me cough. And the air is filled with pieces of ash, floating down, so that the ground is covered with them.

And I'm thinking that maybe I'm having one of those bad dreams that I've not had for a great while, and if I busy myself with something else, Angus and myself will wake up, and everything will be all right again.

So I walk over to take a closer look at the dairy. But my foot catches against a basin with a big hole in it, and I nearly go flat on my face. I move forward some more, feeling the heat on my cheeks, and now I can see that the shed roof is all fallen in on itself, and where the inside of the dairy should be, there's not a trace of shelves, let alone the other basins for the milk and cream. They've all gone, every last man of them.

I go back and sit myself down beside the dog, and bury my head in his fur. And I howl and howl, until the snot and tears are running down my face, and I've no breath left for any more.

After a while, I get to my feet, and give my nose a blow on the edge of my shawl.

Though I can't think that even Kate can make Angus start moving again, or put the roof back on the shed, I still long to feel her arms about me, and hear her telling me to stop making such a fuss.

It's as I'm turning to go down the track, that I look over into the ditch on my straw-foot side. One of those big crows goes hop-hopping away, and then I see two boots sticking in the air. Even from where I'm standing,

I see they've a great shine to them, so I know they don't belong to Barney or one of the Ten Aunts, because theirs are always covered in mud.

I go tiptoeing over, and when I look down, I see a man lying in the ditch, having a bit of sleep, like Kate and I used when we were walking the countryside. His face is turned away from me, and one hand is behind his head and the other is across his chest.

I look over my shoulder, but there's no one else about, so I scramble down. It's when I kneel beside him, that I see it's the Drummond man's jacket with the orange and green squares across it. One of his eyes is staring up, and where the other should be is just a big hole. And around his neck is a piece of shiny red ribbon and when I go to touch it, my fingers come away all sticky with blood.

I scramble out of that ditch as quick as wink. I'd like to run, but my legs are shivering away, so I stand under the tree, with my breath going pant-pant, in and out of me.

And in my head I can hear Kate's voice. *Get away from here, Brede! Run as fast as you can. Because what'll Mister Henderson say when he hears about the Drummond man? And the dog? And what about Missus Henderson? She never minds one or two broken dishes, but what about a whole shedful? And after she and Mister Henderson have been so good to us.*

Beside me, there's one, two big crows hopping around Angus, and taking a peck at his eyes. I wave my arms at them, and they move a little way off, watching me. My blanket's back on my bed, so what I do is this: I take the cheese bag from round my neck, and lay it across the dog's face, so the birds can't get to him.

Then I give him a last pat, and turn my back on him and on the shed. But I'm not heading back to the house, because who's going to want me there after I've let all this happen? So I start climbing the other way, along the side of the cattle stalls, and onto the track that leads up the mountain. Sometimes my foot trips on a stone and I fall to my knees, so my skirt gets all tangled up, but still I keep on going. Because I need to get as far away from here as I can.

And when I stop to draw in my breath, I can see the smoke still rising from the milking shed, and a fat man that looks like Barney, coming up the slope towards it.

And way below him, a big man on a white horse is riding like the clappers along the track that leads to the Thompsons' house.

And all the time I'm thinking that not even Kate can make this all right. And that maybe nothing will ever be right again.

THIRTY-ONE

I'VE NOT BEEN ON THIS PART OF THE MOUNTAIN before, and it's a fair old scramble over the rocks, that get bigger the higher I climb. My feet keep stumbling into all these hollows in the ground, and the brown bits of heather go scratch-scratch against my legs. Already my shoes are wet through from the streams of water running past, and over my head there's nothing but grey clouds.

I've been going a good while, but I daren't slow my pace for fear of Barney coming chasing after me. Every so often, I glance down the slope, but there's no signs of him yet.

My side feels as if someone's stuck one of Missus Henderson's sewing needles into it, so I stop to catch my breath. Everything is very still and quiet – just one of the birds that Kate says is called a Curl Ewe calling way above my head.

And now I'm thinking that maybe I've just dreamt everything up. Until I look below me, and give a shiver, because those black posts are still there all right, sticking into the air, with the smoke rising around them. I can make out two fellows, one of them stout enough to be Barney, standing beside them so I tuck myself into a big hollow in the ground, where there's a slab of rock to peer out from.

I'm glad to be having this bit of a rest, but my belly feels terribly empty after all this scrambling and climbing. So I take Angus's breakfast out of my pocket. It's as I go to take a bite that I remember: He's lying down there under the tree, with the cheese bag over his eyes, and his chest with that red patch on it. And when I look at my fingers, they're covered in blood that tastes all salty when I give it a lick.

I don't recall hearing the saints having any dogs living with them, but even if they do, that's no good to me at all, because Angus won't be eating his breakfast ever again. And when I think of the two of us running up the track together, and how he always gives his tail a wag when he sees me, and what great friends we are, I don't feel hungry any more.

So I toss the bread into the air and it goes bouncing away down the slope. Then I give the sore patches on my legs a rub and curl myself up.

A while later, I hear voices in the distance, and I'm thinking that if I just stay nice and quiet where I am, I'll not be found. Because I can't begin to think how cross the Hendersons will be over the dairy, as well as over their

321

friend, the Drummond man – maybe so cross that Kate and I will be put out on the road.

And I just want all this worry to go away, so I lay my head down and close my eyes.

'Brede! Brede!'

It's a man's voice, making me jump. I turn onto my belly, and take a peek over the edge of the hollow. The slope is very steep and with the rocks and brown heather covering it, it's hard to see anything properly, let alone the person who's calling me. But way below, there's one, two, three fellows making their way along a track, and there's more of them spread out on either side. And I know it's me they're coming for, to take me away to the Poor House. So I crouch down again, and squeeze my eyes tight shut.

When I was very small, and playing hide-and-seek with my brothers, I used to think because I'd made the world go away, it couldn't find me either. But I know better now.

I open my eyes again, just as someone says, 'She surely can't have come up this far?'

I give a jump, because it's Kate's voice, and when I take a look, there she is, peering ahead into the valley. Although she's quite a way below, her voice carries through the air.

I'm about to leap up, when a man says, 'What have we here, then?' Mister Henderson is walking towards her, so I stay quiet as a mouse.

He stoops down. 'A piece of soda bread.'

'Brede always takes some for the dog. Do you think—?'

'It could have come from anywhere.'

'You're right – probably dropped by some bird.'

I wish the pair of them would move off, so I can have a hunt around for that bread, because my belly is growling away again.

'You look tired out, Kate. Let's rest here for a while.'

'Over an hour searching, and still no signs of her.' She gives a sigh that makes me all sad inside. 'We really should keep going.'

They're sitting with their backs to me, so I lean over the edge to have a listen.

'The Ten Aunts, as well as the farm hands, have joined the hunt. Try not to worry so. It'll be a sorry thing if between us all we can't find her.'

'I can't think that anyone but her would have put the cheese bag over Angus like that,' Kate says. 'But why didn't she come straight back to the house?' There's an edge to her voice that makes my insides twist around. 'Just wait till I get hold of her!'

'She may have seen poor Drummond also.'

'Of course – please don't think I was putting the animal before your friend.'

'I never imagined that for a moment, Kate.' He shifts closer to her, and it puts me in mind of the time Dermot drove us away from the Thompsons, and him and Kate were side-by-side in the front of the cart. I didn't like that one bit, any more than I like the way the two of them huff-huff away together when they think I'm not looking.

Now I wait for Mister Henderson to put his arm about Kate, but he stays right where he is.

'It's a terrible business, all right. And one for which I'm afraid I'm in some way to blame.'

'Surely not, Mister Henderson?'

'I've been planning to let out one of the fields, so I suggested Mister Drummond come up to the dairy, to see the lie of the land.'

'Well, that's hardly your fault!'

'All the same.'

'So, who do you think's to blame?' Kate's voice has a wobble to it. 'Could a Feen Yun really do something as terrible as this?'

He heaves a sigh. 'More than likely. But they're bound to be caught, given time.'

'And then what will happen to them?'

'A hanging, no doubt. But you're trembling, Kate. Here, take my jacket.'

'Oh, I couldn't—'

'No – I insist.'

He puts it around her, and I wish it was me sitting beside him.

'Though one thing does puzzle me.'

She shifts away from him. 'Oh?'

'There've been plenty of farm buildings burned before now, but this feels different. None of the cattle were harmed for a start, and why would anyone want to kill poor Drummond? They always go for a landlord, or someone involved in polly ticks.'

'Maybe he saw something he shouldn't?'

'Maybe.'

I look down at my hand that has the blood all over

it. Perhaps it's the Drummond man's. I give it a wipe on my apron, wishing I'd never spotted him in that ditch, or seen that fellow galloping off on the horse only Mister Thompson is allowed to ride.

But now I go all cold inside, because Kate says, 'Mister Henderson, there's something I have to tell you.' She starts to cry, and my chin is going wobble-wobble, because I'm thinking it'll be about all the dishes I've broke, or the milk I've let Angus drink from the pail, so he'll know all the bad things I've been doing.

'Now, Kate. Whatever it is – and I think I can guess – there's no need for you to upset yourself.'

'Please, Mister Henderson. Just hear me out.'

He passes her his handkerchief. 'On condition that you dry your eyes.' He puts his hand on her arm, and this time she doesn't move away. So I'm thinking it won't be long before they have a lie down together.

'It's just that my being a Carth Lick means I've had to do things that I'm not proud of.'

'Kate! Kate! For anyone to imagine those things – whatever they might be – bear any resemblance to what's happened here is well – beyond belief!'

'But…'

They're so busy talking they don't notice Barney and another fellow crossing the side of the mountain towards them. Then Barney cries, 'Oh, there you are, Mister Henderson! I've been calling away to you…'

He jumps up, and Kate along with him. 'We were just taking a bit of a rest.'

The fellow with him gives a laugh that ends in a cough.

'I came to say there's still no sign of the girl, Mister Henderson. Do you want us to keep looking in the same area?'

'No – let's try round the other side.'

'Very good.'

'Kate, you go on back to the house, in case Brede turns up there.'

'I'm so sorry, Mister Henderson, for causing all this trouble.'

'Try not to worry. She'll appear in her own good time. You wait and see.'

When I poke my head out again, the four of them are walking away, and soon I can't make them out at all, because the mountain swallows them up.

I wait a while and when I've had a wee, I start scrambling down the slope, my feet catching on the stones, and my skirt all muddy and torn from where I have to slide over the steep parts.

And all the time I'm trying to work out how cross Kate is with me. Because one minute her voice is all worried, and the next she sounds as if she can't wait to give me a slap – or send me to the Poor House.

But now I'm thinking that I could do with a bit of a fire to warm me, and no one to tell me off for all the terrible things I've let happen.

So I go arse-over-tip down that mountain, and then I run along the track and into the lane. And when I'm by the fewsher hedge, I draw in my breath, and take a run at the door, and go flying into the house.

Missus Purdy is in her seat by the range, and when she

sees me, she lets out a shriek. 'Lord above, child! Would you look at the state of you?'

But all I can do is throw myself on the floor, and howl and howl. And I can't stop, even when she stoops over me, and says: 'Sit up now. I've a nice drink of tea for you, and a piece of fresh barm brack.' But I just carry on crying worse than ever, and I'm sure that nothing in all the world will make me stop, because this is a day as terrible as when my mammy and da were took with the sickness.

And then I hear Missus Purdy walk across the room, and all goes quiet. And after a while I take a peek through my fingers, and see that she's left me all alone. So I start crying harder than ever.

And I don't know how long I'm lying there on the floor, wondering when I'll get the strength to go back up on that mountain, because I'll not be wanted at the Hendersons' place, that's for sure.

But then I hear steps coming in again, so I lie very quiet. The feet are too heavy to be Missus Purdy's, and before I know it, a pair of arms scoops me up.

'I'll take her back to the house now, Missus Purdy.' And my insides give a flip because it's Mister Henderson's voice. 'Kate will be that relieved to see you safe, Brede,' he says. 'As we all are.'

'Poor Mister Drummond, what a terrible carry-on,' Missus Purdy says. 'I'll be locking my door the night, I can tell you!'

'I've asked two of the men to keep watch along the lane,' Mister Henderson says, 'and in a few days' time the militia will be carrying out a search of the houses in the area, so I promise you, Missus Purdy, you can rest easy. Now, I must see this girl to her bed.'

And the next minute, he's carrying me out of the house, and I have my arms round his neck, and I can feel his jacket all rough against my cheek, and breathe in the good outdoor smell of him. And suddenly all the bad things that have happened don't feel so bad any more.

'Did you think we were cross with you, Brede?' he says. 'Because of course we weren't. Though Kate's been half out of her mind with worry.'

But I don't care about any of that. There's a bit of a moon showing above the trees and an owl going hoot-hoot in the distance. And all I want is to go on being carried along the lane with Mister Henderson's arms about me.

And although it's not far to the house, and I'd like to stay awake, I'm so tired out with all the running and scrambling I've done, that my eyes won't stay open a moment longer.

And the last thing I remember is Kate's voice saying, 'Oh, Mister Henderson, you've found her! Thank God!'

And him saying: 'Didn't I tell you, Kate, that everything would be as right as rain?'

THIRTY-TWO

'MORNING ALL!' SAM COMES IN THE DOOR WITH A pail of milk in each hand. 'And how are you gorgeous women doing the day?'

'That's quite enough lip from you,' Margaret says.

He gives a wink, and I'm thinking he's almost as tall now as Mister Henderson, with a load more hair on his chin, and his voice has gone all dark-sounding. And just looking at him makes my insides turn all warm.

One, two, three days have gone by since that terrible morning when I found the dairy all burnt up and Angus lying stiff as my board under the tree. No one speaks of it, but Kate says I don't have to go for the milk anymore. So now it's Sam who brings it to the house, along with the butter and cheese. It's grand that he's the one doing it, and even grander that no one is cross with me, except for Margaret, when she catches me crying as I look over at Angus's kennel.

'Sure the Hendersons will be getting another dog. So stop this carry-on, Brede. It's putting me off my food.'

She and Kate and myself, along with Molly and Annie, are at the table finishing our breakfast. I swallow down my piece of bacon, and Molly starts telling us about a fellow in town who's taken a fancy to her. 'Buck teeth, and not a day under sixty!' she says. The others laugh, but I can't see what's so funny about looking like some old rabbit. And for a moment, I'm put in mind of the Drummond man, but I won't think of him and his huffing with Missus Thompson.

The door opens, and in walks Mister Henderson. Although it's not a Sunday, he's dressed in the waistcoat and jacket he wears when he goes to the Prod church.

'Put the kettle on, could you, Kate? There's a dozen soldiers coming along the lane, and I'm sure they'll be glad of some tea.'

She drops her knife on the floor. 'Soldiers? Whatever do they want with us?'

'After the recent events, it's been decided to carry out a search of properties in the district.' He gives a smile. 'Purely routine.'

'But what would they be looking for, Mister Henderson?' Annie asks.

'Who knows, Annie. Weapons? Secret drawings? Whatever it is, they won't find any here.' Then he turns to Molly. 'If you could make sure young Rory stays upstairs, Molly? We don't want him getting under everyone's feet. And, Annie, would you see to the front door, while Margaret gives Kate a hand with the tea?'

I wish it was me opening the door to the soldiers, but I'm left watching as everyone moves about. Only Kate, whose face has gone pale as milk, stays just where she is.

Mister Henderson walks over to her. 'No need to look so anxious. They'll be gone before we know it. You stay here with Brede – we don't want her running off again.'

I give a smile, thinking of how he came to fetch me from Missus Purdy's house and wishing he'd put his arms about me again.

'Ah, there you are, William.' Missus Henderson has on the brown frock that suits her so well. I'm hoping that when I'm grown, maybe I'll be given one just like it.

We hear a rat-a-tat coming from the hall. 'That'll be them now,' Mister Henderson says.

'I'll be in the parlour if you need me,' she says.

Then Annie is in the doorway, puffing away with the excitement of it all. 'If you please, Mister Henderson, a Captain Woods is here, along with his men.'

'Show him into the front room, would you, Annie? I'll ring for anything we need.' And out he and Annie go.

I've never come across a captain before, and with Margaret busy at the range, and Kate staring out of the window, now's a good time to have a peek.

I tiptoe along the passage into the hall. Annie is by the door, and Mister Henderson is shaking hands with a man, who has a white beard and a big stomach. But what I can't take my eyes off is his hat that has points at each end. And he has a red belt on him and bits of gold on his shoulders, and very long black boots.

'You'll take a drop of something, Captain?' Mister Henderson says.

'Thank you, Mister Henderson. I've given orders for the men to start outside. Hopefully we won't inconvenience you for long.' He continues talking as they go into the front room. 'These rebels – no fools – we'll not find anything –'

I run back to the kitchen, wondering what in the world use there is in searching for something that's not there.

Kate's still at the window, and Margaret has one, two, three teapots lined up on the table. 'I wondered where you'd got to,' she says. 'Fill the big jug with milk, and take care not to spill any.'

Annie comes back in. 'The captain says the tea won't be needed until the men have finished their search. They're going through the barns now.' She looks across at Kate. 'Can you see anything?'

She turns. 'What?'

'The soldiers?'

'Oh – yes. There's two of them in the yard now.'

They have red and black caps on their heads, and grey-coloured jackets with buttons down the front. The nearest fellow has a curly moustache on him, and as we watch, he pushes the handle of the pump, and water spills over his legs. He steps back, shouting something. The other soldier is on his hands and knees peering into the dog's kennel. The rooster is behind him and anytime he gets a chance, he takes a peck at the fellow's boots.

'Did you ever see such a pair of eejits?' Annie says.

'Well, I wouldn't mind one of them warming *my* bed!' Margaret says.

They'd only make it all wet and muddy, but Annie says, 'Ssh, would you?' and gives a look at me. 'Are you all right, Kate? You've gone very quiet.'

'I'm fine. Just my sore head again.'

Margaret pulls out a chair. 'Well, you sit yourself there. The child and I will see to the tea.'

Kate lifts a chopping board onto the table. 'Fetch the apples from the pantry, Brede. I'll peel them myself today.'

When I've put them on the table, she starts removing the skin, and I wait for her to tell me to clear the rest of the dishes, but she says not a word.

Then we hear feet coming tramp-tramp along the passage, and in come the soldiers who were in the yard, followed by the captain. 'If you women could wait outside,' he says, 'while we take a look around.'

'Well,' Annie says, 'I hope you'll not go breaking anything.'

The captain has a very stern face on him. 'And you are?'

'Annie Laverty, sir – the housekeeper.'

'Well, Annie, you have my word for that.'

So Annie, Margaret, Kate and myself go into the yard. One of the soldiers is by the gate. I'd like to take a closer look at him, but Kate has hold of my hand, and is squeezing it so tight, I can hardly move. She's still very white-looking, and I can hear the breath coming in and out of her. The kitchen door is open, and one soldier is pulling out the drawers of the dresser, while the other has his head stuck inside the turf store. I feel Kate go all stiff. It's where Dermot and Francis put those old tools. Though it beats me why she's so bothered about them.

The soldier lifts out some of the turf, before kicking the pieces back, and closing the door after him.

Kate gives a big sigh, and lets go my hand. The next moment, the captain comes out. 'That's all fine,' he says to Annie.

So she calls to Margaret, and back we go into the kitchen.

Mister Henderson is by the range, holding out a piece of paper to the captain. 'This is the list of names you asked for.'

'Thank you. I take it you employ no Carth Licks in the house?'

'Only our cook, Kate.' Mister Henderson smiles across at her. 'I can recommend her baking, if you'd care to sample some?'

The captain is staring at her. She's moving in a very jerky kind of a way, and when she picks up the knife for peeling the apples with, I can see her hand is shaking.

I wait for him to tell her to stop looking so worried. Instead, he narrows his eyes. 'I always say that the innocent have nothing to fear. Isn't that right, Kate?'

'Yes, indeed, sir,' she says, but her voice comes out all trembly.

'Kate's not been herself all morning,' Annie says.

'Is that a fact?' the captain says, but he doesn't stop his staring.

'I'll just fetch the scones,' Kate moves forward, glancing at the turf store, and then away.

My belly twists about at the thought of anyone looking in that cupboard again when it's plain as day that's the last thing she wants. So I go and place myself in front of it, with my legs spread wide, and my arms folded over my chest, the way she did when she tried to stop Dermot putting those old sacks inside.

'Come away from there, Brede!' Kate's voice has gone all high and sharp.

The captain raises his hand. 'Just one moment.'

I'm not going to budge until he leaves us alone, but then he turns to the soldiers, who are by the door. 'Phillips and Smith, I want that cupboard searched again.' As they go towards me, he says, 'And be sure to take everything out of it.'

They push me to one side, so I have to steady myself on the table.

'Do you really think—?' Mister Henderson begins.

'Please, Mister Henderson. Leave this to me.'

We watch the soldiers scoop up armfuls of turf, and pile them by the range. Bits of black are flying around, just as they did when Francis emptied that store. And the pile grows and grows until it's the height of my knees. And I'm thinking what a job Kate and myself will have cleaning it all up again.

She's standing so stiff and still that I want to go over and hold her hand, but all of a sudden I'm too afraid to move.

When all the turf is in a great pile by the range, Curly Moustache goes on his hands and knees into the cupboard. Then he gives a shout. 'There's something here!' And out he comes, dragging one of the sacks after him. When he's done that, he goes back for the second one then the third, and then the last.

'Well, go ahead then, Phillips,' the captain says.

The soldier takes a knife from his belt, and cuts open each sack. Then he lifts one after the other, and there's a great clanking noise as all the tools go crash-crash onto the floor. Only it's not tools inside. It's a load of guns, some of them like the long one that Mister Thompson uses to shoot rabbits with, and other smaller ones, along with a load of little black balls.

Mister Henderson stares down at them. 'My God!'

And I put my hand to my mouth, because I know this is a very bad thing that's happening. And I wait for Kate to tell everyone that it was Dermot and Francis that hid the guns, but she says not one word.

'Mister Henderson,' the captain says, 'could you get all the servants to assemble? Phillips, take four men and begin rounding up the farm workers. Smith, you stay on guard here.'

Curly Moustache puts his hand to his cap, and goes out.

Margaret begins to cry. 'Tell him, Mister Henderson! Tell the captain that none of us here had any part in this!'

Mister Henderson runs his hand through his hair. 'I'm sure the captain doesn't believe for one moment that anyone in this household is responsible, Margaret. Any more than I do. But we must give him all the help he needs.' He stops his pacing. 'I can tell you now, Margaret, that we're after the men who murdered poor Mister Drummond.'

'Oh, my lord!' she says.

'The same ones who slit the throats of the cattle?' Annie asks.

'Very possibly, Annie.' He heaves a sigh. 'And I'm afraid we'll not have to look beyond some of those new men I took on last year.' He glances out of the window. 'The rain's setting in, so we'd best assemble in the dining room. If you and Margaret and Kate would go on through, and push the table against the wall, we should fit everyone in.'

'Very good, Mister Henderson.'

Kate still doesn't give me a look, and the three of them go off along the passage, so I'm left all by myself, with just the captain for company.

THIRTY-THREE

MISTER HENDERSON IS BACK IN THE KITCHEN.
'You really feel it necessary to question the servants?' he says. 'As you know, all the Ten Aunts are Carth Lick.'

The captain strokes his beard. 'Whoever's involved in this, must have had access to this room. And I imagine that rules them out?'

'Well, I suppose one of them might have sneaked in at night. But I agree with you, it's unlikely. I suppose that just leaves the cowman, Barney, and Sam, the lad who helps about the place. But both of them are Prods.'

'So the only Carth Lick is your cook?'

'Kate?' Mister Henderson gives a laugh. 'She's totally devoted to us. Why, she more or less delivered our baby daughter single-handed!'

The captain sighs. 'I've had a deal of experience of

these situations, Mister Henderson, and if I've learned one thing it is that we must never underestimate the kind of low-life we're dealing with. So, as I've already informed the servants, there will have to be some rigorous questioning of them. You do understand?'

'Whatever it takes to clear up this whole wretched business. I thought you could use the front room for the interviews?'

'Thank you.'

'And perhaps another drop of whiskey before you begin?'

'That would be grand.'

And off they go down the passage.

My belly is rumbling away, and I'm just wondering whether to find myself a piece of bread, when Annie, Margaret and Kate come back in.

'What a carry-on!' Margaret is saying.

'I just want these blessed interviews out of the way,' Annie says. 'Mister Henderson says I'm up first.'

'And I'll be next,' Margaret says. 'I keep telling myself there's nothing to be nervous about, but I wouldn't want to get on the wrong side of that captain.' She turns to Kate. 'And you'll be after me, along with the child.'

Kate sits herself down. She's still moving in a jerky kind of a way. 'I wondered, Annie,' she says, and she's speaking very soft, 'if you would mind taking Brede in with you? I've such a bad head, I'll manage better on my own.'

Annie gives Kate's arm a pat. 'Certainly – no problem.'

I'd rather stay with Kate, but she's looking so poorly, I can see why she needs her rest.

'To think of those guns, right under our very noses,' Annie says. 'It's enough to make anyone ill. You just stay quietly here, Kate.'

Curly Moustache appears in the doorway. 'Captain Woods will see the housekeeper now.'

'Well, that's me,' Annie says. 'Come along then, Brede.'

I'd rather stay with Kate, but she's still taking no notice of me, so I follow Annie and the soldier along the passage, and into the front room where the big tree with all the lovely candles stood at Christmas. And I'm remembering how we all stepped forward to be given our presents, and how I had those gorgeous ribbons off Missus Henderson. I've mislaid the pink one, but the others are safe enough in my special drawer.

Now there's just a soldier standing in the corner of the room, and he waves for us to go over to where the captain is sitting behind a desk. There's a load of papers on the top of it, and he picks up a pen and writes something. Kate says that one day, when we have a bit more time, she'll teach me my letters.

The captain gives a nod. 'You seem a sensible woman, Annie, and as I said earlier, there's nothing to be afraid of if you've done nothing wrong.'

'I can assure you, sir, I have not.'

He begins writing again. 'So you've been in this household for how long?'

'Nigh on forty years.'

'And you know nothing about these guns?'

'As God is my witness, today was the first time I clapped eyes on them.'

They keep talking away, so there's a chance to take a good look at the picture that hangs behind the desk. It's of the front part of the house that I saw the very first time Francis drove Kate and myself and Missus Thompson over in the trap. I've not been round there since, but I remember the rows of shiny windows, and the plants growing like a green beard up the walls.

Annie gives me a nudge because the captain is pointing his pen at me. 'And what about the girl?'

I shape the words in my mouth that tell him it was Dermot and Francis who hid those guns, but it's no use – just spit runs out of the corners.

Annie hands me her handkerchief. 'Sure, she can't say a word. Between you and me, sir, she's not quite right in the head. But she's harmless enough.'

'And you'd swear to that?'

'I certainly can.'

He starts writing again. Then he looks up and smiles. 'That'll be all, then, Annie. You're both free to leave.'

She gives a curtsey, and I do the same, and as we go into the hall, a soldier comes towards us, with Margaret following behind. 'How did it go?' she asks.

'Just answer his questions, and you'll be fine. Now, I want to check if Mister and Missus Henderson need anything. So go on back to the kitchen, Brede.'

The place is still in a terrible mess, with the cupboard doors wide open, and lumps of turf scattered about. The guns are still in a pile on the floor, with a soldier standing beside them. It's no wonder Kate has such a long face on her, because it'll not be easy clearing this lot up.

When she sees me, she gets to her feet. 'My niece and I would like to go to our room for a little while.' She smiles across at the soldier. 'If that's all right with you?'

'Well, I suppose it's all right. A few minutes only, mind.'

'Thank you. The quiet will do my head good.'

We sit side-by-side on the bed, and I stare up at the Sacred Heart, wishing I could ask Kate if anyone will ever find Him some shoes.

Then I give a yawn, because all this bother and excitement has left me tired out. But Kate starts speaking, and her voice is so quiet that I have to lean close to hear her properly.

'Now, Brede. Whatever happens, you're on no account to let on about who left those sacks in the turf store.' She takes my chin in her hand, and looks straight at me. 'Because if you do, I'm telling you now that the Sacred Heart will be very angry. So angry that He won't keep an eye out for you anymore. And I won't be at all pleased with you either. Do you understand?'

I give a nod, because even worse than losing Him as our friend is to have Kate cross with me.

She puts her arms around me, and I press my head against the softness of her, and breathe in her flour and onion smell.

'I hate having to tell you this, Brede,' she says, straightening herself again, 'but there's no way round it.' She reaches forward and strokes my hair. 'It's just I'm having to go away for a while.'

I open my mouth, but not a sound comes out.

342

'I don't know for how long, but however long it is, I promise I'll come back for you.'

But now the tears start running down my cheeks, because if she cared enough, she wouldn't be going. And who will look out for me now?

She puts her face very close to mine, and kisses me on the forehead. 'None of this is your fault, Brede, so no matter what's said to you, always remember that. But if you're ever asked about Dermot or Francis, you're just to shake your head to show you know nothing about them. Can you do that for me?'

It makes no sense at all, when they're the ones who should be ending up in the Poor House.

Kate watches me a moment. 'I've no choice, Brede. I'm hoping Mister and Missus Henderson will see you right. So you're to do as they say.' She takes out her handkerchief, and wipes my nose. 'Never forget that you mean the world to me. And we've had some great times together, haven't we? All the talks and laughs, and the dancing. And—'

There's a knock on the door, and Curly Moustache puts his head round. 'The captain will see you now.'

So Kate takes hold of my hand, and we walk back to the kitchen.

'I've made a start on the lunch,' Margaret says. 'So off you go, Kate.'

At the doorway, she turns and gives a smile, but I can't smile on account of my lips being all trembly.

'For goodness' sake,' Margaret says. 'She'll be back before you know it, and then everything will be right as rain.'

I look through the window. It's fairly tipping down, but I can't see what's so right about it.

'You can give me a hand finishing these apples, Brede. Though the dear knows when we'll get our dinner today.'

I pick up the knife she hands me, and start taking the peel off the nearest apple. I make a ring like one of the queens of Ireland wears, but it doesn't stop the terrible feeling I have inside me – as if I'm slipping off the side of the mountain, with no one there to catch me as I fall.

THIRTY-FOUR

CURLY MOUSTACHE IS IN THE DOORWAY. 'YOU women are wanted in the dining room.' Then he turns on his heel, and walks out again.

Margaret puts down her cup. 'Some people have no manners.'

We've got through two pots of tea while waiting for Kate to return. I kick my feet against the table, wishing she was here to tell me that her going away is all a big mistake.

'Well, whatever that captain wants with us,' Annie says, 'I hope he's quick about it, because I've still the upstairs to sort.' She turns to me. 'Come along then, child. I'm sure you'll find Kate's in there waiting for us.'

Right enough, when I walk into that dining room, she's at the far end, with two of the soldiers against the wall behind her. I run over and place myself beside her, and Annie comes next to me, with Molly and Margaret on the other side, so we're all in a row, like at Christmas. Only with no fire in the hearth, and no table with all those glasses winking up at us, it feels very dull altogether.

Kate is staring straight ahead, and it's the same face she has on her when she's thinking about her steps. But when she still doesn't give me a look, leave alone a smile, my belly starts twisting around again.

And then there's a clump-clump kind of a noise, and the outdoor men come filing in, and line themselves opposite, along with Barney and Sam. He winks across at me, but my insides are too unhappy for me to pay him any heed.

'No Ten Aunts,' Margaret whispers to Annie. 'That's strange.'

'Maybe they'll be along shortly,' she whispers back.

And I'm thinking it's strange too that no one gives the outdoor men a telling-off for coming in here in their muddy boots, when there was all that fuss over those slugs.

Then I feel Kate go all stiff beside me as the captain walks in, with Mister and Missus Henderson following.

They have very long faces on them, but they'll soon cheer up when Kate tells them it was Dermot and Francis who hid those sacks.

Then, at a nod from the captain, Curly Moustache shuts the doors.

Some of the men start shifting their feet around, but I don't need Kate telling me to keep still, because all of a sudden I'm too scared to move.

The captain clears his throat. 'We've called you together like this because it's important you all see what's about to

346

take place. And what's about to take place –' he glances around him – 'is a public confession from someone in this very room. A confession to a serious crime – a hanging offence, no less.'

Molly begins to cry and Margaret, who looks near to tears herself, passes a handkerchief to her.

'You'll all be well aware of recent events.' The captain carries a stick with a silver end to it that he taps against his other hand in a way that I don't care for at all. 'The murder of an innocent Protestant, Mister Robert Drummond; the destruction of Mister Henderson's milk shed, and the killing of his dog; and now the discovery, under this very roof, of a sizeable quantity of arms. These bear the hallmarks of an organised gang. For it's my considered opinion, and that of my superiors, that these crimes are all linked.'

He starts walking up and down the line of men, staring into each of their faces. Sam twists his cap in his hand, and the rest of them gaze at their boots, and I'm just glad it's not me he's looking at in that way. 'Let none of us here forget the dangers we face in dealing with such vermin. Those callous enough to murder innocent men, women and children in their beds – those who will stop at nothing to put this land of ours under Popish rule.'

I give a sigh because that's another rule I've not heard of.

The captain comes to a stop by the door. Then he turns. 'You may well be asking yourselves why we don't simply haul the criminal off without further ado. Well, I'll tell you why. It's because we want you to see for yourselves the traitor you've been harbouring in your midst.'

Mister Henderson is tugging on his moustache, and only stops when Missus Henderson lays her hand on his arm.

'In a moment, I will ask the criminal to confess publicly to these crimes,' the captain says. 'And then you'll be free to go about your work – safe in the knowledge that you can rest easy in your beds.'

He stops speaking, and a kind of humming noise fills the room. It gets louder and louder, and higher and higher, until it sounds just like a scream.

Annie is shaking me so hard my teeth rattle together. 'Stop that!' she hisses. The noise dies away, and in the silence, a clock chimes out the time – ding-dong, ding-dong.

The captain taps his cane against his boot – rap-rap, rap-rap. 'I will now ask the person responsible to step forward,' he says.

No one moves.

Kate is staring ahead of her, as if there's no one else but her in the room. When I follow where she's looking, I see through the window another soldier walking up and down outside, his shoulders hunched against the rain that's set in.

There's a smudge of flour on Kate's cheek, but when I reach up to pat it away, she gives me a push.

Then she takes one, two paces out from the wall.

'Is your name Kathleen O'Hagan?'

'It is, sir.'

She's speaking so soft, I have to lean forward to hear.

'And do you admit, Kathleen O'Hagan, to the concealment and possession of weapons in this house

348

– namely, six muskets, three handguns, two knives and twenty-four rounds of ammunition?'

'I do.'

Molly lets out a gasp, and Annie cries, 'Oh, my God! Whatever were you thinking of, Kate!'

'Indeed,' the captain says, 'that's something we might all ask ourselves – and a court of law certainly will – whatever was she thinking of? How could Kate O'Hagan have accepted Mister and Missus Henderson's care and protection, whilst all the while plotting to murder, not just Mister Drummond, but them and their children? How could she look them in the eye, knowing herself to be part of a fiendish plan to kill their dog and destroy their milk shed?'

He continues talking away, and I'm waiting for him to stop so Kate can explain about Dermot and Francis. And while I'm waiting, I count up the number of soldiers in the room. And then I count the pictures on the walls. And I'm just starting to count all the ones in the room, because Kate says I need to work harder on my numbers, when the captain goes rap-rap again with his stick.

'Take O'Hagan through to the kitchen,' he says to the soldiers, 'and keep her under close watch.'

Two soldiers step forward and grab hold of her, one on either side.

I want to run over to her, but she'll only get all cross. So I stay right where I am.

The captain looks around the room. 'The rest of you servants are free to go.'

Kate and the two soldiers start walking to the door, and in my head I'm calling to her: *Tell them what happened, so everything can be all right again*. But she keeps staring ahead of her.

Suddenly, Missus Henderson rushes forward. 'How could you do it, Kate?' she shouts. 'Accept our care and protection, whilst all the time planning to murder us in our beds?' Then she lifts up her hand, and hits Kate hard on the cheek. 'For Rory,' she says – and then, as she hits her again – 'for baby Is a Bell.'

Kate stumbles back, so the two soldiers have to keep her from falling. And then, never mind about staying nice and still, the next moment I'm rushing forward, and beating them with my fists, and kicking out at them for all I'm worth.

'Seize the girl too!' the captain shouts, 'for assaulting Her Majesty's soldiers!'

So they drag me across the hall, and into the kitchen, but at least Kate and I are together. And we sit at the table, looking at the guns on the floor, and the peeled apples that are turning all brown. And we go on sitting there for a very long time, and I'm waiting for Kate to explain it all to me, as well as to the soldiers, but she says not one word.

And then there comes a very bad moment – worse even than the time I saw my mammy and da still as stones in their bed, or when I found poor Angus and that Drummond man with all that blood on them – when two more soldiers come into the kitchen.

Kate puts her arms about me and kisses me. 'I'm going now, Brede. Remember what I've told you.'

She goes out, with a soldier on either side of her and, after a moment, I follow them into the yard. The rain is still tipping down, and there by the gate is more soldiers, and beyond them a big carriage with two horses.

As she moves towards them, I run forward. One of the soldiers reaches out a hand, but I'm too quick for him.

Kate is stepping into the carriage, but when she sees me, she stops and looks across.

And inside my head I'm shouting for all I'm worth. And then suddenly – like when Dermot pulls the cork from his bottle – the words come pouring out of me in the way they used. 'Kate! Kate!' I shout. 'Don't leave me!'

I can see the astonished look on her face, and then she starts to cry. 'Oh, Brede,' she says. 'My poor Brede!'

One of the soldiers gives her a shove into the carriage, and as I go to move closer, the one nearest to me pins my arms to my sides, so I can't move. And all the time I'm crying too, because I don't understand why Kate can't stay here with me, and why the grand life we have can't just go on as before.

Then her head appears out of the window. 'Dance for me, Brede!' she calls. 'Promise to keep dancing for me!' And she's having to shout even louder, because the horses' feet are going clop-clop along the ground, as the carriage moves away.

I throw back my head, and roar at her for all I'm worth. And my new voice comes out, strong and clear. 'I will, Kate! I promise I will!'

And then Mister Henderson comes striding up, and says to the soldier holding my arms, 'For God's sake, man! You can surely let her go now!'

The soldier nods, and steps back.

Mister Henderson doesn't move. He stays right beside me, and I can hear his breath coming in and out of him very fast.

I reach for his hand and, after a moment, he takes it in his, and his skin feels all warm and friendly against mine. But when I look into his face, there's a load of wet running down his cheeks, and I'm thinking that this must be what everyone means by the wrong kind of rain.

The top of the carriage is moving along the lane, and a fat, brown bird rises into the air in front of it, and goes *rick, rick, rick.*

But Mister Henderson and I just stand there until the carriage turns the far corner that leads to the mountain road.

And then it's gone.

1908

THIRTY-FIVE

'Now,' I say to Kate, 'there's some things you need to explain. Because people are still not understanding, though God knows, I've tried hard enough to drum it into them.'

Straw foot: hop, heel down, change, heel down.

'So this is what you need to say: First: You'd never harm a hair of Mister or Missus Henderson's head, leave alone Rory or Is A Bell's.'

Other foot: kick down, lift back 2,3.

'Second: The Dermot fellow said those sacks just had a load of old tools in them.'

Straw foot: hop hop down, kick up 2,3.

'Third: He promised there'd be no trouble. And just look where that's landed us.'

Straw foot: Hop back, 2,3.
Other foot: hop back, forward.

Jesus, Mary and Joseph – I have the order all wrong!

'Remember to count, Brede – and mind your language!'

I know Kate's busy watching my steps, but what's the point of having my voice back if she won't listen? Because any eejit can see the sense in what I'm saying.

I look out of the window to where the lane meets the moor. The cows were driven past for milking a while ago. I like to hear their hooves going clatter-clatter along the track on their way to the new milking shed, their bodies rocking from side to side – as if they've had a swig from Dermot's bottle.

This is the exact same spot where Missus Purdy and I used to stand, talking away to one another. We had a grand time of it until the saints took her one, two Christmases ago. I mislaid that gorgeous looking-glass she gave me, though I still have the box it came in.

I don't miss her as much as I thought I would because Mister Henderson comes calling each week. His moustache and hair are frosted over, but looking at him still makes me feel all warm inside. He tells me that Missus Henderson and Is a Bell are doing just fine and young Rory has grown into a fine-looking fellow.

'He's due in just a while,' Kate says. 'So remember to whet the tea and put out the plates and knives.' And I'm so busy that before I know it I hear the garden gate go click-click and next moment young Rory is in the room. When he sees me, he gives a grin, so that I picture him clear as day, perched on Kate's knee in front of the range, or placing a stone on one of them towers we used to build together Today he has some girl with him. 'You remember Ray Chell?' he says.

Her hair's the colour of butter and perched on the top of it is a hat shaped like a pancake. She has on a white blouse and a skirt that doesn't cover her legs properly. And I'm thinking that there's never been anyone with such gorgeous frocks as Missus Thompson.

Rory hands me a basket. 'Margaret asked me to give you these.'

When I take a peek, there's a load of scones inside, along with a big square of butter and a meat pie. Margaret's been doing the baking for a good while now, but her pastry's never a match for Kate's.

'I'm afraid Ray Chell and I can't stop long,' Rory says as the pair of them seat themselves at the table. 'We've tomorrow's meeting to get ready for.'

I start whetting the tea, leaving the pair of them talking away together.

'There'll be a really big crowd then?' she asks.

'More than two hundred of us.'

'Will your father ever give up, do you think?'

'Him?' Rory shakes his head. 'He's like a terrier with a rat. Although my Uncle John' – that's Pea-in-the-pod – 'says Home Rule came near enough to scare the life out of everyone.'

There was a time when I was scared out of my life too, thinking that Dermot would come walking into this place, dragging a sack of guns after him. But the Sacred Heart, who hangs on the wall here, always looks after me, just as Kate says He would. Because no one's set eyes on

Dermot or Francis since the day the soldiers were here.

And as I pour the tea, suddenly I'm recalling the big meeting in the barn, with Missus Henderson's beautiful banner pinned to the wall and all those men in their mushroom hats jumping up and down. And there's something else I want to remember, but sometimes it's hard to form the words, so I have to roll them round on my tongue before they come out right.

'The one who caused all that trouble,' I say. 'What was he called again?'

'Who do you mean, Brede?' Rory says.

'He had a fancy-sounding name.' I wipe the spit on my sleeve. 'I've got it – Sir Enda.'

Ray Chell gives a laugh. 'She does say the strangest things!'

'Never mind, Brede,' Rory says. 'I know it's hard for you to make sense of it all.'

And as I put more water into the pot, I'm thinking that maybe I'll never know what happened to that fellow.

'Your grandmother will have arrived at the house by now?' Ray Chell says. That's the Bosom woman she's talking about.

'She will indeed, along with my two aunts. Please God we won't have to stay long because now Aunt Adelina's had to move in with my grandmother and Aunt Nora, a more miserable parcel of women you'd not wish to find.'

'Wasn't there some scandal about that aunt?'

Rory looks across at me, but I busy myself giving the sink a wipe.

'Yes, and it caused quite a stir at the time. Because the

minute my cousin, Peter, was born my Uncle Alexander upped and left her. But we're not meant to talk about it.'

'Goodness,' Ray Chell says, 'and she so lovely looking too!'

Young Rory lowers his voice to a whisper. 'Brede here came up with some cock-and-bull story about Peter being Bob Drummond's child.'

'The poor man who was murdered up at the old dairy?'

He gives a nod. 'She also kept insisting that our cook, Kate, was forced into hiding the weapons they found. I was only small at the time, so I don't remember much about it. Other than the excitement of seeing all the soldiers about the place.'

'And they never caught the men behind it?'

He shakes his head. 'The housekeeper mentioned some red-headed fellow she didn't like the look of, and one of Aunt Adelina's servants disappeared around the same time, but no one's been able to prove anything.'

'But that's terrible!'

'Yes – and there was no getting Kate to give any information, though my parents were of the opinion that she knew far more than she was letting on.' He lets out a sigh. 'I remember how much I minded when they took her away. We were all really fond of her, especially my father.'

'To think of those Feen Yuns still out there, planning their attacks. Does it not frighten you?'

'That's what this meeting is about.' He reaches forward and grips her hand. 'Don't be scared, Ray Chell. "Ulster will fight!"'

"'And Ulster will be right!'" she says, and they both start smiling away.

I've never cared for all this talk of fighting, so I'm glad when Rory says: 'Thank you for the tea, Brede. I'll be up to see you again before long.'

I wave them off at the door, and as they go down the path she whispers: 'So what about the woman who was arrested?'

'Brede's mother you mean?'

I'd like to shout after them that Brede's not my mother, but where's the point? Even if you have a voice, no one listens.

He jerks his head in my direction. 'They spared her the hanging, so as far as I know she's still in the Crumb lin Road.'

It's the first I've heard of that road, but all this talk has given me an appetite. So I put on the bit of bacon I've been saving, and while it's frying away, I stare out of the window again.

Before the frightening things came along, there was nothing I liked better than to be up on top of the world on a fine morning. On quiet days like this, the mountain looks like some big creature – a bear or a lion that Kate once showed me pictures of – curled up asleep on its side. It seems harmless enough, but I know what can happen up there.

'For goodness' sake,' Kate says, 'what's done is done. And doesn't that bacon need seeing to?'

However would I manage without her? For it's not as if she's really gone anywhere. Not while I can still talk to her in my head.

'But oh Kate,' I say. 'Wouldn't it tear the heart out of you to think of our old times together?'

'For God's sake, stop all this carry-on!' she says. 'And how are you getting along with that reel?'

The bacon is still sizzling away in its pan, and the kettle will soon be boiled, ready for my next brew. So I move to the space by the stove to show her.

'My back's as straight as old Mister Henderson's flagpole,' I tell her. 'And I'm pointing my toes.'

'Just get on with it!' she says.

So I draw in my breath, and start moving across the room, my feet going tap-tap, tap-tap over the floor, as I turn around and around and around, in time to the music.

HISTORICAL NOTE

- In 1885–1886, when this story is set, there was no separate Irish parliament. Irish MPs sat at Westminster, along with their English, Scots and Welsh colleagues.
- The problem over how Ireland should be governed – 'The Irish Question' – evoked bitter debate and division between those who passionately advocated an Ireland free to govern herself, and those who equally passionately believed she should remain a part of the United Kingdom.
- The proposal for Ireland to have a limited form of self-government – Home Rule – was endorsed by the Liberal leader, William Ewart Gladstone, but strongly opposed by the Conservatives, under Lord Salisbury.
- In order to win the General Election of November 1885, Salisbury agreed to back proposals for Home Rule, so gaining the needed votes of the Irish Nationalists,

led by Charles Parnell. However, many of Salisbury's Conservative colleagues viewed this deal as a betrayal, and withdrew their support. The Liberals regained power, and in February 1886, Gladstone was re-elected Prime Minister for a third term.

- Gladstone had long declared that his mission was 'to pacify Ireland'. However, the landlords of Protestant Ulster remained strongly opposed to any form of Home Rule, and the Liberals among them crossed over to the Conservatives.
- In August 1886, the Home Rule Bill was defeated, and the Conservatives were back in office.
- Re-elected for a fourth term, Gladstone introduced a further Home Rule Bill in 1893, but both it and a later one in 1912 were defeated.
- It was not until the Anglo-Irish Treaty of 1921 that Ireland's independence as the Irish Free State was recognised, with the six counties of Ulster remaining a part of the United Kingdom.

FOOTNOTE

In writing the novel, I have been helped by a number of sources, including:

Donald Harman Akenson: *Small Differences: Irish Catholics and Irish Protestants 1815-1922*, Gill and Macmillan, 1990.

Roy Jenkins' masterly biography of one of my heroes: *Gladstone*, Pan Macmillan, 1996.

The fascinating account by Ruth Dudley Edwards of her time with the Orange Order: *The Faithful Tribe – An Intimate Portrait of the Loyal Institutions*, HarperCollins, 2000.

ABOUT THE AUTHOR

E J Pepper grew up in Worcestershire and Co. Donegal and now lives with her husband on the Surrey/Sussex border. She trained as a marital therapist and as a magistrate and has an M.A. in Creative Writing from the University of Chichester. She is the author of 'Flight Path,' published in 2020, and is currently working on her third novel.

For exclusive discounts on Matador titles,
sign up to our occasional newsletter at
troubador.co.uk/bookshop